I0612549

The Witches of Wildwood
Cape May Horror Stories
and Other Scary Tales
from the Jersey Shore

First Edition

By Mark Wesley Curran

NMD Books
Simi Valley, CA

Library of Congress Cataloging-in-Publication
Witches of Wildwood: Cape May Horror Stories and Other Scary Tales from the Jersey Shore
by Mark Wesley Curran
ISBN: 978-1-936828-49-4 (Softcover)

First Edition March 2017

I'd like the thank all who helped bring this manuscript to fruition, including the wonderful beta readers at Goodreads.

A very special thank you to book editor Danita Mayer, who went above and beyond the call of duty in pointing out to me the many ways in which the English language can confound, frustrate and mystify the fledgling writer, but, once mastered, has the power to move worlds.

I am grateful to you all.

— Mark W. Curran

The Witches of Wildwood
Cape May Horror Stories
and Other Scary Tales
from the Jersey Shore

By Mark Wesley Curran

Table of Contents

The Girl In The Attic 1

Dante's Inferno At Castle Dracula 45

Neptune' s Revenge 55

Night of the Wildwood Dead.................................... 72

Captain Harvey 's Wildwood Seafood Palace......................... 90

Showdown In Anglesea... 120

The Fortune Teller Machine 137

Jersey Devil 191

Werewolves Of Dennis 205

Swamp Beast Of Grassy Sound 219

The Witches of Wildwood.................................... 246

The Girl In The Attic

"I don't ask no questions," Gracie hissed through what I believed was emphysema, "I got two rules. Pay the rent on time and no drugs," she'd say in her thick Jersey accent. "Other than that, I don't give a shit."

Gracie always talks like that, but deep down, she's really a den mother. She's my landlady at the *Ocean View*, a boarding house where I stay when I work summers in Wildwood, New Jersey.

The Ocean View is a crumbling Victorian just off Surf Avenue, two blocks from the beach. It's a three story job with an exterior stairwell on the right side of it that leads up to each floor. A rusty sign hangs out front in peeling faded letters that says *Ocean View Apartments*, but there's no ocean view and the apartments are old and decrepit, kinda like Old Gracie.

All that stuff is just incidental, though compared to the thing that freaks me out the most, and that concerns the girl living in the attic and why I killed her. I'll get to that in a minute, once I set the scene for you, because it's important.

Now, Gracie feels like all her renters are her kids. I imagine she was probably a hell-raiser and a pretty hot piece of tail when she was younger. Now she's on the backside of sixty and looking pretty beat. Too much time in the sun, too many cigarettes and too much hard living can put the mileage on you. When you are in your late teens, like me, you don't give much thought about age until it creeps up on you and hits you square in the face.

Old Gracie owns the place and runs it during the season. She's by herself because her two daughters have lives of their own and don't bother with her anymore. Sometimes I go down to the kitchen on the first floor where Gracie's apartment is and pay my rent. She never stops talking.

That's how I first learned about the girl in the attic.

* * *

"When my Earl died, he left me this dump to run," Old Gracie rasped, "and it's been killing me ever since." A lot of times when she'd finish a sentence she'd go into a coughing fit before lighting up another Virginia Slim. "I'm gonna sell it next year," she'd say, and start coughing up phlegm.

She always says that kinda stuff about selling the boarding house but I don't think she'll sell it, even though the building's seen better days. It's a firetrap long past code. It was built back in the thirties but looks like something out of the last century. It's got thirty units, ten per floor. Each room has a sink, a bed, a dresser, a small stove and a tiny refrigerator from the fifties that always needs defrosting.

Teens come down the shore for the summer and get jobs on the boardwalk or in one of the many restaurants and bars around town. Vacationing families also rent rooms and stay for a week, since it's only a few blocks from the beach. The shower stalls are out back, though, which is kind of a drag, but you get used to it.

Before I get any further into my story, I guess introductions are in order. My name's Cody Myers, and I live in room 301. My unit is the first door on the left on the third floor. Most days I work a game booth on the boardwalk, two blocks up.

Some nights I lie awake and can hear the clatter of the roller coaster on Fun Pier off in the distance through the heavy window that opens out on Roberts Avenue, through the rusted screens facing the Atlantic.

When I'm not working I lie in bed a lot and think about stuff. My mother tells me my imagination is way too active and I think up things are happening that aren't true. She tells me I should write fiction stories because if I keep the stories in my head I'll go nuts.

Anyway, let me tell you about the creepy girl in the attic.

Her name's Victoria. She's blonde and very young, maybe sixteen, tops, and sexy in a tom-boy sort of way. She dresses weird and wears her hair spiked out, a real Gothic kinda look. You know, one of those heavy metal chicks into AC/DC and Sabbath. She wears a lot of heavy purple eye shadow, loads of mascara and has a pierced nose with pea-sized stud in it. She probably has tattoos and piercings in places only her lovers know about.

I'd been thinking a lot lately about where those tattoos and piercings might be and what they might look like.

According to Old Gracie, Victoria only came out at night and slept during the day. A nocturnal creature, yes, which added greatly to her mystique. Gracie says she's an artist or photographer of some kind. Other than that, Victoria is pretty much a mystery.

The first time I spotted her was a weeknight, maybe two in the morning. I'd left my room gone down the hall to take a whizz. In the boarding houses, everyone on the floor shares a communal john, which is a toilet installed in a space the size of a closet. While I was in the john I heard her footsteps coming down the creaky stairs that led to the attic. By the time I'd flushed and stepped out into the hallway I could see the back of her.

She was short in stature, with long straight blond hair down to her ample waist, sexy ass, studded spike wristbands and an intoxicating perfume that reminded me of dead roses and whiskey.

It was a heady fragrance both forbidden yet incredibly sexy, like maybe there was pheromones or something in it.

She wore tight jeans that hugged her body like a latex glove, and a black midriff tee that had a *MEGADEATH* logo in white with a lightning bolt over it. She always carried a camera, a small metal job that clung tightly to her body at the end of a thin black leather strap. It was one of those German jobs that cost a fortune, the kind the street photographers use. She walked fast and was out the screen door at the end of the hallway so quickly I'd barely gotten a glimpse. I was intrigued.

* * *

"She's a whack job," Vince said between bong hits, his face lit up in the dim room as he torched the bowl with his Bic.

"She don't work no job, I seen her out on the boardwalk at night, taking pictures. She develops them up there in the attic, I saw her carrying trays and chemicals up the stairs. I've never been up there," he said, looking at the ceiling almost as an afterthought, inhaling, holding it, his face going red.

"I'm gonna try to get into her panties," he said, and burst out coughing and laughing, the smoke shooting out of his mouth and nostrils.

That's my buddy Vince and he lives next door, in the room next to mine. He's a stoner and an okay guitarist. He I get high together a lot. I go over to his place and we shoot the shit, smoke some bowls, and sometimes we do shrooms. Vince is no movie star in the looks department, with that horsey face and all, but somehow he does pretty good with the girls. I think it's because he's a good talker.

He's always talking about philosophers I never heard of but one he always talks about is a guy named Spinoza. Vinnie's whole philosophy on girls is to divide and conquer at all costs, and he's pretty ruthless. He'll tell a girl anything to have sex with her, and by the sounds of things over there at night, the method seems to be working pretty well for him.

I'm always hearing him over there yakking away with different girls, and when the yakking stops, it's usually followed by a short length of silence and then I'm hearing all kinds of moans and screams from whatever girl he's got over there.

He picks them up off the boardwalk and on the beach, but he does pretty well in the clubs, too.

"I don't know, man," I told him, "you really want to get involved with a girl who has a wingnut loose?" Much to my own surprise, I found myself trying to discourage him.

"Who's talking about involved, Tonto?" he grinned slyly, "I'm talking and krumpets not marriage."

I must admit, I'd been watching her come and go and had been fantasizing about her a lot, and I wanted her to myself.

At least I have my fantasy, and the thought of Vince banging her made me jealous.

He seemed to sense it and was amused. Guys like Vince see chicks as a game, and he figured he could compete with any guy for the poon.

"Babes are like postage stamps," Vince would say. "Lick 'em and stick 'em and send them the hell out the door." He lit the bowl again for another try at what tasted like some wicked Columbian gold. I'd even seen him score with girls that had long time serious boyfriends - sometimes with the boyfriend sleeping a few rooms away. Vince had no shame when it came to game.

I could never understand how he did it, or what psychology came into play, but I have to admit I was envious. I wanted what he had that could get girls like that. My problem was I was too nice of a guy, and I think girls sensed that. They always seemed to go for the kinds of guys that were dangerous, or tough, or a challenge. I myself was no slouch in the looks department, I didn't think, and I'd occasionally get lucky, but it was much too rare for my liking.

"I know you have your eye on her, cuz. If I score I'll see if she'll be open to giving you a mercy fuck" he laughed.

"Fuck you!" I laughed back at him as I lit the bowl, but deep inside I was bugged.

* * *

I was coming back from the *Fluff and Fold*, a laundromat on Pacific one night around 1am. I'd climbed the rickety stairs up the front face of the *Ocean View* with my pillowcase filled with semi wet clothes and took a deep breath of the salty moist air coming in off the ocean. I had my key in my door and was just turning it when I sensed her standing there next to me.

It was creepy, because she seemed to appear out of thin air, and she scared the shit out of me.

She had cold eyes. There was something sad about her. But pretty, her skin so smooth, young and vibrant. She had a killer body for a girl so short. She lifted her camera and clicked so swiftly it caught me unaware. She shot from the hip, never even focusing. I didn't even hear the shutter click. She laughed a kind of playful, almost kitten-like chuckle, turned with a little high-toe pivot on her black Keds then bounded down the hall toward the john.

"Hey," I managed to stammer, "Aren't you the girl that lives upstairs? What's your name?"

I felt like a schoolboy. She stopped but waited a few seconds too long to turn around. It was odd. It was like she was debating even answering.

"The name's Victoria," she said, finally, then turned and continued on down the hall. She turned and looked back at me before she bounded up the stairs to the attic. "I'll see you around," she said, only the slightest smile on the corner of her lips. Those luscious ruby-red lips.

Then she was gone, disappearing up the stairs into the attic.

I went inside my room, dropped the sack of clothes next to my bed and cracked a Molson's Light. I sat in silence.

I spent the rest of the night fantasizing about what it

would be like to make love to her.

* * *

Most days working the booth were hot and boring. Families weren't coming down the shore as much in recent years, preferring to stay home and watch cable TV in air-conditioned comfort. If they didn't stay home, I was hearing that a lot of folks were taking their vacations in more exotic locales like Hawaii, or opting for Florida.

I ran the bottle game. Let me tell you about that. There's these flat wooden paddles cut to look like bottles. They're lined up in neat rows at the back of the booth on a shelf. You get three balls for buck. Knock one of those bottles down you get a prize. Sounds easy, yes? Well, it isn't. That's the whole idea. It took me a good six solid hours of practice with Pops to learn how to knock those bottles down and make it look like a walk in the park.

It works like this. A punk comes along with his squeeze in tow. He's feeling cocky and wants to impress his girl. I draw 'em in with my bark, lay out the shtick, and pull a dirty baseball out of my apron pocket. In one toss I knock a bottle down like it's the easiest thing in the world. *Here, you try it.* The punk takes the ball and I take his buck and now he's on the hook.

Most guys miss all three tries. I do it again in one toss. *Here, try again, buddy, you're just gettin' warmed up.* Rinse and repeat the routine until he runs out of pride or money, or both. On average a guy will spend nine bucks and maybe he gets lucky once and takes away a stuffed animal that costs maybe a buck. That's da biz, as Pops would say, like taking candy from a baby.

There wasn't much action at the boardwalk booth. I'd get a few stray couples here and there and I'd lure them over with my shtick bark

'I set em up - you knock em down - walk away with the big prize - easiest game in town.'

'Three balls for a buck - step up and try your luck,'

These I'd shout these these phrases in a hypnotic tone anytime I had potential customers within earshot. They were taught to me by Pop Turner, the owner. He'd been in the carny biz since he was a kid and he was pushing seventy now.

"Patience lad, don't jump too fast - reel 'em in - let 'em come to you. It's like fishing," he'd say, and he was an old pro at it.

If he worked the booth he'd reel in twice, maybe three times the people I could on any given hour, day or night. "Don't try to read the rubes," he'd say. "Don't vary your pitch," he'd rasp, "most of the time what your head tells you ain't true. Go with your gut."

I'd learned a lot from Pop Turner. Back in the day he'd been a hell-raiser, and some days he'd regale us with stories of his days on the road with one of the many carny shows that used to criss-cross the country.

He'd had his share of wine, women and song, he'd said, but now he seemed content enough just running his booth during the summers and spending his winters in Florida. He'd sure never lost his edge when it came to money. One hot afternoon when the boards were slow, he stopped by to check the till and drop off a few boxes of prizes.

"Hey Pops, I need some advice about a girl."

"Whattaya wanna know kid."

"There's this blonde, lives in the attic of my building where I stay. I'm hooked on her and want her but I'm too shy to ask her out."

He laughed that knowing chuckle of his, and his eyes narrowed in a way that suggested hard-fought wisdom. He also seemed pleased I was trusting him for advice.

"You gotta set up a mystery 'bout yourself," he barked in that Brooklyn accent. "Play hard to get. Show some interest then pull back."

"What if that doesn't work?"

"Then she's a naw-suss-sist, in that case, fuhget about it. There's a lot of fish in the sea. Don't get hooked on one fish, specially not a shellfish." That's Pop's slang for a selfish chick, he called them shellfish, which I guess sorta fits. I think he saw I was tense. He smiled as much as Pop Turner could manage a smile, which wasn't much, but it was there. He patted me on the back like a Dad.

"Don't spin, kid, your head will take you places you don't wanna go."

With that, he was gone, down the boardwalk ramp, waddling like a duck, carrying the old canvas till bag that had *'Cape May Savings and Loan'* printed on it in faded letters. The bag was empty.

That night in my room I couldn't sleep. All I could think about was Victoria. She was probably up there right now, I thought, sitting alone. Was she fantasizing about me? Was she boinking some guy she'd met at a club? Or was that weasel

Vince up there right now banging her brains out? Funny how girls and their behavior can drive a man crazy. They just never acted in a manner that was consistent, was how I looked at it. Had it been that way since caveman times?

I twisted and turned in that dank, rooming house bed. The dripping from the faucet in the corner sink became louder with each passing minute. I stared at the peeling paint on the ceiling, watching the shadow of the old ceiling fan spinning in the darkness. I hadn't been sleeping well for what seemed like weeks.

I had to get up, move around.

Against Pop Turner's advice, I decided to go up to her lair and see for myself.

If she was there, I'd invite her to get high, I reasoned. I'd make conversation with her. Yes. She'd be open to that, wouldn't she? My heart was thumping in my chest, blood pounding in my ears just laying there thinking about it.

I arose in a sweat, pulling on my best tattered jeans. I fished a clean tee out of my bag, the nice one with the Madonna photo just starting to fade. It looked hip but lived in. I ran a brush through my hair, pulled on my sneaks and steeled my nerves.

It was time to find out what made Victoria tick.

* * *

I opened my door slowly, sticking my head out into the hallway. It was quiet, like something waiting. The corridor seemed longer now, dimly lit, an old bare light bulb dangling from the ceiling near the end. There were old Victorian glass lighting fixtures every ten feet lining the gray walls, like flower vases in a crypt. They hadn't worked since electricity became the norm. Now that hallway looked like a place I didn't want to be at night. It gave me the creeps.

I checked my flashlight, a small penlight job I'd won playing skeet-ball at the Fun Pier Arcade.

Check.

I stepped quietly out into the hallway. I don't know why I was being so stealthy, maybe I didn't want to wake the dead, but it felt right. I looked at my watch. Three thirty four. I pulled the door gently shut, the click of the latch echoing down the dimly lit hallway. It reminded me of one of those New York tenement hallways you see in movies where the drug addicts live.

I padded down the hallway past the door to Vince's room. Inside I could hear the muffled sounds of a young woman in the throes of an impending orgasm. I stopped next to his door and listened. The sound was a moan, coming slow and long, like something caught in a trap and about to die. Then I heard the girl from inside somewhere scream a long low moan... "Vince! Oh God yesssss!"

I swear it was the voice of Victoria.

I felt the heat rising from my chest, my face burning red, the prickly heat sensations of shock and anger. *Victoria*, a maniacal voice in my head whispered. *Are you cheating on me?* Of course, these were crazy thoughts, fueled by jealousy. A lack of sleep, I reasoned. The constant thinking about her in the humid dark. Her sexy body. Her whole incredibly enticing package.

Let it go. She's a whack job, man. Forget her.

But something inside made me want to push on toward the stairs. I had a mission. I had to find out more about her. She had me hooked like one of those boardwalk rubes. I reached the entrance door to her stairs, the ones leading up to the attic, and I paused, pressing my ear to the door. I waited... and listened. There were no sounds coming from within.

I was almost certain she was not up there. She was often out all night, not returning until just before dawn. She mostly always used the back entrance, the one with the stairs that led down to the shower stalls out back.

Still, she could be up there. Was she with a guy? Or was she now in Vince's room, with his hands all over her perfect body? Was he taking her to places of ecstasy she'd never experienced before?

It made me angry and jealous just picturing it - her with him. I could see that little smart-ass grin of his, probably thinking 'I'm sending this one out to you, Cody old buddy" while he was plonking her. I could almost picture his pale white rump rising and falling in the dank room, catapulting my lovely Victoria to the outer planets.

I shook these thoughts from my brain and tapped on the door.

If she was up there, she probably wouldn't have heard me, anyway. If I knocked too loud, I might wake everyone up on the floor, or worse yet, have Vince and whoever was in there with him poking their heads out into the hallway. And what if it was Victoria in there with him?

I tapped again, this one a more insistent rap of knuckles. I listened again, waiting. Nothing was stirring from up there, no movement at all.

I looked down at the wrought-iron doorknob, worn down by the ages. Christ. it even used a skeleton key.

What if it were unlocked? I thought.

I stared at it a long time - my thoughts racing. This was crazy. I reached down and turned the knob. Locked. My hand stayed on the knob. I turned hard, hoping to break it free. It would not budge. I released the knob and stepped back. Sweat trickled down my back. *This is crazy, Meyer. You're stalking some strange chick you don't even know.* I stopped and listened. It was dead quiet in the hallway. Something in my head spoke to me. *Try it again, Meyer. Go ahead.*

I gripped the doorknob again and slowly turned it. To my astonishment, it turned as I ever so slightly pulled back the door. It stuck for a moment then the old oak door creaked open as if on high tension strings.

I froze, not breathing, like time itself had stopped. Had someone heard me? I listened intently. Silence, like ghosts waiting in the corners. Looking up those stairs I swallowed hard. They ascended up into the darkness of the loft, disappearing into the unknown.

My heart did double flips. Was she up there sleeping? Would she come awake startled at the intrusion? Start screaming bloody murder and send Old Gracie running up those stairs with a shotgun? Was she sleeping with a samurai sword at her side, would she hesitate to use it?

Perhaps she was trained in martial arts and was capable of dispensing with perceived attackers with deadly dispatch? Was she one who possessed ninja warrior moves designed to take down and permanently immobilize much stronger opponents?

All these things and more ran through my mind as I peered up into that nothingness, frozen like a statue on those stairs - paralyzed with fear. Once I started up those stairs I'd be in total darkness, since I'd have to shut the door behind me. I didn't dare turn on the light. That would alert her if she were up there, and if she wasn't up there, it would be a sure sign someone was upstairs if she came home.

Then I remembered the penlight.

It was back in my room at the end of the hallway.

I looked up into the darkness again.

That's when I remembered my lighter. I fished the Bic from my right jeans pocket, flicking it twice. It was running low. I shook it and tried again, the flame was small, even at the highest setting. It would have to do.

I began my slow ascent up the stairs when I heard the noise from below.

The heavy wooden screen door slammed from the front entrance to the floor, then footsteps approaching fast.

Moving quickly, I tiptoed down the stairs and pulled the door closed till it was only open a crack and waited. All I could see was the dim line of light from the hallway that leaked in around the edges of the door.

I held my breath. If it was Victoria, I was busted.

* * *

It seemed like an eternity, waiting there. Footsteps approached and stopped just outside the door. A shadow moved across the light from the thin slice of white around the edges of the door. A figure. Someone was moving just outside the door. Was it Old Gracie?

I heard the door to the john slowly creep open. Someone seemed to be looking around for something. Trolling. Again the shadow moved back across the slices of light, just outside of the door, inches away. Whoever it was had stopped, listening. My stomach muscles tightened.

Then it was gone.

I heard the footsteps walking swiftly away, moving down the hallway in the direction of the back stairwell. I heard the light banging of the screen door leading down to the shower stalls and ground floor, footfalls on the stairs now fading away in the distance.

I breathed a great sigh of relief.

It had probably been Old Gracie, policing the halls as she often did on nights she couldn't sleep.

The coast was clear!

Swallowing hard I began my slow ascent back up the stairs toward Victoria's lair.

As I ascended up into the loft of the attic, the first thing that hit my senses was the smell of her sweet yet bitter fragrance. It was a dangerous smell, yet one that invited and seduced - something forbidden and ancient. I don't know why but the fragrance carried with it the promise of eternal life.

It reminded me of when we'd visit my uncle who was interred in the mortuary. Dead flowers. I was overwhelmed by another odor that was familiar - a chemical smell like acid and Clorox. I'd remembered that smell from my days in high school at the Vo-Tech hall where students took their photography classes and developed their own black and white photos. It was photo processing equipment, I was sure of it. I didn't dare flick the lighter for fear of waking the dead. I squinted hard through the darkness, trying to adjust to what little light was there.

It was an open loft, one large bedroom space against the sloping open rafters of the Victorian, with two small windows facing out toward the street below. The ghostly light from the streetlamps below were barely visible from up here, and through the tattered flimsy curtains which softened the harsh shadows, the entire space was illumined by a soft mist of light. I scanned the blackness quickly.

She was messy, Victoria was. The whole place was an unholy mess.

Her clothes everywhere; on the floor and even on the dresser, piled high with bras, panties - girly stuff. Strung across the length of the loft were thin lines of wire, from which hung eight by ten photos, some of them still glistening with the wetness of chemicals. I didn't immediately focus on the photos - it was her bed I was concerned with. I scanned the room and held tight on her large bed, barely a mattress on a box spring, upon which lay her huddled mass beneath a crumpled and dirty sheet. It looked like she was asleep. I instinctively backed away, back toward the stairs, trying to squint through the darkness.

In this light I couldn't tell if she was deep in sleep, or was she laying awake with her eyes open, waiting? I held my breath and listened for her breathing. It was completely quiet - the still summer night holding its breath as I did mine.

Silence.

I crept over to the bed and was now able to see the crumpled heap on her bed were her pillows tangled within the sheet, giving the illusion of someone laying there. Victoria was not in the bed. For the moment. I flicked the lighter and extended my arm, the room now a host of shadows as I panned around the room.

In the corner she had fashioned a small darkroom workbench, on which rested plastic jugs of chemicals, three developing trays, and hoses extending from a tiny sink. There was a red light on, a darkroom work light, which emitted an eerie glow, throwing the corner of the room into a red haze.

As I moved closer to the photos I was shocked to see my own face, in closeup, on one of the photos. It was a photo of me. It was the one she had snapped out in the hallway days earlier. There was a look of fear in my eyes in that photo. She'd captured something. Terror.

There were photos of people strung along on the wires, drying. They were faces and figures of tourists, most of them of guys she'd taken up on the boardwalk. Some of them looked like they were taken in some of the nightclubs around town, most of them teens with scared faces. In each there was a deep focus on the eyes, as if her ability to capture what lay inside the windows of the soul was her birthright. She knew fear, she knew how to capture it in a way that only the most gifted photographers can. Something about the photos was disturbing, yet mesmerizing, something drew you in but you didn't know why. Further down the workbench were stacks of photographic paper sealed in boxes, and then there was a painters easel on which she had tacked one of the eight by ten photos.

It was the photo of a young man she had photographed on the beach in close up. You could see the Ferris wheel from Fun Pier towering in the distance behind him. He appeared to be a homeless sort - a look of bravado and swagger yet the fear in his eyes told another story.

She had several paint brushes and small inkwells of red paint. What struck me was the neck of the young man in the photo. Though the photo was in black and white, the only color on the photograph to be seen was from two small bullet hole puncture wounds on his neck, and two small trickles of blood running down the neck from the wounds.

My mind fought for an explanation, the illogic of it all too overwhelming for my senses to handle. I stared at the photo for what seemed like forever, but nothing was making sense. Those long rows of photos which ran down the wires hung like sleeping bats. They were waving gently in the slight breeze caused by a small electric fan which swept the room. It was like a gallery of the dead.

I continued to scan the room with the lighter when my eyes caught something large and wooden propped in the corner, something which sent me into shock.

It was a coffin.

* * *

At first it didn't register. Like my retina sent the signal to my brain but my logic refused to process it. When it hit me, I stumbled backwards like I'd been hit in the stomach. I didn't want to light the lighter again, not wanting to believe what I knew I'd seen.

My nerves were on their jangled edge as I swallowed hard and rolled the flint wheel of the the lighter again, extending my arm toward that dark corner. It rested in the corner next to her bed, laying flat on its back, the lid closed. It was an old oak job, looked like, and was so over the top steam-punk it resembled a throwback from an old Dracula movie.

It was oblong at its ends, the kind they used to use in the latter part of the eighteenth century. It was old, no doubt, like it had been dug up. It was dingy and dinged like it had seen it's share of use. I shuddered just looking at it. The only thing missing was fog and a crucifix, and it gave me the goddamn creeps.

I stood with the Bic flame burning, trying to process what I was seeing, the flickering flame throwing eerie shadows against the slanted rafters. It smelled old up there - a place where memories go to die. The flame coughed out and I flicked the flint wheel again, this time touching my thumb against the hot silver lip of the lighter.

I reflexively jerked my hand back and yowled in pain, tossing the lighter. It shot across the room, hitting the workbench, then skittered across the wooden floor.

Great move, Myers. Now you are in the fucking dark.

I stood breathing hard in the dim gray of that place, alone with a goddamn coffin. The only thing I could see clearly were the neat rows of white paper, hanging from the wires like miniature pillowcases, and the faint weird close-ups of those black and white faces. No way I was staying here. I forced my feet to move in the direction of the stairs, feeling my way blindly across the room. My sneaker hooked into the bottom of something sharp and wooden, my forward momentum taking me head over heels and landing on my back.

It was an old antique rocking chair, probably left up there from ages past.

Now it lay on its side and I was staring up into the rafters having what I was sure was a cardiac arrest. From below on the stairs I heard the scraping of a skeleton key turning a rusty latch and the door to the attic creaking open.

I was trapped like an animal.

Victoria had returned.

* * *

A series of images in a dark hazy dream.

A forest. Gnarly trees with giant branches like arms reaching out and strangling me, abrasive bark scratching and tearing at my skin, my limbs, my face.

A tiny girl stands in a clearing of smoke. She is dressed like little red riding hood, except her hooded cloak is black. Her face is young and beautiful and I see it is Victoria. I'm moving closer and closer like a camera on a dolly track floating and flying at her and just before I crash into her, I am floating in mid-air in front of her.

We are face to face and then I see her mouth now forms an evil smile, something that beckons me to come closer and I want to kiss her. I float even closer and her mouth slowly opens and it is then I see her fangs.

One on either side of her upper middle teeth, two

perfectly formed razor sharp pointy fangs, longer than the rest of her teeth, perfect for feeding on unsuspecting victims looking to get a piece of ass and getting a big piece of unholy eternity instead.

As I float, the teeth begin to drip blood, oozing from the ends of the fangs, dripping down her chin and now her neck, disappearing under the robes.

The cold eyes and perfect face turn into a rotting corpse and then I am bursting through her face like an arrow hearing the rotted flesh tearing and brittle old bones cracking then I explode inside of her like a giant white exploding ball of energy.

The pieces fly apart and float outward into a vast sea of space and stars, then orbit one another and begin to form small planets and then I feel awareness, now, stifling fear, claustrophobic, air sucked out, like being buried alive in a coffin.

I came to consciousness tearing at the empty air in front of me.

I was in a hospital bed - flat on my back staring at an antiseptic white ceiling. Noise out in the hallways and a muffled voice over a loudspeaker paging a doctor. A young nurse gently grabs my arms and looks into my eyes.

"Whoa cowboy," she says, "calm - be calm. It's okay. You are going to be okay. Shhhhhh.... calm"

Her manner was warm and immediately disarming. The room came into focus and light and sound seeped back into my awareness like oxygen after a near drowning. Her dark hair was short and straight, her olive skin smooth and pretty against her pastel nurse uniform. There was an intravenous tube taped to my arm leading up to a hanging plastic bag of clear liquid.

I could see a dark figure seated in the corner of the room at the outer periphery of my vision.

The nurse's face was large and comforting above me as she placed my hands gently at my side and spoke in soothing tones.

"You're in Atlantic City Memorial Hospital," she said slowly. "You've had an accident."

* * *

Whatever had happened came back slowly in traces. Wisps of weird scenes seeped up from the aquifer of my unconscious as isolated fragments. A scene coming into clarity as if in a dream: me laying on my stomach on the cold damp shingled roof of the boarding house, wet with sea mist - the beach waves crashing off in the distance. Things starting to come into focus.

Fragment one: The broken, ratty dark shingles of the roof pressing against my skin.

Fragment two: A car full of hooligans rushing past below, radio blaring, now gone, the sound trailing off up Pacific Avenue.

Clarity of thought just a dream - fighting for some semblance of reason. Memory coalesces, stars and gases forming solid mass. At the edges of my vision, filling in slowly from blackness, the scene before me.

I realized where I was. On the roof of the Ocean View

Apartments. The gabled roof allowed access to the lone window of the attic loft. Victoria's lair. The style of these homes were such that even standing on the roof, a window jutted out at an angle. A window into the soul of the house.

I lay motionless squinting through the dirty window. The same window moments ago I'd barely gotten open and slipped through. I'd no sooner gotten it closed as her pretty blonde head rose quickly from the stairwell into view. A bare light bulb clicked on inside the attic loft - watching Victoria come into the loft from the stairs.

Watching Victoria stop and listen, as if she sensed I was out there.

She stood there, head half cocked, as if listening to the universe itself.

She closed her eyes, began running her hands up her thighs, massaging herself. She swayed, as if listening to some sensual music, far away in some distant place, rocking back and forth, she began to slowly undress. It was slow striptease, long and sensual. She seemed to be enjoying herself, reveling in her body. It was as if she enjoying something that she instinctively knew she would not have forever, something temporary, a changing skin.

She stripped down to nothing and continued her slow dance - never once looking at the window, never once opening her eyes - her eyelids were themselves as sensual and smooth as her perfectly formed body. He breasts were small and tight, her curves athletic yet sexual - like an exotic dancer that had once been a gymnast. She danced that way for a few moments, seconds that stretched on into some glorious eternity.

Moments I never wanted to end.

Even in my fear and revulsion of what I knew she was, I still desired her with all of my being, would have, at that moment, given my life to her gladly for one moment of pleasure with her. It was a love that existed beyond all understanding.

As she danced, she slowly pulled on a white nightie - flipping her hair back over the neck. I heard a faint knocking from below, watched her turn, as if hearing the knock, and then watched as she disappeared down the stairs.

Someone was at her door. Sudden images flooded my thoughts. Images of things I'd seen only moments ago. The photos. The blood. The coffin. The certainty, now solidifying, fast becoming a reality - the terrible assertion and the horrific implication that Victoria Martin was a vampire. That the photographs proved such a fact - a gruesome record she lovingly had created, even reveled in as grim trophies of her conquests? It defied all logic, of course, but didn't all things that defied science?

Nobody had ever proven vampires actually exist in human form. But did that mean they didn't exist? Wasn't the world believed to be flat before proven otherwise? Were not all the great discoveries of man previously thought not possible?

Yet, I could not turn away. I watched through the window, a voyeur in my own horror movie, far above the street, trapped out on a roof and peering through the window of a girl whom I now knew was a vampire. I was now focused on her visitor.

He was a punker, maybe 18. His spiked hair and leather vest punctuated by an ear stud, and from my vantage point outside the window, looked like he had a tattoo on his right bicep, but I could make out what it was.

He was tall and thin, he towered above her like a stalk as they walked with their arms around each others waist to the center of the room. They kissed a long slow mouth kiss, then began to slowly dance, his hands dropping from her waist to her ass. I could see her face when they circled, her eyes lost in some faraway place, a deep pool of tragic finality. They danced like that for awhile, this silent ritual going on, kissing several times, the dance becoming slower and more sensual until they stopped, she looked deep into into his eyes.

He seemed as if in a trance - his eyes were glassed over like his brain and his vision were walled off from one another. He offered his neck to her, a submissive, almost sad ritual I imagined she by now had done countless times. She sunk her mouth into his neck, and stayed there for several minutes, feeding.

When she pulled away, two small puncture wounds the size and width of her incisors marked the naked flesh of his neck, two clean lines of blood traced a glistening red pathway downward. For a few moments he stood there, dazed, then dropped to the floor.

She wiped her mouth clear of blood, picked up her camera, and began slowly, ever so methodically to take photographs of him.

* * *

Everything from that point on was a jumbled blur. I remember vaguely rolling sideways from the window, shocked by what I had seen; repulsed as if kicked in the stomach.

A succession of images in slow motion; losing my balance. Rotten shingles sliding down the steep gabled roof. I heard them landing far below as the surf crashed angrily off in the distance.

The Ferris wheel and roller coaster off in the distance in the dark; silhouetted against the night sky, dark and eerie, stars tumbling. Everything going downside up as I slid down the roof, unable to regain my footing. I clutched at breaking shingles, before feeling my legs shoot out over the edge of the roof. I felt cold steel at my fingertips and grabbed tight, then the groan of rusted nails pulling away from rotted wood. Dangling now three stories up - from a rain gutter that had twisted free from the edge of the roof. That was the last thing I remembered.

* * *

From the hospital bed, I looked down and saw my bandaged hand, the scratches on my arms. There were bruises everywhere that were slowly throbbing to life. My head pounded as if there were men shooting off cannons inside there. My mouth was dry and my eyes ached.

"You're very lucky, Cody Myers," the nurse said reassuringly. You've had a quite a fall."

Things were coming back in fragments.

Old Gracie sat in the corner, and lighting up a Virginia Slim.

"Dumb shit!" was all she could manage. "What were you doing on the roof, pervert!"

She forced a laugh, but I knew she'd been worried. and

went into a coughing fit.

"I'm sorry, maam, there is no smoking in the rooms," admonished the nurse, and with that she walked over, took the cigarette from Old Gracie's fingers, and walked it over to the sink, extinguishing it.

"The doctor is going to run a few tests," the nurse said, checking my vital signs. "Hopefully you can be discharged tonight, but I can't promise anything," she said, and then was gone. Cute, that nurse.

"You pull a stunt like that again," Old Gracie warned, "you're gone. I don't need this shit." She wasn't smiling anymore. "And another thing. The damage is going to be added to your rent, due your next paycheck."

I could only manage a nod. Everything hurt. They kept me overnight.

The prognosis was a mild concussion.

* * *

It started raining when Old Gracie's battered Ford Fairlane rattled onto the Garden State Parkway on-ramp. She didn't say anything for a long time, even after the skyline of Atlantic City disappeared behind us.

Old Gracie chain smoked all the way back to Wildwood, me riding shotgun, and her dripping the wheel with her left hand clenched tight around the wheel in a white knuckled death grip and me slumped in the passenger seat. Rain fell in gusting sheets, the wipers banging frantically but doing little to help visibility.

Old Gracie punched the dashboard lighter again, placing

a fresh filter-tipped Slim between her chapped lips. The battered Fairlane clunked and wheezed as faster cars whipped past. The engine was not in the best of shape, seeming to miss a stroke every other millisecond. Either the timing was off or she needed new spark plugs, or both.

The dashboard lighter popped out and Old Gracie grabbed it, puffing the Slim to life. She never played the radio, if it worked at all.

"I'm going to call Dixie to come fix the rain gutter and whatever else we can patch up there," she coughed. "No more cavorting out on the roof, Cody. I mean it."

"What the hell were you doing out there on the roof? Peeping Tom?"

I knew she was serious when she called me by my first name. If I screwed up again, I'd be out. It was bad enough I'd missed two days of work at the booth. I had some explaining to do with Pops when I got back, and I didn't know if I still had a job. Then there was matter of Victoria and what I'd seen - something I was still trying to process and doing any kind of processing was exceedingly difficult.

There were gaps between my thoughts. A bland gray fog. Shadows moved around in that fog, back lit by what appeared to be spotlights which glared behind my eyes and pierced my throbbing head like white angry suns.

Far as I knew, Victoria wasn't aware of my roof excursion, she'd probably not heard anything with the window shut like that, and if she'd had her music on she wouldn't have had a clue I was losing my life out there or that I had been spying on her.

Of one thing there was now no doubt.

I'd read stories and seen movies about vampires since I'd been kid. Once they bit you, that was it. You'd walk the earth in a kind of twilit horrid existence, seeking out human blood for eternity. A vampire's victims, once bitten, would suffer the same fate. The scourge of the undead would spread like the black plague, except its victims would never die.

Victoria Martin was a vampire.

I was sure of it.

She had to be stopped.

* * *

Pops was in the booth running the game as I approached. I could tell he spotted me coming, just like all good carny men he seemed to be aware of everything around him yet maintained a cool focused gaze. A military kid was walking away from the booth, frowning, most likely nine bucks lighter.

"Welcome back Myers. I was beginning to wonder if you'd gone AWOL for good." He didn't look up as he pulled a few stuffed lions from a cardboard box under the counter. He glanced up long enough to see my bandaged hand and battered body.

"Looks like you got in a fight with a wildebeest," he cracked, "what was her name?"

"I had an accident," I told him. "I fell off the roof of my rooming house."

He smiled and shook his head. You could tell by his expression he knew it had something to do with a girl.

"You ready to go back ta wawk?"

"Yeah. I was kinda hoping I could," I said.

He took a long time to answer.

"Be here tomorrow at nine ayem sharp," he barked, finally, and he wasn't smiling anymore.

"I appreciate this, Pops." I appreciated more than he could ever know. Getting a job mid-season was just about impossible and I was broke.

"Watch yusself," he mumbled, before launching into his pitch.

Within seconds, he had a young couple gravitating toward the booth.

Pops was the best.

* * *

She hunted at night and I followed her.

She'd walk the streets of Wildwood once the sun went down. She was the perfect hunter because she used herself as bait. Being alone and attractive, in a town like Wildwood, a young girl, properly attired, could rack up incredible kills, if she put her mind to it. From the looks of her photos, she was good at it. Everywhere she went she carried that camera. I watched her stand in the middle of crowds, freeze, and snap shots of people passing by and they'd never even notice.

I walked the boards after dark, sometimes late at night. The crowds were thinning. It seemed each season brought fewer tourists. The town was starting to look aged and worn, like an old hooker used up and left to die.

I spotted the earring guy, the one that had been in Victoria's room the night of the accident. He was sitting motionless on one of the wooden benches facing out toward the ocean, his feet up on the rails. I approached him, his eyes, sunken deep in their sockets, were pools of emptiness. He stared dead ahead, out in to the blackness, not moving.

He didn't look good, like he'd been shooting crystal meth or maybe even heroin. His skin was blotched and pale, his hair was greasy and dirty. It didn't look like he'd showered in a few days. I stood at the rail and casually turned over toward him.

"You okay, buddy?" I ventured.

He just stared dead ahead - a zombie in some nightmare netherworld.

I didn't stick around.

I walked half the night that night, all the way down the end of the boards and back, at least twenty times.

Scanning the faces I saw their emptiness, their tiredness. Every now and again I'd see faces like the kid's. Eyes sunken in their sockets, devoid of feeling. Eyes like Victoria's.

My mind swam with dark thoughts all the way back to the *Ocean View*.

Something had to be done.

* * *

In the days to follow, I couldn't sleep. The humidity never let up. My K-Mart box fan did little to move the damp air around my room; the ancient sink in the corner dripped. Down below on the street carloads of kids hissed by, stereos blaring. Summers here were an endless party and the great next something was always a second away. I lay on that musty old mattress, staring at the chipped peeling paint on the ceiling.

Listening. Thinking.

It was quiet next door. Maybe Vince had gone up on the boards in search of yet another conquest. I hadn't seen him since before the accident. I doubted he had even heard about it. The night it happened he was probably humping away in his room with some babe while I had swung precariously one story above him, moments from my impending death. That's one inconsiderate bastard for you.

At least I knew it hadn't been Victoria in there with him.

Then a terrible thought crossed my mind. What if Victoria had done him in?

It seemed like forever, but my eyes eventually grew heavier, the room growing dimmer.

Thoughts swirling in my head, the darkness closed in.

* * *

I stood in the hallway - night blackness. The hallway was dark. Victoria stood at the end of that hallway, backbit by the light that leaked in from the backstair screen door. She wore that white nightie again, except it looked old and tattered and was stained with blood. Her long blond hair fell in dirty straggles down to her shoulders, also caked in blood. Her eyes were red, like a possum caught in the headlights on a desolate back road.

She vanished in thin air.

Above me from the attic rooms upstairs the rhythmic thumping of footsteps, like ritual walking, ten fifteen people, maybe, the sound growing louder and echoing down through the walls and hallway. I could hear men crying, muffled cries of pain. People dying and being resurrected.

Blood ran down the walls from where the wall met the ceiling leaving long trails of streaking crimson. running down the walls and disappearing into the floors below. The light fixtures lining the halls were long dormant, most of them busted, now sparking to life and flickering on and off, throwing weird shadows across the hallway. I heard screaming from the attic, the screams of men in terrible agony.

The door to the attic was cracked just slightly, the dying fluorescent tube lights were coughing and spitting their last throes giving off an eerie yellow-green hue that leaked out from the edges of the door. I could hear the buzzing of the tubes, the electrical noises of insects being zapped by bug lamps.

I'd was the chosen one to stop her. That conviction was clear in my mind. In my left hand was the thick handle of a short, heavy object. A large wooden mallet, the kind we had in shop in high school. The kind I'd seen in the hands of vampire hunters in the movies.

In my right hand, a wooden stake. A thick, medieval thing fashioned from a white pine two by four with a whittling knife, its end tapered down to a deadly pointed spike. Someone fashioned that stake with a great deal of conviction, for it bore the craftsmanship of an artisan. It felt cool and solid in my hand as I walked steadily down the hallway toward the attic door. Muffled cries of pain and anguish drifted down from the attic loft.

The way up the stairs was lit by the flickering neon. The smell of burning ash assailed my nostrils, a sickening smell of smoldering pine bark and pine cones. At the first sounds of my footsteps on the creaking stairs, the cries stopped as if the weight of my advance had quelled them. One by one I crept up the stairs - the mallet and stake in hand. I felt fear but my courage drove me forward.

The neon light zapped out with one last dying spasm. Silence. I held my breath and listened. Something was waiting. I felt it as surely as I knew I was going to drive stake through Victoria's cold heart.

The musty attic smell turned to something rancid. A heady mix of dead salt air creatures and tombs. A stifling stillness which ratified the August heat. Sweat trickled down my back. My grip on the wooden stake so tight my knuckles were white. I felt the veins bulging in my neck.

The attic room lay just above the stairs as I ascended toward the loft. I crept slowly. Above me at the top of the stairs was bathed in the haze of the red darkroom work light.

* * *

I could smell the chemicals of the photo developing trays mixed with the remnants of old perfume. I stopped and listened. Was she up there? Was she dancing slowly in the middle of the room with her next victim, hypnotizing him. Had she already sunk her fangs into yet another innocent man's neck?

I listened again.

No, it was too quiet. Perhaps she was asleep in the coffin. Or worse, perhaps she was laying in wait for me.

I climbed the stairs, each one creaking beneath my wait,

each groan slicing my heart knowing it was a dead giveaway I was coming.

Once my eyes became level with the floor, I quickly surveyed the room. Her clothes were everywhere, bras, panties, old T-shirts strewn across the wooden floor. There were photos drying on her clothesline - some still slick and glistening, still dripping.

My vision scanned the close up faces of her victims one by one - I saw a photo of myself, one

she'd taken of me on the boardwalk when I hadn't been looking. I'd turned to see her just as she clicked the shutter. Right then she'd captured a fear in my eyes, in that subtle instant. It shocked me to see my face now, so vulnerable and scared.

My eyes moved from photo to photo.

The photos were a macabre gallery of horror. Teenagers, mostly, some adults, all male. Some just studies of fear, others with their necks exposed, black and blue markings, suck marks, various levels of fang puncture. It was hard to see detail in the dim light of the red work light, in only the few second I had to see them before I heard something behind me.

Slowly turning, I saw her.in mid-air behind me, large black wings spreading wide, but they were not the wings of a bat, but angel wings. Black angel wings running the length of her height, the tips towering several feet above her, spreading and stretching out. I saw the detail of the membrane and the perfect structure of her wings.

Her face was cherubic, but the eyes dark - the pupils giant black grapes, her mouth twisted up in an evil grin. The wings flapped and kicked up an enormous amount of wind in the stifling chamber as she slowly rose, floating, flying several inches off the floor. Her arm lifted slowly and her index finger uncurled like a bony hook and pointed directly at me.

My fingers involuntarily released my vise-grip on the mallet. It fell to the floor, soon followed by the wooden stake. I could not move a muscle. Her laugh echoed through the chamber, a long insane laugh, mocking and hateful.

Her teeth were showing now, but her white pearlies were no longer. They were stained dark brown, like old coffee stains and ancient parchment. But the fangs were still there, oh yes. The dripping photos were flapping on the line as if in an Atlantic tempest, frantic paper, some of them pulling loose from the clothespins and flying around the room, some sticking to the walls and the slats of the slanted ceiling.

"I am going to make you immortal," she screamed, floating toward me, "and you shall join my army of the undead."

That was the last thing I remembered before the darkness closed in.

* * *

The dream had left me shaken and shell shocked My breathing came in short bursts, my entire body was sweating. Light was seeping in through the curtains. I lay on the mattress, breathing heavily.

My bandaged hand throbbed along with my brain. Spasms of pain spider-webbed and ached. I pulled myself out of bed and shuffled to the mirror, fingering my neck and throat. No fang marks. It had indeed been just a dream. But there was no doubt in my mind it could have happened the very same way for real.

The nightmare had been an omen, a foretelling of things to come as prophetic as a gypsy card reading. How Victoria became a vampire was something beyond my concern or understanding. The world of science was unable to explain many things. Things which defied logic, things dark and mysterious. Things that reached into the deepest recesses of fear. If what she had become was true, then she was creating an army of vampires just like herself.

Hungry. Immortal.

I shuddered at the thought of those teens on the streets. I knew it because I'd seen them, wandering aimless and distant, their eyes dead. Deep bags under their eyes, unkempt like homeless junkies, existing in a world of eternal terror. Their victims would in turn seek other victims and perpetuate an underworld of vampires, eventually turning all of the living into the monsters they themselves had become.

Something had to be done.

I had to kill Victoria Martin.

And the only way to do it would be to drive a wooden stake through her heart.

* * *

It would have to be done quickly. It would be messy and difficult to explain, but once done I had enough evidence to show anyone that killing her was for the greater good of mankind, and most certainly would stem the tide of vampires now growing in their number with each passing night.

The photos of her victims were solid proof of her pedigree, and an examination of her dead body would seal the deal. Her fangs. The stomach contents would reveal the blood of her victims. The coffin. All of it was there and would exonerate me when the homicide was investigated. That was provided I was not killed in the process of eradicating her from this earth.

Having no possession of a wooden stake with which to accomplish the deed, I scoured my room for the raw materials from which I could fashion the weapon. There was nothing in that spartan room that would work.

It was then I hit on an idea. I opened the door slowly, sticking my head out into the hallway. It was dark and empty. The only sound I could hear was from the distant waves crashing on the beach.

I crept down the hallway to the john. Sitting right next to the toilet was a rubber plunger with a long wooden handle. Grabbing it, I ran back down the hallway to my room and disappeared inside.

* * *

Crafting the wooden plunger into a razor sharp stake had taken some time. I popped the rubber cup off the end of the stick and whittled it down using the paring knife which I'd found in my utensil drawer of knives, spoons and forks.

By the time I'd finished, I had a thin but effective looking stake that would get the job done. A small pile of white pine shavings at my feet,

I scoured the room for anything that would work as a

functional mallet. There was nothing. A mason jar, and empty Jack Daniels bottle - a flower vase? All might break in the heat of pounding a stake through someone's heart. I needed something heavy, something that would hold up to the task.

That's when I spotted the cast iron skillet.

* * *

I doubted I'd made the most salient looking vampire hunter as I crept down that hallway, clad only in my white cotton undershorts. Though shirtless, my physique was unimpressive, my battlefield footwear merely dirty white socks.

Armed only with a toilet plunger stake and a large rusting iron skillet I am certain I looked more laughable than threatening. Yet, I felt my calling as a chosen gladiator of the modern age.

I knew the story well - I'd seen the movies and TV shows - vampires, unstopped, would rage a bloody scourge across our land, converting helpless victims into killing machines that would not stop until the earth was populated with the thirsty undead.

If nothing else, allowing such a scourge to continue would certainly damage the tourist trade in Wildwood, and attrition and the times had decimated that enough without driving a stake through its heart. If word got out, families would surely stay away from a town infested with vampires. Yes. I was the chosen one - I felt the rage and the power rising within me and the unstoppable conviction my calling was to stop them.

It was getting light now. She would be sleeping in her

coffin and would not know what hit her until the stake pierced through her chest cavity.

I pulled the door open slowly to the attic.

It did not creak this time. There seemed to be no sound at all, as if I were walking on the moon, there was no ambient noise, nothing. Wild eyed and crazed, my eyes bulging from their sockets, I crept stealthily up the stairs, taking each step carefully and slowly. Above me was a whisper of illumination.

Reaching the top of the stairs and held my breath as my eyes adjusted to the darkness of the loft. A haze of ambient sunlight leaked in from around the shades which covered the window. The smell of chemicals had subsided, now overtaken by the aroma of dead flowers.

The first thing that struck me as odd was the coffin still lay open and empty in the corner.

Then I spotted her.

She was asleep on the bed, laying on her back. She was asleep. She was fully clothed, her jeans and tee-top slightly unkempt, An *Ozzy Osborne* tee-shirt neatly tucked in at her waist. The black leather belt with nail studs glistened in the darkness.

Next to her on the floor was an empty bottle of vodka. She had passed out. As I approached her bed, my heart felt like a jackhammer in my chest. Her angelic face smeared with old makeup, her black mascara caked and faded to a dull gray.

Her skin seemed translucent though oddly, she was showing signs of age for a girl so young. Crinkly lines had formed faint crows marks, and though she looked like a hip young version of a new age vampiress, time would not be kind to her. A thought flashed into my mind.

Vampires aren't supposed to age. They are eternal.

But there would be no concern of that, for she would be dead in but a few moments.

I placed the stake directly above her heart and brought the skillet down hard.

Here eyes opened wide in terror. her arms came up, her hands wrapping instinctively around the stake. Her right hand grabbed my wrist, her long fingernails breaking as they dug into my flesh.

Her screams were loud and disturbing, her strength and resolve were admirable, all things considered. Though she struggled mightily and tried to fight me off with every bit of strength she could muster, it was to no avail. It took four poundings to drive the stake completely through her heart.

Blood gurgled up from her throat as her screams turned to wet choking spits, bright red blood filling her mouth and pouring from her nostrils.

When her twitching stopped, she was completely still. Her face was frozen in a suspended mask of shocked surprise and horror.

Victoria Martin died with her eyes open.

* * *

Old Gracie discovered Victoria dead at ten twenty in the morning. Her wheezing screams came from the attic rooms above me with surprising intensity. I'd been sitting in the chair in my room in silence, covered with blood, for probably the better part of two hours. There was sadness at the loss of the girl with whom I'd had a crush, yet a sense of victory in a death I knew had saved countless others from a horrific fate.

Not long after I heard Gracie's screams, frantic voices came from the hallway, then a scattering of footsteps overhead, muffled voices, shouting, and people running about in what sounded like a lot of panic and confusion.

Then came the sirens from far away, drawing closer. Within seconds the sirens arrived, tires screeching to a halt out on the street downstairs.

I would explain to the police what had happened.

I would tell them about the coffin, show them the photos of her victims, give them a full confession. Surely with the proof so plain to see, they would exonerate me, perhaps even reward me for my bravery in the face of such adversity. For saving mankind. For striking a blow against the scourge of vampirism that would soon wreak havoc across the land if not eradicated now.

Voices entered the hallway outside my door. EMT's hustling their equipment through the screen door, the commotion of people filling the hallway. I could hear Vinnie's voice outside – he was alive. Thank God Victoria hadn't gotten him. I heard his voice out in the corridor.

"He's in there. I think he's in his room."

Then a loud heavy knocking on my door. The voices of unrecognizable men, men of authority.

I could not move. Try as I might, I felt as if glued to that chair, a strange resistance and apathy rising within me.

The knocks became louder, more frantic and insistent.

They would break the door in and find me sitting there,

catatonic and dazed, covered in Victoria's tainted blood.

Images scatter as in a dream. Snatches of voices as they arrest me. I learn Victoria Martin was not a vampire at all. It had been a terrible mistake, what my mother called a fatal turn of an overactive imagination, fueled by jealousy, paranoia, and lack of sleep.

As they place me in the back of the cruiser, my hands cuffed behind my back, I see the shocked, accusatory faces of Vinnie and Old Gracie, shocked by the monster I had become. I sit behind the closed door, gazing out of the window, in a daze. Neighbors gather on the lawn, craning their necks to get a glimpse of the man in the back seat.

The blazing Wildwood sun rises from the end of the street.

Dante's Inferno At Castle Dracula

Anthony 'Dante' Petrillo saw the smoke in the sky long before he pulled Engine 338 off the Garden State Parkway onto Wildwood Exit 4. The call came in from Wildwood PD at 10:51am. Dracula's Castle on Nickel's Midway Pier was going up in flames. If there was going to be anything left of it to save, every available engine needed to *haul ass now.*

By 11:06, three engines responded, all three from Wildwood; Holly Beach, North Wildwood and Wildwood Crest. Dante brought the big water guns and ladder with Engine 338, and with the six man crew on board, hoped they'd be able to make a dent in the inferno.

It was much worse than expected.

Castle Dracula was a major boardwalk attraction for many years. Since the 1960's it had gone through several incarnations and finally, the owners, the Nickels family, decided to transform it into a haunted house attraction.

A giant gray structure which towered over the boardwalk, it resembled a set piece from a Cecil B. De Mille epic. Its medieval turrets and high fortress walls were topped with flapping yellow flags. Its entrance-way a drawbridge like a gaping maw inviting the throngs of boardwalk-goers into Hell itself.

It became known as Drac's Castle, an iconic centerpiece to Fun Pier and a source of fond memories to many boardwalk families who experienced its magic. It held special meaning for Dante. He and his brother spent many hours traversing and exploring its mysteries. It held a special place in the hearts of many. Seeing it being destroyed before his eyes was painful in ways even Dante could not explain.

The roof of the castle facade was completely engulfed by the time Engine 38 pulled into the coned off section of Cedar Avenue and Boardwalk. Dante was shouting orders before the truck had come to a halt.

"Ferko! Prepare extensions and run the lines out to the water!" he shouted.

Men with heavy firefighter rain coats and hats, axes, long hoses and big boots were running everywhere. Ferko hit the ground as the truck skidded to a halt, already pulling hoses and connectors from their compartments. Engines and flashing red and blue lights, a helicopter circling overhead and a large group of spectators, all locals, added to the chaotic scene.

The men ran the hoses and lines. Dante stood across the blaze, assessing the situation. Brinkman, the newbie, appeared by his side, awaiting orders. *He was just a kid,* Dante thought. *What's a kid want working fire when he could lead a regular life.* But Dante understood why most kids like Brinkman wanted to be a fireman. To make a difference. To save lives. Same reason that he himself had gotten into it when he was Brinkman's age.

"Stay clear of falling debris," Dante rasped, not taking his eyes of the flames. "Watch for shifting wind, it's unpredictable coming off the ocean." Below his breath, more a thought than a whisper, Dante afterthought surprised even him:

The beast can turn on you in a heartbeat.

Dante looked over at the kid. Brinkman seemed scared. *But he covers fear with false bravado,* Dante thought, and gripped the handle of his axe tightly, like a warrior about to go into battle.

Dante heard traces of distant screams coming from inside the burning structure. They were faint as a whisper but he knew he'd heard it. An urgent voice of a young male, in his teens.

"You hear that?" he asked Brinkman. The kid paused. There was silence. "No," Brinkman responded. Dante drew a deep breath and listened again. *"Ohhh God plllease..."* the voice cried... Now Dante was sure of it. Someone was yelling for help from somewhere deep within the soul of the burning castle. It was a vaguely familiar voice. A voice he'd not heard since he was a teenager.

It was the haunting voice of his dead brother.

* * *

Dante lifted his axe bolting toward the gaping entrance to the dark ride, one that was part of his youth; one that held memories of danger and lost innocence and the longing for summers gone by.

The January sky was bright, but smoke billowed in toward the boardwalk with alarming thickness, the air biting cold and the spray from the hoses freezing in the air. Ladder 338 had already gone up; he could see Wally O'Hara perched high in the bucket, the long silver nozzle shooting sea water into the blazing roof. The entire top of the roof was aflame, an angry, otherworldly deep orange, with dark black smoke roiling in coils just below it.

Dante trudged across the boards swiftly, breaking through the firemen who stood all around the base of the building. He jumped up onto the platform, ran up the ramp and kicked in the boards which planked the entrance to the castle.

As Dante entered the smoky, fiery inferno, he switched on his helmet light and placed his oxygen mask on. Peering into the nightmarish, glowing sea of smoke, he was immediately plunged into a netherworld of memories. Faces beckoned to him – some were fiberglass recreations of torture scenes and witchery, of inquisition and religious persecution, others were frighteningly familiar.

As Dante moved through the morass of smoke and fire, mirages appeared before him, flickering like a movie reel in Sixties Kodacolor, Super-8 fuzzy focus imagery; his mother taking he and his brother down the boardwalk as the yellow tram car train rolled by; the fudge and pizza shops, the circling gulls overhead.

His brother's face shifted and changed to an older version of himself, the sixteen year old Vincent Petrillo just before he died in the boardwalk fire. Dante saw images of he and Vinnie, under the boardwalk, smoking weed, making time with girlfriends they just met.

"He's my kid brother," Vinnie told Rosa, the pretty nineteen year old girl he'd picked up just hours earlier on the boardwalk. "But he's alright." He said it with affection, but it still irritated Dante. Dante looked over at his own prize, Rosa's best friend Alana. Alana rolled her eyes, indicating she wasn't taking Vinnie seriously. The teens had all gone underneath the boards to catch some reefer before spending the day on the beach.

Dante snapped out of his flashback in a startled daze.

He tried shutting the images out of his brain as he swam through the smoke and flame – peering forward as the shaft of white lantern sliced through the smoky darkness. As he walked the creaky floorboards, he heard the groaning and falling of smoky timbers in the unseen floors above him; he knew the ceiling could give way at any moment. His radio crackled with warnings to exit the building immediately. He reached down to his radio, switching it to off, then fought his way through the haze and flame.

He fought hard against the images; the memories as ghosts floated around him; he saw visions of his father, a fifth-generation firefighter, his tough, angry face floating disembodied on a thin veneer of white smoke. Then the image of his father: lying in a casket in a Northeast Philly funeral home, looking like some strange wax figure from a horror movie. The embalmers and makeup people had done the best they could but there was only so much that could be done with burn victims. It had been a fire in Manyunk, a section of Philly, that had taken his life.

Dante fought against the exhaustion and inertia he'd been feeling for months now; tried putting it all out of his mind; the divorce from Kathy; losing the custody battle; losing their home to the mortgage crisis. Guilt and depression had dogged him for the better part of his life, but a man had to remain strong, to fight his way through it, that's what his parents and friends had told him. *It'll pass,* they said, in the meantime, *man up.*

But they could not know the debilitating effect of depression, how it freezes you and turns your life into a living nightmare of psychic pain. He'd tried sleeping it off, twelve hours a day; he'd tried drinking it away but it only made matters worse.

Snap out of it, they all said. *Tough it out, Petrillo, suck it up. Yeah, he thought, if I don't snap first.*

The roar above his head was an angry crescendo; it sounded like a thousand railroad trains thundering over his head. He pushed forward into the oily black smoke and the ominous arms of orange and yellow flames that reached out all around him like angry beckoning spirits.

There was crashing overhead as sections of the burning roof fell into the floor above him. It did not slow his resolve or lessen his courage, he simply pushed the fear down below the surface He heard voices ahead of him. He stopped dead and tried to ignore the ghosts. Ahead of him in the glow of flame and smoke was Gracie-Lynn, his mother – the strong, silent pillar of strength that had endured so much before she'd died.

For years she'd dealt with his father's unspeakable anger, the deep bouts of depression, the unexplained rage that would erupt in a split second into violence. She did what most women of her generation did; she endured in quiet grace as a martyr nailed to a cross, suffering the crucifixion of his father's fury.

When she was diagnosed with cancer nobody said anything, his father didn't react except with thinly-veiled resentment that somehow if she died she took the easy way out. His father couldn't bring himself to hit her after that, as if her cancer had transformed her into an untouchable.

Dante saw her face in front of him, tolerant and peaceful as the nun he'd seen at Catholic school. An ageless timeless peace on her face, a wisdom and solace that transcended time itself; Gracie-Lynn's face floated in front of him and her arms reached out to him like the hell-flames that surrounded him. The roar of fire that shook the building with its ominous power was the timbre and key of her voice, a disembodied, eerie monotone as she called to him, her arms outstretched.

Antonio I am waiting for you.

There was longing in her eyes, a yearning for God, an expression he'd seen on cemetery statuary, desire not of this earth but born of divine ecstasy. So many things remembered; so many things lost, a past full of regrets and repressed memories, Dante squinted against the darkness and the image of his mother disappeared in a flash of smoke and falling embers.

He could see the tall cloaked figure of Dracula, the wax face resembling his dead father's; then the tuxedo and cape bursting into flames. *Just like all my childhood dreams,* Dante thought. He saw the faces of the firefighters that arrived that Christmas night to quell the boardwalk fire, their determination to stop the beast that was older than mankind, older than the planet itself.

That goddamned night that would never stop replaying itself in his brain. The night when three rowdies from Wildwood High had set fire to the boardwalk, he and Vinnie had run beneath the boardwalk to escape the flames that had raged so quickly out of control, and Dante remembered vividly how his brother had fallen as the boardwalk collapsed, pinning him beneath concrete, steel and burning wood.

Dante remembered the horrific sound as his brother's screams disappeared behind him as he ran. The same way he'd run from anything or anyone that would ever try to get close to him again. He could hear those screams now, somewhere in the rising flames and thickening smoke of Dracula's Castle, a place where he'd spent many hours of his youth just trying to escape his past.

He could see the terrible fear in Vinnie's face as he looked back, and that fear was in the ghost of his brother's eyes; the same eyes that floated before him now, his face a twisted mass of taunting laughter.

Dante ambled forward into the smoke to a large entrance-way in the center of the room, which opened out into a high ceiling. There were dark castle-like brick facade sheets melting to the walls, the dark metal chains falling as the pieces burned into smoldering wisps of black spiderwebs.

His comrades were outside. O'Reilly, the fire captain probably going nuts on the radio that Dante would not answer. He swung his silver axe into the frame of the doorway, taking out the jamb in one mighty swoop, pulling back and ripping the wood from the hinges.

As he entered the main cavity of the structure he felt the floor weakening as he walked – a slight spongy feeling as water poured down from the burning roof above. The place was toast – there was no saving it. The faces roared out of the darkness like banshees in a haunted church. Faces of people long dead. Relatives. Classmates. People who had died in accidents, and people who had fallen to time.

He pushed forward, trying to block the visions from his consciousness, trying not to see the ghosts of a thousand shattered lives spinning around him. The sounds of the dying structure were deafening and it felt like he was dying with it.

Nobody but the doomed and firemen knew the sound of fire when it consumes a building; it was like standing in the center of a cyclone – the sounds of walls caving in on themselves, nails and screws being rendered loose from their anchors – giant bones squealing in agony while the apex implodes in on itself; a ship being torn apart by the tempest.

He secretly feared, – yet was fascinated by – the flames. In playing with death he felt like some God conquering a demon; it was what drew him to the fire. A far-away disembodied voice screamed off in the distance. Vinnie's voice, sounding like it came from a place Dante never wanted to be. *"Help me Antonio... I'm trapped....."*

He saw a flash to his right, then standing right next to him was Brinkman, the newbie – oxygen mask on grabbing Dante's sleeve – pointing up to the ceiling and indicating for him to retreat. Though the oxygen mask Brinkman's eyes were a model of terror.

Get back. We've got to get the hell out of here, Petrillo, are you fucking nuts?

Brinkman waved his arms frantically toward the exit. Above them, the ceiling was erupting as cascades of water poured down through the sooty smoking blackness, patches of blue, sunny sky poking through the billowing smoke and flame.

Side by side, the two men stood at the edge of a cavernous opening. Dante waved Brinkman back, indicating he wanted him to go no further. The newbie paused for a moment and their eyes met through the fireproof masks. The look in Dante's eyes was that of a man already dead.

Floorboards moaned. The ceiling crashed down in a mountain of flame. With split second timing, Dante thrust his right arm backward, throwing Brinkman out of harm's way as the roofing came down, taking the floor beneath Dante's feet along with it, crashing into the furnace of burning embers below.

Trying to regain his footing, Dante stepped backward with one foot, catching the edge of the precipice; throwing his balance into a precarious tilt and in that moment time seemed to stop. He thought to pull himself backward from that edge of darkness, from Hell itself.

The faces peered up at him from the flames, some of them screaming in agony, some of them calling to him from some twisted dimension that knew no time or space. He saw his life rushing past him in a crazy tilted boardwalk arcade of grinning clowns and laughing, evil children.

As Dante's foot dangled over the edge, he saw a giant cauldron of fire churning below his feet, felt the immense energy of a blast furnace below him, then was blinded by the brilliance of an orange-yellow ball of flame that threatened to envelope him like some angry malevolent Sun.

He felt the heat of incineration as he catapulted forward over the edge, into the maw of orange flames. The distant voice of his dead brother screamed ever closer as Dante went over, falling and tumbling forever into the abyss of terrible fire.

Neptune's Revenge

ack in the mid-80's I used to play horn, bari-sax down in South Jersey, at the Club Avalon in North Wildwood. (In Philly we pronounce it 'da hawwn') I only worked there for two seasons. It was a crappy payin' summer gig but I got six nights, on account of my old man used to bar-tend for Cozy Morley. Cozy owned and ran the place. It was a dump.

Back in them days the clubs was still going strong, back before they screwed it all up with insurance regulations, drinking age restrictions and all that stuff. Back in the day. Back before a lot of folks figured out Wildwood had gone to hell in a hand basket.

People used to flock to South Jersey in huge numbers, especially Wildwood. Even on the back-end of the eighties when biz was already starting to slide, you could drive up Pacific Avenue on a Saturday night in the summer season and it would be packed with party-goers. The place was alive. Bright colored clothing. Big hair. Neon lights and thumping music seemed to be everywhere. And the babes?

Well, anyways, back to my story.

The only place that had live music on my off-night, which was Monday, was a high-octane rock club called *The Tempest*, on Pacific Avenue, just off Spicer. The place was cramped and dark , always smelled like vomit, whiskey and piss.

Everyone called it *The Temp*.

At *The Temp*, it seemed like inside or out, there was always a fight happening or waitin' ta happen. I liked it because it had kick-ass rock and roll with an edge – and Mondays was two for one night, so the, whattaya call it, ensent-tiv was there, ya know?

Outside the joint was these violet purple neon lights that went around it framing it, top and bottom. In broken neon over the wall leading to the main corner entrance was the name spelled out in broken letters, 'T M P S T'. The 'T' in 'Tempest' was a green neon palm tree that was also blacked out.

The babes that hung out in the place were kinda rough and not really my style, but if you got past the tattoos and leather, after a coupla drinks you sorta loosened up to 'em. Anyways, there was an unusual band playing *The Temp* that first summer I was working the Club Avalon in North Wildwood. They called themselves *Neptune's Revenge*.

I'd heard they were good. I read an article about them in *SHOUT!*, the local club paper. They were a five-piece hard-rock outfit from Canada. They gigged the Eastern seaboard during the summer months. The group landed a gig for two weeks at *The Temp* as a pickup date on the their way down to Florida. Like a lot of them eighties bands, they had a chick singer, but other than that, I'd never seen or heard them until I'd hit the club on my night off.

* * *

The night I went to see them, lines of people snaked around the block of the club, even though it was a Monday night. I parked on a side street near Spicer and walked over. From a few blocks away I saw lines of unruly metal-heads waiting to gain admission.

As I neared the entrance, a lethal looking ape blocked the door, his burly arms threatened to burst through the seams of his black tight t-shirt. He used a small flashlight to check ID's before admitting them to the cashier just inside the door.

Parked motorcycles, mostly Harleys, lined Pacific Avenue and down the far side of Spicer, their chrome shinin'. All the wheels was turned in, like sleeping dragons. I stood in line with the rest of the club-goers, listenin' to people yakkin.'

"Heard they rock, man, the lead player is phenomenal..."

"The singer... total fox, man."

"Somebody said she's Norwegian, the rest of them they're from Toronto."

"Lead player is from Germany, Hans Shredder. Heard he sat in with Zeppelin a few times in Europe."

"No shit – total monster band."

I took all this in as I neared the ugly bastard bouncer. Some of the leather jacketed girls, wearing tight jeans, mini-skirts, and lots of makeup and lipstick, stood in groups in the line, chain smoking cigarettes. I always dug the smell of cheap perfume and cigarettes, and they had it in spades.

One of them, a Joan Jett lookalike, hair jet black, stared at me and then said something to her blonde bitch girlfriend. Both of them were chewing gum, and both were looking at me up and down like something that should be exterminated. They turned, looked at one another and laughed and turned back around. *Cokeheads,* I thought.

When I got to the ape-man, I showed him my ID. He looked at me with a cocked eyebrow, handed the ID back to me and said "Pay the lady the kuv-va, just inside. Two bucks. Get your hand stamped," he uttered mechanically in a thick Philly accent.

I went inside and gave my two bucks to a platinum haired lady with a Tammy Wynette hairdo. She looked totally out of place. She stamped my hand with a rubber stamp, putting a little letter 'T' on the back of my hand in purple ink. "Go inside, have a seat, two drink minimum," she snapped, and I wondered if the bouncer was her son.

I walked through the tiny bar. It was already crowded. Lotta underage kids. *Faked ID's,* I thought. All the tables were taken, while other club goers stood two deep at the bar. The cocktail waitresses were already hustling, moving like bees through a busy hive.

Like a lot of the dive clubs, this place smelled like old piss and whiskey. The closer you got to the toilets the stronger the smell of piss and vomit. These places was always smoky, so it covered up the stench some, but I never got used to it.

I found a seat in the back of the place and ordered two double jacks from the waitress. The stage was set in dive-bar black – a black platform made of plywood covered in rat-nest carpet, and black torn draperies pulled across the back of it. Ppatches of old duct tape stuck to the stage floor in a buncha spots. Tons of wires and guitar pedals.

The drum set was a Ludwig Octa-Plus, polished, new heads, eight drum heads all positioned perfectly surrounding a drum stool buried in a crap-load of cymbals and backed with a bad-ass gold Chinese gong, which hung behind the drum throne on a tubular aluminum stand. In the center of the gong was the band's logo, the head of a Norse goddess with flowing black hair, wearing a Viking helmet.

The keyboard setup was equally as impressive – racks and rows of electronic keyboards and synthesizers, and a dark purple baby grand piano, polished like a gleaming jewel. It, too sported their logo. The plush white piano bench, done up in that thick upholstery with inlaid buttons, added a nice touch of class.

Sitting on guitar stands, like proud trophies, were an array of guitars that would have made Hendrix jealous. A double necked axe appeared to be custom built, 'cause the inlay on the fretboard was the guitarist's name spelled out in pearl.

In front of the lead guitarist's singing microphone were all kinds of effects pedals, and they all sat neatly in a case that simply opened up on the stage and could be snapped shut and carried out in a flash.

The lead vocalist's position was dead center. Hanging from the mic stand was a silver headless tambourine. The stage was lit with the warm glow of multi-colored par cans, made even more dramatic looking from the smoke that was already in the air.

As showtime approached, the excitement built up as the volume of the background music rose with the conversations and crowd noise. The smoke had gotten thicker and I was already buzzed because some of the tattooed biker women were starting to look sexy.

The house lights went down fast. The keyboard player walked out onstage, dressed in all leather, long blonde hair down to his waist, and white snakeskin boots. He looked rough, like he'd been down a pretty bad road, hard lines etched into his face, but there was still a glow about him. He looked damned serious and didn't smile. He sat down at the piano and the place went dead quiet. A follow spot hit him in a tight focused circle and he began to play.

The piece was classical, and though it sounded familiar, I knew it was original. It was kinda movin', like, what them writer guys call pathos — that's what my Dad used to call it when he listened to something classical that made you all achy feelin inside, except my Dad had a Philly accent and it always came out 'paddoes.' *It got a lot of paddoes,* he'd say.

The song also had something distant and icy — it reminded me of them *fee-yords,* them ice-packed snowscapes and something I couldn't quite put my finger on. It was movin,' man and powerful, as if it belonged in one of them Doctor Chivagus movies or a Viking picture or somethin'. He played with a kinda style I hadn't seen in guys twice his age, and I been around and seen a few in my day. This cat had chops and had studied classical, but he had a sound so different I'd tell it was him if heard him again on a record or somethin' like that.

There was this recurring theme in the piece, and as he played, one by one, the other band members came out and began to play along with him. First the lead guitarist entered, a tall, rail-thin biker looking dude with long stringy black hair and a goatee and an evil looking intense stare that reminded me of Frank Zappa. I knew from what I'd heard this was Lars, and the inlaid fretboard pearl confirmed it.

He picked up an acoustic 12-string and finger-picked in classical style. What he laid down fit what the pianist was playing like a tight, silk glove. Not single note out of place from either of them. Interwoven, baby.

Next, the bass player came out, a strange looking cat with a hook nose, like the wicked witch in the Wizard of Oz, set off by a large, black cowboy hat with a purple feather sticking out of it, nothin' faggy, just classy yet hip.

This guy sorta reminded me of Stevie Ray or maybe Lemmy in Motorhead. He played these long single notes that were like a warm bed waiting for lovers. He was feeling the notes – his eyes were closed. He wasn't looking at the frets but simply going into that zone where I guess those Indian yogi guys do when they meditate.

There were two tall conga drums downstage stage left – polished up real shiny like. Lights threw splashes of purple and yellow down on them giving them the look of new toys under the tree and making me feel like a kid on Christmas morning.

The drummer came out in long strides, calm with an edge, walking ram rod straight but he had the balance of a ninja. His hair was wiry, a white boy Dylan afro – maybe a Jewish kid but he had intense slits for eyes and I guessed him to be some kinda intellectual.

He stood before those congas and laid down skin, barely touching the heads at first, touching them like a man caresses a women's body, slowly warming them up, *Deek-da-dok, Deek da-Dok*. The trance like rhythm was this spell-like thing, and it was tuned perfectly with the bass.

The crowd was into it, man. The band weaved a spell that was loose yet sexy and precise. In the pocket. It lulled and pulled, it throbbed and pulsated. Everybody was sorta grooving to it, but it seemed weird for these biker-types to groove on anything. Usually these folks are into Black Sabbath and death-metal.

That's when I first caught sight of her.

She came out from the back, through a black curtain, long straight blond hair down to her waist, in a long white dress. She seemed to glow – her skin nearly whattaya call it. You know, it glowed kinda. She moved very slowly. Everyone in the place was spellbound by her. Even the bartenders stopped their running around and looked up at the stage at her. People were stunned. Like that deer in the headlights look but more like just after the deer has been hit by a semi. I knew from the article I'd read her name was Vixa.

Her eyes were shut, her mouth a sensual pout. Her body was thin, she seemed slightly emaciated, dark eye shadow and a deep hungry look I could not place. She walked to stage center just slightly swaying to the beat – that hypnotic snake dance rhythm taking her over. She surrendered completely to it. There was no rush, no hurry, like Eternity was hers.

None of the members of the band ever looked at her, they just stayed in their zones oblivious to anything around themselves. She seemed like a ghost that had slipped back through the time and had came back as a rock n roll queen. She was kind of creepy in a turn on sorta way, something I couldn't quite place but it made me uncomfortable yet – man how can I say it – aroused... at the same time. Yeah. Aroused. *Like a tom cat gets when the puddies are purrin' and puttin' out tail* as my ole' man used to say.

I looked around and noticed the same effect she was having on the crowd. Even the Donnas, rough-biker chicks were caught by surprise – and Donnas aren't generally gals who gather at stage doors waiting for autographs, if you get my drift.

"Holy shit," I heard one of em say, and it was a mixture of jealous rage and admiration. That pretty much said it all, I figured.

Star power is something that's hard to put your finger on but Vixa had it in a way that was different than top forty chicks singing on TV. It was like she was going to live forever, had it all, and didn't care. She knew she had her audience yet she didn't give a shit. She was the chosen one and owned it. She didn't have to say nuthin'. She just projected it.

Vixa stepped up to the microphone and opened her lips, her eyes remaining closed. She was enunciating 'oooooooooo's' as strings of long sweet beautiful notes that were like honey pouring from the reeds of Heaven. It was tonally the most beautiful voice I had ever heard, deeply resonant and full, with complete control and power deep from her chest and abdomen.

She sang them long lines, pausing for sixteen bars between them, for effect. Then she started, like, soaring the lines, up and up like some beautiful winged creature I'd never seen before, then dipping back down, the rising and falling of the phrase weaving through the piece real clear and perfect like. Them words described a frozen place – white, distant cold. She brought a feel to it that was more than a feelin'.

Flying Dutchmen travail roiling seas
Plunder ocean forged their destinies
Cursed boatmen oar hellish spate
While singing songs of Norsemen's fate

Far as I could hear, the song was about a curse placed on boatmen who went out and robbed the sea of its treasure without giving the Gods their due, that was my take on it. Usually stuff like that doesn't appeal to me but she had me at *Flying*.

She mesmerized us with her song yet I felt she was singing it to me – and never once did she look at me or the crowd. She was coming from a deeply sad place, a well of sorrow and longing so deep I felt it in the pit of my stomach.

Like in a movie when there's somebody on the screen you are invested in and they end up getting heartbroken or worse, well, that was the jist of it.

It was like an unquenched thirst, a hunger that couldn't be satisfied, that high lonesome place of the roller coaster as it hangs at the top of the track, suspended in some weightless limbo before the drop. I felt tears forming, but held them back.

At one point during the song Vixa's gaze rests for one second on a guy who was standing over near the back by the pool tables. As she watched him, he walked forward as if in a trance, gripping his beer bottle tightly in his right first. She had a spooky control over him. My old man used ta call it 'she put a whammy on him.' That was the way a hot woman can tempt a man, make him lose his reason. By the look on the man's face, she had him hooked like a fish.

That cats eyes never left hers. He walked forward to the front of the stage and looked up at her towering above him. Now she was singing to him. I was not the only man in the crowd that felt jealous. Even the women were envious and like I said these aren't gals who normally display emotion.

Vixa played the guy like a snake plays the mongoose. She swayed back and forth with cobra-like movements, her wrist bangles making these sexy clinking noises and frankly the whole damn scene gave me a woody.

The cat looked like an average nice guy, probably some Joe from the Philly suburbs, by the way he was dressed my guess is he worked at *The Gap*. He was locked into her gaze and the two seemed to be communicating in some telepathic way.

I couldn't see how this schmoe had anything I didn't, and I didn't get how a woman this hot was attracted to him, but then again this was show biz and maybe she was just playing the part of the hot chick temptress.

When the song ended, Vixa broke the connection and turned away, and for the rest of the set, she never looked at him, but he stayed right there, front and center, and I swear he didn"t move a muscle or drink that beer, he just stood there in a daze. I figured the cat was probably stoned and since she was now ignoring him, it didn't matter anyway. Vixa's voice weaved like a silver thread through a magical tapestry.

Delerium's dream take you away
Sorceress scheme desire sway
Follow me through the sands of time
Partake from me the magic wine

Those words almost had me, too, but I had enough skepticism left from my pending divorce not to trust too much in the seductive whispers of the fairer sex, if you get my meaning.

Vixa was a dead ringer for my ex, Marcie, if you switched out the blonde hair for brunette. That fact made Vixa both a turn on and a turn off at the same time. Marcie and me, we'd tried making the marriage work for five years but she just couldn't adjust being married to a musician. Can't say I blame her but I did anyways.

You know, we musicians are out late a lotta nights playin. We're night owls but I never saw it any different than working a night shift someplace. But Marcie had some idea of changing me into some version of her old man. Daddy'd worked in a shoe factory all his life till he died of emphysema, so those weren't exactly footsteps I wanted to follow.

The memory of Marcie's voice drifted back to me from the past.

Come on, honey. Let go of that music dream and get a real job. We'll be so happy.

I tried shaking off the memories but they were hard fires to put out. That's where the double jacks came in, and mine just arrived.

* * *

When the set ended the band members disappeared like ghosts behind the black curtain at the rear of the stage. Vixa was the last to move through the curtain before she turned and looked straight into my eyes.

What I saw there was scary – like scenes from horror movies is how I'd describe it. You know them old late night flicks with spooky halls, old mansions and graveyards, that kind of stuff. There was an emptiness about her. Sadness. What I couldn't understand was how a chick so hot with all that talent and a great career could be sad. All that from one look in her eyes, so I could only imagine what the rest of her would bring. She fascinated me like a big beautiful train wreck.

She had me hooked but I knew if I stayed there I would never leave and if I pursued her as I wanted to do I'd get trapped forever in some kind of Nordic goddess spell. All this sounds crazy, and it is. It was like her soul was hijacking my thoughts.

I'm outta here, I thought. I downed my jacks and hit the exit.

* * *

I stepped out of the club into the balmy Wildwood night. A gust of salt air hit me and I took a few deep breaths, trying to clear my head of Vixa. There was music everywhere. It pulsed from the clubs and bars and from the porches of boarding houses and motels.

I wanna take you to.... Funkytown! Blasted from a car as it sped past.

I heard the strains of Devo's 'Whip It' from somewhere, and from one of the boarding house porches droned Ozzie Osborne's strange nasal vocals screaming *'Please God help me!'* from Black Sabbath's second LP. I tried to clear my mind of what I had just experienced inside *The Tempest*. Walking up

Pacific Avenue, my head was ablaze with thoughts.

Neptune's Revenge was a group that was awesome in every way. I figured them for major stardom. But Vixa disturbed me deeply. Her resemblance to Marci was pretty damn scary. But unlike Marci, she could sing. Marci only sang in the shower and when she did, dogs howled.

Vixa had the excitement and beauty of a diva, a voice of gold and kickass stage presence. She had The Gift – the IT factor. You know, they walk in a room and light it up, that kinda thing. My old man told me a story once about Frank Sinatra. Once Frank walked into a lounge in Vegas where my dad was playing. The whole place went silent as Frank walked across the room. They was mez-muh-rized It's presence, baby. But there was something else about Vixa that bugged me, something I couldn't place, something about that emptiness in her eyes.

I walked quickly toward the boardwalk. The night air was starting to chill. I felt the wind picking up as the sound of rolling breakers crashed in the distance.

That's when I spotted Vixa. She walked far ahead of me, walking at a fast pace toward the boardwalk. She was still in the white dress, but she was wearing a dark jacket over it, her long blond hair tucked beneath it. She headed toward the beach and she was alone. I kept my distance and followed her.

How she'd gotten so far ahead of me when I had just seen her in the club was a mystery. Perhaps she'd gone on break and jogged a few blocks, I'd reasoned, though she didn't seem to me the jogging type.

Vixa turned onto Baker, which dead-ended at the

boardwalk. As I approached the boardwalk ramp she had disappeared. I climbed up the ramp to the boards, the railings damp with sea-mist.

It was past midnight and the boards were nearly deserted, the orange lights threw deep shadows on the long empty rows of wood. I looked in both directions down the boardwalk, seeing only shuttered storefronts and abandoned snack stands. A low fog had set in, giving everything a nightmarish glow. I stopped and listened, hearing only crashing surf in the distance from the beach.

* * *

Looking out over the expanse of sand which stretched in all directions on the other side of the boardwalk, I could see two lone figures on the beach. Vixa stood near the center of that beach, her hands straight down at her sides, watching motionless as the young man walked into the waves fully clothed. I recognized him as the man in the club who had fallen under Vixa's spell. Now he was walking straight into the crashing waves, as if those waves did not exist – his eyes dead forward.

The scene felt eerie and surreal, out of place from the moment in which it was happening. Vixa stood like a statue out there on that desolate beach. I knew that whatever the man was doing he was doing it of her will, not his own.

My first instinct was to run to his aid, yet my legs were powerless to move beyond the spot at which I stood. My brain was racing but not computing, trying to comprehend what I was witnessing.

The man continued out into the waves until he was up to his neck and without hesitation continued his procession into the crashing surf. Then he disappeared beneath the water.

Vixa was without emotion. She stood there as stone cold in some ancient place.

She began to sing. Her song was difficult to hear over the crashing surf and wind but I caught the sound in waves. They were the long ooooooooooos she had sung at he opening of the sea-song – the notes clear and pure. I caught thoughts of men lost at sea. Longin' and grief, that kinda thing.

I couldn't move. I wanted to save the man but my muscles were frozen. I wanted desperately to rescue the man. Vixa sang the sea-song, a lament of sadness and despair, and the whole damn thing felt like Marcie was sending my spirit into the ocean to drown. There was a ella-ment of destruction in it, something predators do.

My need to help the man was negated by my frozen state. My feet were as if glued to those boards as I watched the lifeless form now wash ashore and lay a huddled motionless mass on the sand. Vixa continued her song as she strode toward him.

She turned back toward me, an evil grin spread across her face. She was far enough away the details were spotty but one thing I swear I saw was two sharp fangs emerging from just below her upper lips. They stood out white and glistening against her dark red lipstick, all of this illuminated by the long throw of warm light emitted by the halide streetlamps that lined the boardwalk.

She opened her mouth wide. I saw the fangs clearly now.

She turned away from me, looked down at her victim and reared her head back. My stomach churned and shock waves shot down through my frozen legs as I realized Vixa was not human.

She swiftly went in like a wildcat on her prey and began to feed.

Night of the Wildwood Dead

Thus be it as God be my witness in the year of our lord, eighteen hundred forty two, as a harpooner on the whaling ship the *S.S. Potomac*, we set sail from Newfoundland with an eighteen man crew across the Atlantic Waters to Port-Au-Prince, Haiti, wherest we picked up supplies and further gear for an overnight stay in that strange and mysterious land of voodoo and sacrificial fire.

The captain of our vessel, Landis W. Crocklander, a Quaker in the finest God-fearing tradition, a rather stoic and careful man, yet weather-beaten as if ravaged against the splintery rocks of time itself, and whose skin hammered tough by the tempest of many violent storms, had steered us over the treacherous waters in search of the mighty leviathan, which had alluded our capture this and some many days from our point of departure.

Alas, our hopes of bounty had been dashed against the reef of despair, since our compensation in gold was only to be the share of the profits which we would reap, and none of any salary whatsoever, it seemed to us we would at some point abandoned our voyage all the more paupers than when we embarked.

As for my own duties on this worm-eaten collection of rotting boards, I was hired as deckhand, a position more venerable than sewage steward, though this was an arguable valuation. Officially I was to be responsible for the hoisting of sails as well as various maintenance tasks, both of which I was horribly unsuited. I'd also signed on as harpooner, in the eventuality of such an opportunity. Though I'd never thrown a harpoon in my life, the extra pay it afforded, though meager, well made up for any foreseeable danger it might bring, at least in my estimable wisdom.

My own motivation for taking such a voyage came at the behest of my father, who, declaring me a ne'er-do-well, made stipulation that if I did not do something with my wasted life other than bury my head in books and writing in my journals I would be stricken from his will and thus deprived of the inheritance of his considerable fortune. It was at the prospect of this unpleasant possibility that I signed up for maritime duty forthwith, for the thought of being left poor and destitute upon my father's passing seemed to me a fate worse than death.

I was warned that whaling was not for the faint of heart or weak of stomach, though it seemed to me, in my foolish hubris, any sort of discomfort such as hunting large fish on the open ocean in the winter would be preferable to being left penniless in the world and having to work for a living.

After a few months, reasoned I, I would have satisfied my father's unrealistic expectations, remain in his good graces, and thus, be the heir to large sum of money which would allow me to live a life of comfort and ease.

As it was, my own father had relegated me, temporarily, to the life of a beggar, thus shutting me out of the house, left forced to survive on my own until such time as I had a change of heart in obtaining gainful employment.

Still, a hearty meal once a day and a few paid restless

months on a tossing ship could be a worse fate for such as we, many of us, as were none the better to be landlocked and in search of an Inn and sustenance beyond what could be found scavenged on the street.

So it was, weak of spirit and short on faith we sailed into the tropical port of Haiti. This, I had read, was a God-forsaken island of poverty, corruption, mad dictators, wild ghosts and shameless idolatry. Our visit would be short' to restock our meager supplies for the arduous voyage ahead.

As I chose to stay in my cabin for the duration of the portage, and work on my journals, the crew made me the donkey-end of ridicule as they went in laughter off the weathered deck on their frivolous drunken excursions into the taverns and places of ill-repute.

"Aye," they would wink at one another with knowing camaraderie, feigning some great conspiracy of inexorable collusion, "It seems young Thistlemeyer is boning up for the priesthood!" and other such barbs meant to sting, but to which I ignored and did not allow to bother me in the slightest.

"Go and make merry, heathens," shouted I at the disappearing backs of them, "and me hopes ye bring back the solace of joy and satisfied soul, and not the stink of syphilis and guilt, for should you return with any semblance of the latter, you'll not find forgiveness nor redemption from me!"

As I cried this in a sing-song manner, happily, this seemed to quiet them for a spell, though they still seemed somewhat bemused and solitary of purpose. Within moments they vanished into the night, they to their mirth-making and revelry and me to my quarters, my quill and my inkwell. It was toward dawn I heard them return to the ship in a loud and boisterous manner, but by that time I had already been fast asleep and in the grip of dreams and contentment for an hour and six.

At the breakfast mess, the men seemed tired and irritable and none the better for wear; old Cobblesox, the sail-master, was in a daze and the rest of the men looked in various stages of drunken hung-over discombobulation, and as I, being the only fresh faced and clear-eyed among them, wasted no time in reminding them of it.

Shortly after a breakfast of foul, egg and somewhat questionable biscuit, we shoved off from port, bade farewell to our landlocked brethren, making sail with strong headwind North back toward the New England states that we might chance upon a catch worthy of our voyage, nigh, any catch for braving the cold wintry waters of the stormy Atlantic which lay ominously ahead.

Over those coming days I did notice with growing concern a strange countenance which had fallen over the crew and Captain since our landing in Haiti, as well as a rapid vexation in their general health. There seemed a growing despondency among all of them, and in not a few I began to notice a faraway look in their eyes that defied description, a chilling, dead look, one that conjured up visions of a netherworld I thought best to quickly shut out of my mind.

Some fears are left to the dark recesses of the unconscious, and what with the furies of the seas and storms, not to mention the ever-present threat of being crushed and killed by a gigantic whale, my mind had already been working hither-thither with considerable aplomb. On many a moonlit night

I would find a crew mate standing on the deck, looking out over the roiling waves as if in some kind of hypnotic trance, completely unaware of anything or anyone around him.

When spoken to, they seemed not to hear in the slightest, and when given an order to hoist a sail or man a rudder, nay, even to hook a simple fish for an evening meal, seemed they not to acknowledge or respond, just looking outward in that dead way. I continued writing in my journals in the evenings and in daytime to stay on deck as much as possible so as to show the Captain and the deck-master I was not deficient in my duties nor mirroring the increasing sloth I observed around me.

At least I could not be subject to a docking of pay or worse, a plank-walking, though my reason stopped me short of the latter in consideration of this being a more civilized bunch than a deck-full of rogue pirates. They were, after all, so my reason said to I, for most intents and purposes, lying Christians if nothing else, and would at least attempt some illusion of civility.

A loss of appetite also seemed to plague my fellow sailors, and as we sailed onward across the increasingly angry, icy waters I was of no small concern they to exhibit a disheveled, unkempt appearance, and to exude a rather unpleasant smell, like that of rotten meat.

This disconcerting state of affairs was further aggravated by the fact we'd spotted nary a whale in our voyage, and those we did glimpse disappeared quickly, and it did seem they had communicated to their blubbery counterparts a ship-full of bad smelling men with sharp harpoons were coming their way, and that a hasty exit might was in order.

At any event we'd come up empty handed with not a single kill to our credit, but rather than haughty discontent, the men only grew infected with the blight that seemed to have thus overtake them all, the Captain included, all of this in the face of increasingly difficult navigation, as if a giant claw had reared up with a mile-high talon and was about to pluck us like a turnip from the sea and hurl us blindly into the raging maelstrom.

* * *

It was on such a turbulent night when I had turned in to my sleeping quarters at around midnight. The stateroom which I occupied accommodated six of us in stacked bunks, on which I was ensconced in one of the uppermost berths.

The five other crewmen had already gone to their slumbers, though all were doubtful of any fitful sleep given the considerable tossing and turning of our ship in the wake of a coming tempest. The sea itself seemed contemptuous of us, not only reluctant to give up its bounty but to punish us for our transgressions upon it. I had lain awake by the glow of my lantern, scribbling with shaky quill in my journal whilst waiting for the solace of sleep to overcome me. When at long last I finally extinguished the lantern, I settled in to the pitch with the resignation of restless, agitated slumber.

As given no light within the chamber, we were all enveloped in the deepest blackness, and thus there being no other light from which to peek from creeping consciousness, was all the more conductive to acquiescence into the netherworld of nightmares. I have no recollection of the passage of any time, but at one point in the remainder of the early morning hours I came awake to an eerie silence.

As I opened my eyes, there was an ambient white glow emanating at a very low and dim frequency like the flickering of a white flame. It appeared to be coming from the center of the room, which I did not have clear view of at the angle of my bunk at the position which my head lay on the bedding.

The stateroom and ship were now completely silent and with no movement of pitch or sound of storm. I was taken as if in a vacuum of the oddest quiet. I moved my head to the edge of the bunk and looked down to the center of the bunk-room, most shocked and astonished to see, standing in the center of the wooden floor a negro woman who appeared to be ensconced in a transfixed like state.

The woman appeared to be in her fifties or possibly sixties, short of stature wearing a print dress of white and robin's egg blue, her hair hidden in a turban or wrapped cloth of the type often used by Haitian women of the time.

She stood erect as a plank in the center of the room, motionless, staring directly at the blank wall into space as if seeing through the walls of the stateroom. It was a this point I noticed all the other men gone from their bunks and thus I was completely alone in the stateroom with the very disturbing vision of this maniacal-looking woman.

I thought myself to be, at that moment in my own awareness, in the throes of some strange dream, a consciousness or realization that would normally trigger my awakening, but thus, that was not the case as I woke up fully and continued to stare at the negro woman, glowing this odd, faint white in the center of the room.

"What is it you want?" I cried, feeling rather silly to exhibit fear of this diminutive woman, yet I should show no such timidity in the wake of a giant killer whale.

The woman appeared not to hear, just stood motionless with that very curious wild-eyed stare I must admit chilled me to my very marrow. In her gaze was something I'd come to recognize in the eyes of the rapidly disintegrating crew, a look which spoke of open graves and corpses, moonless nights and dusty tombs.

I sat upright with the covers clutched against my chest with both hands, peering and squinting at the vision as if pulling it in with stronger clarity would make it disappear, or at the very least give it less animated form.

Then there came the sound I can only describe as a vacuum sound coming from the closed door of the cabin, and then slowly, the sound of pitching and storm came slowly back with a limited movement of the ship.

The image of the woman appeared to dissipate into a bright white-blue smoke, but her features and shape were still clear but coalescing into a vapor like mist which drew itself and stretched like pipe-smoke drifting across the room, her face stretching out of proportion into a hazy mass.

In one swift movement, the image of the woman sucked out of the room beneath the crack of the door, taking all light with it and from the edges of the door I could see the light illuminating then disappearing altogether, leaving me in total blackness.

Fumbling with the lantern, I found a match and struck it, then lit the lantern, climbing down from my bunk, all my senses reeling and my body twitching and shaking from fear.

I turned to see all the men now had appeared back in their bunks, as if they had never left, and all were fitfully sleeping, with one in particular, A mulatto named Riggs, snoring in a most annoying yet welcome fashion.

I walked through the area where the woman had stood, waving my hands through the air as if to check if there were matter to explain the spirit but there was no discernible form to the touch – only empty air.

I opened the cabin door and peered down the hallway with the glowing lantern, but alas, there was nothing to be seen in that darkness and nothing to be heard save for angry winds and the painful creaking of the ship as it cut its way through terrible black seas.

On stepping back inside my stateroom and on seeing the other bunk-mates had remained asleep through this episode, and had not stirred even of now, I climbed back into my perch, extinguished the lantern and lay awake for the next hour before finally succumbing to a most dreadful sleep.

* * *

At the mid-point somewhere near the Carolinas, a winter storm hit with great savagery, threatening to break our meager vessel into splinters with the hurricane force gales and icy winds that chilled us to our marrow. For three days and nights the storm lashed us with its relentless fury, and many times I was certain we would be plunged to our watery deaths to the bottom of the unforgiving Atlantic.

The men seemed with each passing day to grow more despondent and distant; to a point where finally it seemed they simply allowed the storm to take us where it would, and if that meant to the bottom, then so be it. I fought hard as I could to try and rally the Captain as well as my fellow crew-mates, but neither threats nor reason could reach them in their catatonic stupor and rapidly advancing illness.

It had occurred to me that they had contracted some kind of malaria fever whilst we had been docked in Haiti, but my medical knowledge in such matters being most lacking, I was merely at the mercy of guesswork and conjecture.

For those three hellish days it was everything we could do to help keep the pile of boards afloat against impossible odds, and on the final evening of the morning before the storm broke, the ship's cook, Brenton Talmadge, a Nantucket seaman with thirty years on whaleboats, went berserk and tried to strangle the first-mate on the aft-deck.

Their struggle had gone on for some minutes before any of us caught on to the scuffle, and just as one of the harpooners, Johannsen, peeled the rabid cook away from Talmadge, it was apparent the rabid cook had managed to bite off the right ear of first-mate Herbert Bonsall, leaving squirting red meat where the ear had once been.

To make matters even worse, as Johannsen pulled the crazed ear-eater away, the cook turned and grabbed him by the back of the head, pulling him forward and bit the harpooner's nose clear off his face. As you might imagine, this bit of unpleasantness was not received well by harpooner

Johanssen, who covered his missing nose with his hands, screaming in agony. I'd come upon on the commotion just as Brenton Talmadge had swallowed the nose, his eyes crazed and insane, rabid foam leaking from the corners of his mouth, mixed with blood, and looking altogether horrific.

I thought first to separate the men but after seeing the blood and foam, decided against touching any of them for fear of some kind of contamination. A bright flash and *pop!* came from over my left shoulder from above. Within one quick movement the Captain fired a shot into the back of Talmadge, striking him in the upper right shoulder, spinning him sideways and knocking him to the deck.

All of us astonished and somewhat reeling from this strange turn of events, as more crew rushed to the aft deck to ascertain what all the commotion was about, and thus seeing Talmadge lying bloody on the boards, and what with the missing ear and nose he was responsible for, it was a good thing he had been, for the most part, incapacitated.

The problem was Talmadge did not stay down, and presently arose again to lurch awkwardly, eyes in some dead place, blood covering his face and spurting blood from his wounded shoulder, advanced in an oddly syncopated gait toward another of the crewmen, presumably to bite off whatever he could sink his rotting teeth into.

The Captain shouted fair heed for him to stop, but he would not, and thus shot again, this time the iron pellet-ball striking Talmadge's opposite shoulder, causing a terrible wound which splintered both shirt and bone in a spray of crimson gore, knocking him once again to the splintered boards. So much to our utter shock and horror that he once again arose from his lying position, and, struggling in a most pervasive manner, managed to balance himself back on his feet.

At this point the wounded, yet wobbly image of Talmadge advancing o'er the deck with two spurting shoulders, now making a most disturbing gurgling and groaning noise, such as a dying moose upon the tundra, and thus continued to swing out in all directions wildly with his arms, as a blind man might whilst fending off a swarm of angry bees.

The Captain, he himself awe-struck yet baffled by the seemingly unstoppable and monstrous Talmadge, did shout out again another warning in a tone which now seemed doomed to extinction, and aimed again this time to the head, and in another loud *pop!* and spray of further gore, the figure of Talmadge now lay motionless on the pitching deck.

A communal silence of bewilderment overcame all on deck who had witnessed this scene. Even the most callous among men who would massacre the innocent leviathan could not feel some sense of empathy for one of their own.

Though he himself seemed distant and lethargic, our ship medic, a one Artemus J. Bradshaw, he of mousy and bespectacled persona, did rush to examine the bleeding corpse of Talmadge but was warned off by the Captain, who ordered the immediate removal of the corpse to be thrown overboard by two of the whale men, but only with the precaution of bandanna-covered mouth and nose, and with adequate gloves to cover their hands so as to avoid contamination.

Bradshaw immediately tended to the wounds of the

stricken men, taking them below deck to the infirmary, where it was hoped that through stitch, suture and antiseptic, both men would survive their mutilations, alas not without permanent scar and handicap. With the body of Talmadge safely disposed of at sea, the lot of us still in shock and loathe to discuss or even explain the strange phenomenon which had just occurred, went back to the business of the management of keeping the ship afloat in so severe a storm.

* * *

Over the course of the next several days the storm raged without mercy. No less disturbing was the deteriorating state of my comrades, which had escalated into several more incidents of attack both below and above deck. Both Johannsen and Bonsall had become increasingly agitated, their wounds festering and opening into a hideous sight of disrepair. Their demeanor became unmanageable, nigh, their attacks against the other men resulting in wounds which did ooze with strange colored pus.

Our ship now pervaded with the acrid smell of rotted flesh, all of the men, with exception of myself and the Captain, had become cadaverous and rabid, several of them requiring rather inhumane restraint by rope and chain. I was convinced in my ongoing observation and so surmised the men had contracted a horrid disease upon the island of Haiti, once which rendered them nearly invincible to blows or bullets, unless the latter were aimed directly into the brain itself. This was made all the more difficult when faced with a decision to kill one's own shipmates or be killed oneself.

I felt myself in the grip of panic and despair, nigh, even paranoia, feeling as if a terrible fate were about to befall us. Somehow I had the notion it was connected to the ghost-woman who'd appeared in our cabin in Haiti, whom, I was now certain, had cast a demonic spell on the lot of us. I'd read accounts of Haitian sorcery from published stories of wayfaring seamen, but had previously heretofore paid them no heed. I'd tossed them of to be, at best, the imagined fictions of fevered minds. Now standing at the brink of uncertainty and death, I was not so sure these accounts were entirely untrue.

In the midst of these horrors, and that final, terrible night of storm, while I had locked myself alone in my quarters, an epic lightning display of savage intensity raged in the dark, stormy skies over our bobbing cork of a ship as we were tossed relentlessly about on the tumultuous waves. A low rumbling sound like that of an earthquake caused me to spring from my bunk and climb the stairs, entering out onto the icy cold of the storm lashed deck.

The very waters seemed to shake in a maelstrom of deep resonant sound. The skies lit up all around and created a giant flash out across the dark sea. It was if God had taken a photograph and I could thus see the distant horizon if but for a split second then pitch darkness again. Another lightning bolt cascaded down from the clouds, giving an eerie blue-white glow, and I could feel the intense heat of it against my face.

In one gigantic clap of thunder and a blinding flash of lightning so intense it enveloped the ship, this brilliance dissipated and there was only rain as it pelted the now-still ocean as I looked out over the water to see a sight of astounding impossibility.

Ahead of us on the distant shore was a land mass, a string of lights like a chain of pearls along it, with some of these jewels brighter than others, but those jewels not like unlike the light of fire, orange, but perfectly round like gas lamps in a long solid procession across the entire coast, unbroken but for a few mile gaps between chains. There were also moving lights along paved streets, though their source could not be seen from this distance.

I rushed to the galley where I found an eyeglass and scanned the distant shore but could not make sense what I was seeing. It was if we had sailed out from the hellish storm through some passage of time into another world.

As we drifted closer to the shore, Captain Crocklander stumbled from the wheelhouse. He seemed quite ill, taken of the same symptoms observed in the other men, and as he shuffled to the edge of the deck, staggering.

He gazed out over the water in disbelief at the shoreline which loomed before us, then promptly lost consciousness, thus falling to the deck at my feet.

I dared not touch him for fear I might contract the hideous disease afflicting him, thus torn between helping him and saving myself, but my inner conflict broken by the fire which erupted from inside the wheelhouse behind him.

* * *

A fiery blaze raged in the wheelhouse. By the sounds of explosions below deck, it was apparent the lightning strikes had ignited our flammables. Lo we had become the damned of both disease and hellfire. Crocklander struggled to his feet, but could not stand properly, and when he turned his face towar't me, I was shocked to find it now exhibiting the same tell-tale pallor and spreading black-rot which had afflicted the other unfortunate souls aboard.

As he ambled toward me, his limbs stiffening, his arms plunged out straight-head of him like a sleepwalking ghoul, I was thus obliged to pick up a nearby shovel and swing it mightily into him, catching his head in a splattering of steel and blood. I swung the spade several times, to little avail, for Crocklander (or what he had become) continued toward me in that awkward gait of the dead, as our ship neared further to the coast of the God-forsaken land before us.

Stepping forward toward him, in one swift movement I removed the pistol from his waistband, pulling it free, pointing it at his head and pulled the trigger, a flash erupted, sending him sideways against he railing, where he fell backwards into the dark, roiling sea.

When the ship finally ran aground, it was a flaming mountain of fire, the remaining men, many of them in the throes of the terrible affliction, jumping oer'board into the chilly waves. They desperately swam toward shore, flames reflecting behind them in the black mirror of ocean.

Before the inferno forced my final retreat, once I had unchained all the restrained men, I too dove into the wildly swirling, reflecting sea and set stroke to shore, where already I could see my water-soaked ship-mates, their clothes clinging to their skins, dragging themselves up on the sandy beaches.

Off to our right, jutting outward on an extended wooden platform, was a gigantic web of steel, a skeleton of white which had curves and turns on it, and what appeared to be narrow gauge steel tracks, where a wheeled cart might ride.

Standing off to one side of it was a giant wheel with what appeared to be spokes, and seats where people might sit. There were colorful booths and metal frameworks which appeared to be some kind of circus.

As I neared closer and pulled myself ashore, I could see a large painted sign.

It read:

Welcome To Morey's Fun Pier! - Wildwood, NJ.

* * *

There are many things logic and science cannot explain. That which can be seen with the naked eye and in the light of reason is but one perception. I cannot venture a reasonable explanation for how we came to be shipwrecked on some futuristic New Jersey shore.

I feared it was related to some evil spell cast upon our lot by the mysterious Haitian ghost woman I had sighted in my cabin, something we had picked up from that devilish voodoo-land. I had heard astonishing tales of voyages made by seafarers to strange and distant shores, ones which defied the laws of nature and space as we understood it. I surmised that somehow we had sailed into sliver or doorway forward in time. Through some hexing of occult intervention we had forced passage to a void which transcended time and space.

As I struggled across those stormy sands toward the

elevated platform of wood and stairs leading up to the walkway, I looked behind me to see the last vestiges of flaming timber of the ship falling in slow motion into the ocean waters. Ahead of me, the remaining survivors of our perilous fate shuffled in wet and torn clothing down boards lined with shops and amusements, devoid of any life but for confused looking sea gulls.

I watched in horror as one Charles A. Winthrop. once an able sailor on the mainsail rigging crew, accosted an old man who appeared to be pulling trash out of a receptacle near the railing, grabbing him and ripping out his throat with his stained and rotting teeth.

The old man fell to the ground, a bloody heap, grasping at his bleeding throat with his old, weathered hands, then fell still and silent. As Winthrop, now a walking cadaver turned away I saw the old man's eyes open wide, reanimated to life by the hideous curse with which he was now afflicted.

Having lost my firearm in the swim to shore, I was helpless to terminate the scourge which would now spread across this doomed land. More of the walking dead were struggling toward the stairs from the beach, coming up out the water like drugged tortoise, while before me more of them making their way down the boardwalk promenade.

Still others had found their way down the ramps and stairs leading to streets which were lined with Victorian homes, futuristic looking shops, and what appeared to be large smooth glass structures with small balconies overlooking the sea.

It would now be only a matter of time before the terrible cataclysm of this hideous scourge would spread onto the continent.

Captain Harvey 's Wildwood Seafood Palace

Gus Harvey's reputation as the happiest man in Wildwood was beyond reproach.

Back in the sixties, when folks had only three choices for channels and a color TV show was a luxury, you could catch Gus in a wacky comedy show every week on NBC called 'HOOKS AHOY!' where he played Artemus Rumm, an old salty sea captain on a fishing boat who supervises a crew of bumbling misfits who become lost at sea. It ran for eight seasons. You can still catch it on cable. It's still funny.

What wasn't so funny was Gus had a crappy agent in Los Angeles and when he signed the contract to do 'HOOKS AHOY!' he made union scale but never saw a dime in re-run residuals. Those kinds of things used to happen all the time in Hollywood, and it's one of the reasons Gus came back to Wildwood, New Jersey when the show had run its course.

Gus was frugal, and of Scotch heritage, saved his money, and had invested well in real estate. By the time 'HOOKS AHOY!' was canceled, Gus had set himself up with a tidy little nest egg, and headed back East.

One of those investments was a broken down old shack of a restaurant he bought in Wildwood, on Rio Grande Avenue, just as you come over the bridge. The place had seen better days back in the thirties, but by the time the seventies rolled around, it was ready for the wrecking ball.

He'd bought the place when it was called *SAL'S ITALIAN GROTTO*, owned by Salvatore Spiotti, a former gangster and bootlegger. Back in those days it has been a hangout for the mob and their families when they came down the shore from Philly or Atlantic City.

Cozy Morley, a popular entertainer on the island, used to joke that if you went to Sal's back in the day and ordered chicken in a basket, when it arrived at your table all the legs would be broken.

After Sal's body was found in Grassy Sound (and his head was found in Margate), the building had gone to hell and eventually Gus bought it. The place still had a speakeasy he loved to brag about and show people after he told a few gangster stories.

(The speakeasy held up better in the stories than in person, though, since now it was only a musty storage area.)

The story was, Gus Harvey, whom everyone called The Captain, high-tailed it out of Hollywood and came right back to where he was born and raised, right in Wildwood New Jersey.

Gus often said Cape May County was his true home, and no matter how far he traveled around the world, the Atlantic Ocean ran through his veins, and Wildwood ran straight through his heart. If he ever left Wildwood again, he'd said, he'd do it in a box.

Gus built a great restaurant business based on great food, personable service and the ability to schmooze his customers. During the heyday years, Gus became known as the happiest man in Wildwood. Even now, in 1985, the restaurant still did decent business, though it never equaled its glory days.

He was involved in the Chamber, gave freely to local charities, and could be counted on to help any local he learned of who was in need, especially fisherman's families.

He knew how hard it was to make a living from the sea, for he had grown up in a fishing family that used to make their meals from the catch they brought in from the waters just off Corsen's Inlet. There were pictures of his family hanging on the walls in the restaurant, in the hallways leading back to the rest rooms, in the booths – everywhere.

There were many old black and white photos of his parents and grandparents and kids and grand-kids fishing, standing next to giant catches on rickety docks, and in general looking like they were enjoying life a helluva lot. Gus had a great family, and he didn't mind letting people know about it.

Gus fixed that old restaurant up and turned it into a famous local eatery, specializing in seafood, of course. He loved kids and families, and always seemed to be in the restaurant, dressed in his trademark sea captain's hat, white boater pants and an anchor-crossed short sleeve light red crew shirt, the same outfit he'd worn on the TV series.

Always good for a joke and a beaming smile, his crinkly old eyes and forever tanned skin were a welcome and familiar site to all who came down the shore each year for their family vacations. He did little magic tricks for the kids and when it was just him and the adults, he could weave a dirty story or two from the blue side of things. Captain Harvey had a bit of the devil in him as well as the angel.

He'd invented all kinds of dishes for the menu, named

after characters from the *'HOOKS AHOY!'* show. There was *Darby's Stroganoff* a hearty noodle casserole dish named after Darby Kincaid, his bungling first mate on the TV show.

There was also the classic favorite *Desiree's Dreamboat Platter*, a seafood combo plate named after Desiree Vance, the busty brunette from the series.

He'd even come up with his own drink called *The Sea Serpent*, a rum concoction that supposedly had eight kinds of booze in it and was served in an oblong glass shaped like a strange mutation that looked like the bastard offspring between a mermaid and a Loch Ness Monster. After a few of those potent cocktails, it was said, a man could get lost at sea without a rudder.

There were special burgers, like the *Ahoy May-tee*, made with three different kinds of cheeses, a triple stacked toasted sourdough bun, and a secret sauce only he knew the recipe for.

Served with a basket of onion rings spiced with sea salt and cayenne pepper, those burgers were the largest on the island, and most people could not finish a whole one at a sitting, so there were always boat-shaped to go boxes brought with each order.

Captain Harvey's Seafood Palace had become an institution in *The Wildwoods*, and by the 1980's, even when the crowds had thinned considerably from most shore eateries, his place was always crowded, even off season.

There was a dock behind the restaurant where people could tie up their boats and come in and have drink or three, or bring in fresh catches of the day, which were immediately put up on the old chalkboard menu, the one with the smiling shark at the top of it.

Sometimes a fisherman would have one too many *Sea Serpents* and forget to untie the ropes on the way out, and on more than one occasion you'd see Gus out there with his toolbox, making yet one more repair to the perpetually damaged dock.

It was a happy place, and it showed.

Well, on about the mid-80's the local newspaper, the *BEACH REPORTER* over in Cape May hired a food critic to write a weekly restaurant review column.

Blemus K. Fritch was a fussy, bespectacled dorky guy in his thirties, wore polyester suits with a signature polka dotted bow tie. He'd come down to Cape May from New York after being canned by the New York Times.

He'd left New York on the heels of a messy scandal involving a gay accountant, the details of which were rather sordid and unpleasant, after which the shamed food critic had left The Big Apple for more sedate shores.

Up to that time, however, he was one of the most feared culinary writers in New York, such was his ability to slash and burn with the fire of his criticisms and to lay ruin to the financial fortunes of many a local restaurateur.

He curried the favor of the dining establishment as such fear had garnered a grudging respect, accompanied by continuous perks and gifts of graft. Free meals and drink were an expectation at whatever eatery he chose to park himself, and woe onto thee any waiter or waitress unlucky enough to be at his beck and call at such a sitting.

As was the respect given to gangsters and Third World Country dictators, it was a falsely based and ill-gotten regard, one which Blemus K. *Fritch* relished with all the glee of a schoolyard bully. He'd moved to Cape May, renting an efficiency apartment, and had landed a gig writing the food column for the local paper.

Fritch was a rather odd bird, a moody, opinionated man, now at odds and quite bitter at the hand of cards he felt life had dealt him. He made his living selling his biased opinions as fact, sold to gossip-starved people who could not think for themselves, and had carved out a dubious niche in the field of food criticism.

He was given free reign of his assignments, as per his contractual demand with the *CAPE MAY BEACH REPORTER*, and upon arrival, had asked locals to recommend to him restaurants of interest.

He'd heard favorable things about Captain Harvey's, but had hated *'HOOKS AHOY!'* as escapist drivel, and felt Harvey may have been unfairly capitalizing on his Hollywood fame with a seafood-themed restaurant.

Setting out to establish himself as a force to be feared and reckoned with, to become the same feared critic and defender of the taste of the restaurant going public as he used to occupy in New York, he set out to write a scathing review almost immediately from the time his bags were unpacked.

He set his sights on Captain Harvey's Seafood Palace.

* * *

The night that Blemus K. Fritch walked into Captain Harvey's Seafood Palace, nobody recognized him. He entered like any other customer, waited at the hostess podium for a table, then escorted to a corner booth overlooking the Rio Grand harbor.

Once seated, he was handed a menu. "Your waitress will be Susie, and she'll be right with you," Monique said, a bouncy nineteen year-old working the early hostess shift. Fritch didn't look up, merely sniffed with pompous self-importance as he slid into a booth.

The night was a slow one by normal standards. There were only a few people at the bar, and several scattered couples were seated in the main dining room. Gus Harvey had seen Fritch walk in, but didn't know him.

He ambled up to the fussy little man, who was staring over his spectacles at the menu, barely raising an eyebrow when the old salt stopped at this booth, extending his pink, meaty hand.

"Ahoy, may-tee! Welcome to Captain Harvey's Seafood Palace, where the fish is fresh as caught and dissatisfaction is naught!"

Fritch peered over his spectacles at him, regarding him as an elephant might regard a mosquito.

"We'll see about that," Fritch intimated, ignoring regarding Gus's extended hand. "And you are...?"

"Gus Harvey. You can call me Captain!," Gus said, never missing a beat, his smile wide. He kept his hand extended. As an afterthought, Fritch gave him a limp handshake. A glint of recognition came over Fritch. "I know who you are," Fritch said, "you're the owner. The one from the TV show..."

"Right you are, Mister....?"

"Fritch. Blemus K. Fritch."

"Well I'm mighty pleased to meet you! I hope you enjoy your meal here, Mister Kitsch As I said, everything is good on the menu!"

"Yes.... so you say. Good day. Mister Harvey."

"Captain!" bellowed Gus, still smiling ear to ear.

"Yes. So it is," Fritch said, disparagingly, looking back down at the menu.

A small-framed mousy girl arrived with a glass of ice water on a tray, and placed it in front of Fritch.

"My name is Susie, I'll be your server today," she said cheerfully.

Kitsch looked up at her over his spectacles. "Young lady, when I'm ready to order I will summon you."

Both Susie and Gus stopped in mid-smile at the miserable specimen of a man before them. Monique stepped up behind Gus and whispered sweetly in his ear; "May speak to you a moment, Gus?"

Gus Harvey bowed gracefully toward Blemus K. Fritch and said "If you'll excuse me, I must take a call. Enjoy your dinner Mister Fritch."

"I hope for your sake, I do... *Captain*," he added icily, for emphasis.

Once out of earshot of Fritch Monique said "Gus, do you know who that is? It's that nasty food critic from New York. He's writing for The Reporter now. He's here to do a hatchet job on us!"

"A food critic? Is that so?" intoned Gus softly, his eyes

warm, "once he tastes the culinary delights we have here at Captain Harvey's, there will be no way he could give us anything but a positive review!"

Monique looked worried.

"I hope you're right, Gus!"

"You just make sure he's well taken care of. I'll head back to the kitchen and make sure Igby knows he's cooking for royalty!"

He turned to Susie, walking past him with a forced smile, "Just to be safe, bring him a *Sea Serpent*, on the house!"

As Gus disappeared into the kitchen, Monique walked to the hostess station, stealing glances over at Fritch but she seemed no less convinced. She turned and saw the smiling shark over the chalkboard menu. It seemed like it was taunting her.

When Susie brought Fritch the complimentary drink, he waved it away. "I don't drink. It dulls the taste buds," he said, and looked back down at the menu. "I'll start with the clam chowder bisque," he said, and a basket of the house onion rings."

He snapped the menu shut with the flick of his wrist, handing it up to Susie without looking at her. He pulled a notebook encased in black leather out of his bag, and produced a ball point pen that looked like a piece of fine silver jewelry. Clicking the pen, he began to write.

When the soup and onion rings arrived, Fritch made a show of shaking out the linen table napkin and placing it on his lap with a flourish.

Gus and Igby stared through the crack of the kitchen

door, one head above the other, watching Fritch.

"Jeez, the guy has a way, don't he?" Igby said in his trademark Jersey accent, a cross between Joe Pesci and The Three Stooges.

"Shut up! He's about to taste the bisque!" The Captain hissed, and both men held their breath in baited anticipation the reaction of the fussy critic as he carefully lifted a spoon full of the white, frothy soup to his lips.

Once he had done so, Fritch placed his head back, swishing the soup around in his mouth as a fine wine taster might, then swallowed ever so slowly. He waited a second or two, his eyes squinted tight, then, opening his eyes once again, reached down, picked up the pen and made a few notations in the notebook.

"I know I should have put more garlic in it!" snapped Igby.

"Quiet! He's about to taste the onion rings!"

Fritch picked up one of the golden brown crispy rings, turning it in his hand, then holding it up to the light. He then pulled a jewelers manacle from his top pocket, placed it in his eye socket, and examined the texture of the ring carefully.

"Holy mackerels," Igby whispered, "this guy's gung-ho."

"Zip it!" hissed the Captain, "He's about to taste one!"

Fritch placed the manacle on the table beside him and bit off a piece of the onion ring, slowly savoring the tender yet crispy morsel, that for most people would about now have resulted in an explosion of zingy flavor and oniony goodness.

Fritch stopped in mid-chew, his nose in the air, as if trying to discern an unfamiliar scent, then slowly and deliberately swallowed the remainder of the onion ring. He picked up his pen with his other, grease-free hand and notoriously jotted more notes in his notebook.

"He hates it!" cried Igby.

"You don't know that," snapped the Captain, "he may be concealing his enthusiasm."

"I've got friends that work in A.C, Igby warned, "this guy hates everything. He's closed down restaurants with one review."

"Don't jump to conclusions," the Captain said, just a small amount of doubt trickling into his voice. "It's not over till the fat lady sings."

"I think the fat lady is already dead!," Igby lamented, then disappeared inside the kitchen with a scowl.

The Captain took one last look at Fritch about to eat another onion ring, and joined Igby back inside the kitchen, a little less spring in his normally bouncy step. Out in the restaurant, Fritch ate another onion ring and signaled his waitress with the flick of his wrist. Waiting in the wings, Susie approached cautiously.

"How is everything?"

"How 'everything is' will come out in my column in due time, young lady, " Fritch said menacingly, without cracking even the hint of a smile. "Now bring me the house special, and be quick about it."

"Yes sir!" Susie said, and made a run for the kitchen

By the time Blemus K. Fritch had finished his meal and gotten the final check, the restaurant staff was a collective nervous wreck. Even Captain Harvey, normally a pillar of positivism and jovial hospitality, found himself becoming paranoid.

As *Fritch* paid his check, leaving the waitress no tip as he pushed the little plastic check tray at Susie using the exact change for his meal, Captain Harvey made one more attempt at friendliness.

"I hope everything was to your satisfaction," Gus tried, "And that your experience at Captain Harvey's of Wildwood was a pleasant one."

"We will see, Mister Harvey, we will see. When my review runs this weekend the world will know the truth about this establishment, you can be sure of that."

There was menacing and intrigue in his voice, his stiletto manner even causing the shark to frown.

"Good day, Mister Harvey!"

And with that, Blemus K. Fritch turned on his heel and exited the restaurant in a huff of conceited self-importance.

* * *

That night, as his wife of twenty five years of marriage slept soundly beside him, Gus tossed and turned. He was having nightmares. In one episode he was followed by Blemus K. Fritch but the man's face and head had transformed into a shark's head, and, with teeth bared in its angry snout, was chasing him down the Wildwood boardwalk.

In another dream he was he was driving to his restaurant and when he arrived, rusty chains blocked access to the parking lot, and a swinging sign had been attached: *OUT OF BUSINESS*.

As much as he tried, Gus could not get the thoughts of Blemus K. Fritch out of his mind. Why would someone pick on him like this? He was an honest man, he paid his taxes. He was a shining pillar of the community. He'd even given to the March of Dimes, for goddsakes, why was *he* being singled out?

He knew once the negative review ran, it was only going to be a matter of time before his business would fail. He was sure the bad review would result in diminishing crowds. He would be forced to close down.

Bill collectors would harass him and his family. He'd become the laughingstock of Cape May County. He would be the butt of Cozy Morley's jokes!

How could he sit idly by and let someone take away his livelihood?

Gus quietly got out of bed, stepping into his slippers. Being careful not to awaken Gertrude, who was snoring soundly with her head full of dreams and curlers, he tiptoed to the closet and got dressed without a sound.

Gus stepped out into the humid summer air. It was still and silent as a midnight graveyard. He jumped into his car and drove the dark streets down Atlantic Avenue, then cut over to the bridge and pointed the old Impala toward Cape May.

The sky would normally have been lit by a full moon, but tonight it was hazy and warm, the inland fog drifting in off the Atlantic, making visibility low. When he finally got to Cape May, he took Main Street and cruised along the scenic streets past the old restored Victorians and turn-of-the-century architecture.

Over the past week, he'd tried to reach Fritch at the paper, but the critic hadn't been in. When the girl who answered the phone asked to take a message, Gus told her, "No thanks," as if even then his subconscious had started to premeditate a plan.

All I want to do is talk to him, Gus thought, *let him know how important it was that he not publish a bad review. It could ruin me,* Gus thought, seeing himself pleading with an unreasonable Fritch. It made him feel weaker and in less control than he already was.

Don't let your imagination run away with you, Gus thought, as he drove the damp salty streets, looking for the Mercedes that matched the unmistakable color and style of the one Fritch had driven away in the restaurant parking lot earlier that week.

As Gus drove, he caught a glimpse of himself in the rear view mirror, his eyes wild and paranoid. *My God,* Gus thought, *I look like a madman.* What surprised him more than that was his own answer: *Maybe you are!*

Gus's mind turned like an angry paddle-boat wheel through the dark river of his thoughts. *I've worked so long and hard to get where I am... What will my family do? What if we have to move out into the street? What will the community say?*

These thoughts ceased immediately when Gus spotted the powder blue Mercedes, parked in the parking lot of the Soaring Gull Apartments, just two blocks from the beach off of Surf Avenue.

Gus drove around the block twice, then slowly cruised by the apartment building.

He glanced up at the windows which looked out over the

ocean. Only one bore the sign of any kind of life, a bright light on inside, a semi-shadow moving across a faded yellow blind.

Gus parked a block down the street, wondering why his own actions were so calculated, so careful. *All I want to do is talk with the man,* he reasoned, *why not just park in front and announce his presence for anyone to see?*

But he did not want to think about the answer to that question, not as he silently parked the Impala. He slipped quietly from the car and loped toward the side entrance to the apartment house, making sure he was not seen.

Ocean breakers crashed in the distance. On a clear night, he knew far off in the distance on the sea, he would see the tiny shimmering lights of fishing boats far off in the dark water – but tonight there was only fog.

Once inside the apartment building, Gus made his way quietly up the wide, ancient stairs. Most of the renters had left for the season, by the looks of the few cars in the parking area.

Just a few hangers on after Labor Day, why, he and Fritch would practically have the place to themselves. A stair creaked as he ascended up the dark staircase, and he stopped, not breathing. Silence. Apparently nobody had heard him. *Where was the landlady,* Gus thought. *Probably asleep.*

Gus stealthily walked down the narrow hallway on the second floor, toward the room with the window light he'd seen on from the street below.

He stopped and listened.

He could hear the low soothing sounds of classical music

from the end of the hallway. Creeping to the end of the hall, he pressed his ear to an old oak door, polished to a fine finish, a steel '9' hanging like a question mark on the door. He heard the strains of music coming from inside, and the sound of rustling.

Someone was inside.

Fritch!

He tapped lightly on the door and waited, holding his breath.

"Yes? Who is it?" came the timid voice of Blemus K. Fritch from behind the door.

"It's Captain Harvey. Gus Harvey, from the restaurant."

There was a pause, there was more rustling, then slowly, the door opened a crack, revealing a latch security chain. Fritch peered out from the crack of the door over his spectacles.

"What do you want?" Fritch asked.

"I was wondering if I could have a word with you, Mister Fritch. It's about the restaurant. If you could spare of few moments of your time, I have something I need to discuss with you."

Fritch thought about it for a few seconds, trying to size him up, not sure how to read him. But the Captain was smiling, he seemed friendly enough.

"Very well," snapped Fritch "but let's make it fast, it's late and I have a deadline tomorrow."

Fritch shut the door, slid the chain out of it's track and opened the door wide to admit a smiling Gus Harvey.

Gus looked around the apartment. It was meticulously clean. Fritch had everything laid out neatly, even his clothes for the next day were hanging neatly on a closet door, with a new pair of ironed black dress socks draped with the creased pressed slacks pants and a polished belt.

There was nothing out of order. Fritch kept a clean ship, that was for sure.

Fritch waved him with disdain toward a chair pushed in beneath a small round antique table.

"May I offer you a seat? Something to drink, perhaps?" Fritch asked coldly, in an obligatory manner which suggested insincerity, as he turned down the music.

"No thank you," Gus said, wringing his hands nervously, "I'll make this brief."

"I certainly hope so."

"Mister Fritch as you know my family and I have run Captain Gus's Seafood Palace for many years now. We pride ourselves on a quality dining experience at reasonable prices," he cleared his throat nervously. "I would just hope your review of our fine establishment would be honest and fair."

"I don't think I understand what you're suggesting. Why wouldn't my reviews be anything but fair?" his tone was sarcastic, playing on Gus's fears like a cat with a mouse.

Gus felt a twinge of anger.

"Your reputation as somewhat of a shark proceeds you. Some of your reviews have resulted in putting entire restaurants out to pasture."

An amused smile seemed to cross Fritch's lips as he paced back and forth in front of the red-faced Captain.

"So let me get this straight, you're here to make sure you get a favorable review?"

"I suppose I am here to see if the review you are writing is honest and fair, and that it reflects the quality and reputation we've managed to uphold in the community for many years."

"What might such a review be worth to you, Captain, in terms of dollars?"

Gus could hardly believe his ears. He was being blackmailed by this rat-faced boy, who belonged in a circus somewhere, not writing hatchet pieces on good restaurants.

"Dollars?"

"You heard me, Captain. Dollars. Hard dollars and cents. That's how it worked in New York. I would imagine that it's a language we can learn to talk here. A good review is money in the bank. A bad review means you and your family might as well pack it up and move to Camden."

In the split second that it took for the word *Camden* to register, Captain Harvey dove with both hands straight for Fritch's throat, propelling him backward into the closet door.

Fritch struggled violently to get free, but was little match for the considerably stronger and heavier Gus Harvey, who was now seated on the small man's chest, squeezing his throat with every bit of strength he could muster.

As he choked him, Harvey looked down into the wide open eyes of Blemus K. Fritch – whose face was turning blue, his eyes like giant marbles magnified by the myopic thick lenses of his spectacles.

No words were exchanged between the two men, only the grunts and groans of expended strength, the heavy, crazed breathing of Gus Harvey, and the crushing of Blemus K Fritch's windpipe.

When his struggling ceased, Fritch lay dead on the floor, silent but for the tiny gurgling sounds in his throat as Gus Harvey released him.

There were only the faint strains of *Beethoven's Fifth Symphony* playing as Gus sat for several minutes trying to regain his composure.

* * *

Gus Harvey slipped through the side exit of the boarding house into the crisp night air, acutely aware of everything around him. He was shaking, almost near shock.

He'd searched Fritch's apartment and found the review, typed on three neatly double spaced pages in a kitchen counter drawer. He did not read it, he simply folded it and placed it in his pocket and got the hell out of there.

He was not a violent man, in the normal sense. He was a man who controlled his emotions. Yet when placed in a situation that he felt threatened his financial survival, he had squeezed the life out of another man. He doubled over and threw up into the bushes, wiping his mouth on his shirt.

His hands were shaking as he inserted his key into the ignition, and sat with the motor running, looking out through the windshield at the distant breakers, a light wind coming in off the ocean. Barely able to keep his hands steady and the butterflies in his stomach from beating steel wings against his insides, he drove up Surf Avenue, following the signs to the Garden State Parkway.

Once home, Gus padded into the bedroom and looked over at the dark snoring figure laying beneath a heap of blankets. Gertrude was still in dreamland, and had likely not awoken the entire time he had been gone.

Inside the closet, he slipped into his pajamas, trying to steady his nerves. He wished fervently for a drink; he took long deep breaths, switched off the closet light, went to the bed and climbed beneath the covers.

It would take him hours before he fell asleep, and when he did, all he could see in his nightmares was the horrific face of Blemus K. Fritch in the throes of death, his face bloated and white, his eyes bulging from their sockets.

* * *

The morning's newspaper contained nothing of any murder, nor any body found.

Gus Harvey guessed it would be till at least noon or later when the landlady or maid would eventually gain access to the room and discover the body lying face up, just where Gus had left him.

"How did you sleep?" Gus asked Gertrude, who, with curlers in her hair and bathrobe half tied, looked like she'd been hit with a truck and dragged down forty miles of bad road.

"Like a log," she said, and lit up a cigarette, then, forgetting it, let it burn in the ashtray.

Gus acted as if nothing had happened, but he was dying inside. He dreaded going into the restaurant and waiting for the news of the death of Blemus K. Fritch to be announced.

"Orange juice?" Gertrude interrupted his thoughts, and Gus waved her away. "No thanks, my stomach is not feeling great," he said, and put down the paper. "I'm going into the restaurant early today, I have invoices to do."

"Alright," answered Gertrude, pouring herself a coffee. "Say hello to everyone for me."

Gus showered and shaved and dressed quickly.

Within minutes he was on his way to the restaurant, heading across the bridge into North Wildwood from Stone Harbor.

It was a cloudy morning. The seagulls circled overheard, doing concentric passes over the few fishing boats docked in the harbor. As Gus approached the toll-booth, he looked over at the man seated patiently in the small enclosure, a man he'd seen many times before, and in fact knew well. It was Clancy Dennison, a man who'd worked the bridge for years.

Something was different this morning.

As Gus stopped to pay the toll, the small windowed door was closed, but he could see in. Seated inside the booth, looking dead ahead into the harbor was the ghostly figure of Blemus K. Fritch his face bloated and swollen, eyes bugged out of their sockets.

Gus's heart stopped in his chest, and it felt like the highway were opening below him. *This can't be,* he thought, *you're supposed to be dead.*

Suddenly the toll-booth door slipped open and the stone-cold face of Clancy Dennison peered out, his rough, big hand extended, and a look of recognition on his face brought a half-smile as he saw the horrified, disbelieving face of Gus Harvey.

"Hi Captain. Looks like rain today," he offered. All Gus

could do is stare. Clancy Dennison's eyes narrowed.

"You okay? You look like you seen a ghost."

For Gus, the rest of the day didn't go much better. He tried to look busy at the restaurant, working at his small desk behind a stack of liquor boxes in the old speakeasy, but all he could think about was what he had seen in the tollbooth going over Grassy Sound Bridge.

It was not until that evening the news broke that Blemus K. Fritch's body was found at the *Sleepy Sea Gull Apartments,* cause of death undetermined. Police speculated that suicide might be the cause, but homicide was not being ruled out, according to the Philadelphia News report.

Gus watched the news report seated at the bar, on the small color TV that played above the old sea netting and shell decorations. Nursing a beer, Gus was somewhat relieved the body had been found, but he knew it was just a matter of time before he would be questioned.

The police visited just before eight that evening, accompanied by a short, squat detective named Hastings.

Two uniformed police officers from the New Jersey State Police walked in first, introduced themselves to the Monique, where she pointed toward Gus sitting at the bar. Gus walked over to greet them in his best forced smile.

The taller cop addressed Gus directly.

"Mister Harvey, we understand you might have some information regarding the death of Blemus Fritch. Our detective, Wally Hastings will be here in a moment to ask you some questions. In the meantime, do you mind if we have a look around?"

"I just learned of the most unfortunate demise of Mister Fritch and I'd be happy to answer any questions the detective may have," Gus said, and as he did, he saw the diminutive figure of the detective walking through the foyer of the restaurant, a short, intense man with an inquisitive bent, which fit his vocation.

He approached Gus, did not extend his hand, but flashed a badge and tattered ID card from an old weathered billfold. The photo looked at least thirty years old, for the bright eyed young man in the picture looked nothing like the grizzled specimen which stood before him.

"Mister Harvey," Hastings began, snapping the billfold shut and placing in in his side pants pocket, "Please, Gus," The Captain replied, my friends call me Gus."

"I'd recognize you anywhere, Mister Harvey," the detective said, "from that TV show, what was it? Chips Ahoy?"

"Hooks Ahoy," Gus corrected.

"Pardon? My hearing is kind of bad."

"Hooks Ahoy, the TV show was called Hooks Ahoy."

"So it was. I'd love to get an autograph, I'm a big fan."

Gus could tell that Hastings must have seen a lot of old Columbo reruns.

"I'd be happy to sign a photo for you, Detective. But I'm afraid I won't be much help to you regarding this Finch gentleman."

"Blemus K. Fritch" Hastings corrected, reading from his notepad.

"Yes, *Fritch*."

"This guy had a lot of enemies," Hastings said, "Apparently

had come down from New York with quite a reputation for putting restaurants out of business."

"I didn't know that," Gus lied, "He seemed like a likable fellow to me."

"Very few others thought so. In fact, his editor told me he was working on doing a review on your place."

"Yes, he was here yesterday, we served him one of our excellent meals and sent him on his way. I'm sure the review would have been glowing."

"The review was very favorable. Unusual for him."

"Pardon me?" said Gus, his heart in his throat.

"The review he wrote on your restaurant. The editor of the paper said it was very favorable. It's supposed to run this weekend. His editor said its the least he could do to honor his memory."

"That's impossible!"

"What's impossible?"

"That he wrote a review, that it would run--"

"I don't see why. Apparently he'd faxed the review in from the landlady's fax machine just a few hours before he was found dead."

Gus was dumbfounded. His blood circulation created the sensation of honeybees buzzing through his system.

He felt faint.

"Anyway," Hastings continued, "Did Fritch say anything to you when he was here that might give us a clue as to what happened to him? Did he seem scared, did he say people were after him, anything like that?"

"No, Detective, he said nothing of the sort," Gus

answered, regaining his composure, "He simply said he was looking forward to writing a favorable review of our fine establishment, then he was gone."

Hastings stared a long moment at Gus.

"Yes," Hastings said wryly, "then he was gone."

Hastings held his gaze a second too long on Gus, then, snapped his notepad shut.

"That's all for now, Mister Harvey. We may need you to make statement as we get further into the investigation. If that's okay."

Gus escorted Hastings to the front entrance.

"Anything I can do to help," Gus implored, please don't hesitate to call."

"Here's my card," Hastings said. "Call me if you think of anything else. "

"I will Mister Hastings, I will."

Gus watched Hastings walk slowly across the parking lot, absorbed in thought. Just then, Hastings turned around.

"Oh! One more thing!"

"Yes, what is it, Detective?"

"Could I get that autographed photo now?"

* * *

The days and nights to follow seemed to crawl by for Gus; his days were spent waiting and wondering when Hastings was going to question him again. His nights were restless with thoughts of Fritch; what sleep he did get was plagued by recurring nightmares.

He'd opened the safe in his closet where he'd locked

Fritch's folded papers and read with shocked disbelief the glowing reviews given his restaurant.

The headline at the top of the sheet, typed in all capitals, read:

WILDWOOD EATERY IS THE CAPTAIN OF BEACH SEAFOOD RESTURANTS

It went on to praise the culinary virtues of his establishment, with glowing testimony from the critic on the excellent quality, prices and service he'd experienced there.

In only a matter of days, the review would be published and distributed all along the shore points, as far north as Barnegat Light and even in places as far South as Delaware.

Guilt rode his conscience without end. The sightings weren't making things any easier. On three more separate occasions, while fully awake and in the middle of the day, he'd seen the bloated, ghostly image of Blemus K. Fritch. The ghost's neck was swollen and had purple veins running through it.

One of the sightings was while stopped at the traffic light at Lincoln and Atlantic Avenues, an old lady pushing a shopping cart was crossing the street, her head covered by a scarf, her face obscured.

As she walked in front of Gus's car, she turned toward him – and it was the face of a rotting corpse, half eaten away from rot but still recognizable as what was left of the face of Blemus K. Fritch.

In another incident, Gus had driven up to North Wildwood, parked in the dirt lot of Moore's Inlet and stepped precariously across the breaker rocks, watching the ocean, to try and clear his head.

There, standing on the beach, an old fisherman casting his line in the water turned toward him and again, it was the face of a skeleton, a grotesque grinning skull that bore a striking resemblance to Blemus K. Fritch.

On another occasion, Gus had gone grocery shopping at Acme Market and was pushing his cart down the frozen food aisle when he saw a young man walking away from him with a carry basket. From behind the man appeared to be Blemus K. Fritch.

Gus ran down the aisle and turned to follow him, but when the man turned, startled, it was someone else.

Gus was mess. He was not eating right, he was losing weight. Gertrude was worried about him.

Something had to give.

That weekend, the review ran in THE CAPE MAY BEACH REPORTER, and all hell broke loose. Even off season, the restaurant had to hire extra staff just to keep up with the crowds which now flocked to his door.

One Wednesday night, with a full house, Gus sat at the bar nursing a beer, and talked with Walt, an old timer who had been his bartender since he'd opened. Walt had worked all the big places in town over the years, Kellys.. Delaneys.. Zaberers..

Walt leaned over, propped himself on his elbows on the bar, and looked right into Gus's face.

"Listen boss, you don't look so good. You need to take a day or two off. Take a walk on the beach. Go to Atlantic City. Roll some dice. Do something other than worry, for chrissakes. This place can survive without you a few days. "

"Walt, I can't get over what happened to Fritch. It bugs me."

"Unless you were the one who killed him, I wouldn't shed any sea-salt over it," Walt croaked, "I got friends he put out of work. He ruined a lot of guys and wrecked more than a few families. Don't cry no tears for that *shmoe*," he said, and went to wash the beer glasses.

Deep in thought, Gus finished his beer and walked out to the parking lot.

Getting into the Impala, he drove over the bridge into Rio Grand, the empty closed up shops and broken down strip mall zipping slowly past him. The sun was going down over the bay, a golden light bathing the ancient Sound like melting honey.

He'd turned the car around to go back over the bridge when he caught a glimpse in his rear-view mirror of the man sitting in the backseat. It was pale, ghostly image of Blemus K. Fritch.

Missing the stoplight, Gus Harvey sailed across the intersection, sideswiping a delivery van, then skidded into a utility pole.

When Gus came to consciousness, the delivery van driver was at his window.

"You okay mister?" The man looked more scared than Gus did.

Gus climbed out of the car, dazed. He examined the damage, which was minimal. A fender bender. The driver informed him there was no damage to the truck.

"You scared the bejessus outta me running that light,"

the man said "watch where your going before somebody gets killed," he scowled, and sauntered across the street to his van.

Gus got back in his car and shut the door, taking a deep breath. He looked in his rear view mirror. The back seat was empty.

* * *

Gus drove slowly and methodically onto Route 47, then got on the Garden State Parkway going South. His mind was in turmoil.

He saw himself being led to an electric chair by uniformed guards.

He got off the last exit, the one the locals called Exit Zero.

He drove through the empty streets of Cape May, past the building where he'd killed Fritch. *He deserved to die*, an inner voice kept telling him, but his conscience would not let it go.

After what seemed like hours of deliberation, he pointed the Lexus toward the police station.

He parked in the police station parking lot and sat there for a long time, not moving. His mind raced as he played back memories of scenes from a life well lived. A life marred by one mistake that, in the heat of passion, had changed things forever.

Gus steeled his nerves, then took a long deep breath. He pulled the keys from the ignition.

He looked up and fixed his gaze on the stone steps that led up to the entrance of the municipal building.

What about Gertrude? Did she deserve to be without her husband, left alone to run the restaurant? His thoughts were ablaze with recrimination and guilt.

He began the short walk to the entrance of the police station.

Those would be his final steps of freedom.

Showdown In Anglesea

I'll lay it out as best as I can recall, but if it didn't actually happen the way I remember it, don't take me to task on it. I'm scribbling it out longhand on yellow legal pads, so bear with me. Yeah, my handwriting is lousy, but it's also because my hands shake every time I think about it.

So here goes.

Seamus McShane's Irish Pub stood like a ghostly sentinel through the haze and icy mist of the salty fog drifting in off Hereford's Inlet in Anglesea. A lone sodium-vapor streetlamp high atop an ancient wooden pole cast a sickly amber hue over Wildwood, New Jersey's buildings and streets.

It was the only light out there but for the single blinking yellow traffic light that hung over the crossroads that lead to two dead end streets and the sea. It cast shadows in places you didn't want to look.

A late February night, goddamm cold. Visibility was low; even the year-round old timers who usually walked here from their small bay-side bungalows had stayed in for the night. It was the kind of setting where bad things happen, but you always think of that in hindsight, when it's too damn late.

It was the perfect location for an Irish Pub. An old clapboard Victorian converted to a down-and-dirty bar that had been there since the Civil War. Wildwood locals always teased Old Seamus, about what a toilet his place was, but for down-home comfort and hassle-free escape, you just couldn't beat the place, and with beers for a buck nobody was complaining.

Old Seamus lived upstairs. He'd been there for as long as anyone could remember. It seemed like he was always in the bar or behind it, either nursing a tall Guinness at a table in the corner, or limping back and forth behind the bar. He always kept his tattered old sea captain hat on crooked. More often times than not his right eye would start to twitching; presumably from the foxhole incident I'd heard had happened to him when he was fighting gooks in Korea.

I'm a man of few words and usually kept to myself, but that night I'd decided to spend my evening soaking up the local color, which is a nice way of saying I was going to get loaded on Bushmills at a place where nobody knew my name.

Old Seamus was having none of that. His friendliness always contagious, he introduced himself and gave a brief history of the place. Before long we were getting along like a coupla monkeys in a barrel.

Old Seamus was behind the bar that night, since his regular bartender, Clancy Yarborough had called in sick. There was only one other person in the place, a skinny guy named Andy O' Halloran, also a local.

Seamus limped out from behind the bar and pushed the bar stool to the side and propped his bad leg up on the kick rail, like he owned the place, which in fact, he did. He knocked back a shot, grimacing through his thick white beard. His splotchy face was a road map of broken red on a lunar terrain of bone white, twisted up in a mask that somehow revealed both pain and delight.

His eyes were sunk back in his head. You didn't have to look that close at Old Seamus to see hardship there, like a ship lost at sea. Somebody said he'd taken one in the chest in Korea. He'd earned a Purple Heart after he climbed out of a foxhole with his rifle and shot four of the enemy point blank while two grenades exploded on either side of him.

Shrapnel had pierced his left eye and his right leg. The explosion from the hand frags left him with partial hearing in his right ear. Rumor had it his body was scarred and pitted from conflicts of various kinds, not all of them from the military, and I was curious about it, I'll admit. I wasn't asking and he wasn't telling.

Local talk was Old Seamus could hold his own in a bar fight. He told me he didn't believe in bouncers; if he couldn't handle any conflicts in his own place he had no business owning one. I know one thing, he was twice my age, and I wouldn't tangle with him.

McShane's was decorated in a combination of early Civil War, old world Irish, and Northeast Philly sleaze. It was a quaint, earthy establishment and they didn't serve food for chrissakes; if one wanted to get juiced cheaply without judgment, Old Seamus's was the place. It smelled of whiskey and old wood.

A while back a few guys I met at another nearby bar, Cozy's, had told me Seamus kept two old Civil War dueling pistols in an antique box behind the bar. If a fight broke out Seamus would separate the two men [or sometimes women, as the case may be] and pull out the box to give the disagreement more perspective.

Once presented with the pistols, the two parties would often laugh at the absurdity of their disagreement, shake hands, and become friends. Even if fisticuffs weren't a particular troublemaker's cup of tea, Seamus kept those pistols as a "conversation starter," but I think it was more to discourage dissent before it started.

There was a jukebox that sat in the corner but it never looked like it belonged there. It was a classic '61 Seeburg that played 45rpm records – if you can imagine that now. It was playing Irish folk songs, which is all McShane would put on it.

On that particular night, Andy O'Halloran was throwing darts at a weathered old Guinness beer target that had seen better days. Along the back wall was one of those bowling pin slider games with half its lights out, flashing like a sinking ship.

Anyways, that was the setting the night I'd gone in and by nine-thirty I'd gotten on a fairly decent buzz when the front door opened and a shudder of icy air swept in. Back-lit by that hazy amber eye of a streetlamp behind him, framing the door, a tall, commanding man in a long blue duster coat stood in that doorway, the collar flipped high.

He just stood there, as if for effect as his steely gaze drifted over the empty bar. I was reminded of sepia-toned pictures I'd seen from the Civil War, 'cept now I was seeing it in color and the picture was a real guy. He reminded me of Eastwood in one of them spaghetti movies.

There was something otherworldly and creepy about this character. The long coat and shiny gold buttons only added to the mystery. The cap he wore on his head was even more curious, but I'll get to that in a minute. He had white hair, long and slicked back, like a riverboat gambler. His white beard was full and well-groomed, and he carried himself with the a cadence of confidence and the smoothness of a ladies man. His eyes seemed to see everywhere at once, and in his sharp features you could see history. He reminded me of Ulysses S. Grant, 'cept with a white beard.

Old Seamus, who usually never batted an eyelid when someone walked into his pub, turned around in mid-sentence and looked at the imposing figure standing in the doorway. The guy in the long duster sported a dagger look that said there might be trouble. I didn't want to stare too long. I turned back around and watched the odd man's reflection in the mirror behind the bar.

The ominous-looking man strode across the dusty wooden floor with purpose, a strong steady stride that almost passed for swagger, but fell just short of hubris. He looked around, the ceilings, the walls – taking it all in, the corners of his mouth turned up in a half-smile bordering on amusement.

He walked to the bar and took the Confederate blue cap off. The cap was unusual in that it had a small bronze fixture sewn to it, crossed rifles. He laid the cap on the bar.

His boots were polished and new, his uniform pressed and elegant. But there was something off center about him, something I couldn't quite place, like a puzzle piece that didn't quite fit. Dressed like that, I figured him on being either crazy or maybe a civil war buff. Maybe both.

"I like what you've done with the place, McShane," he said, without even looking at Old Seamus," he paused for effect, not looking at us – or the mirror. He just spoke into the air.

"I'll take a whiskey," he said sharply, like he meant it. There was an edge of danger to his words, but then he added "...if you would be so kind." With a small wisp of a smile, he pulled the bar stool out and sat. He stared straight ahead. I found that odd. I got the feeling he knew something we didn't.

Gave me the willies, that's what it did.

Old Seamus looked at the man in the mirror, and even though his poker face rarely gave away his emotions, the Irishman looked truly perplexed at this moment. His bad eye twitched furiously. I could see his wheels turning – where had he met this man before?

Certainly a character of this curious nature would have stood out in his memory, no matter how many years ticked by. But he was drawing a blank. He turned to face the man, extending his hand.

"I don't think I've had the pleasure, Mister...?"

"The names Judson. Noah Judson," the man said, but didn't turn and never accepted Old Seamus's handshake.

"Have we met?" Old Seamus asked, pulling his hand back like he'd been bitten by a sea snake. His mind was swimming in the darkness for something, anything that would trigger his stalled memory.

Too many shots, too many drinks over the years could make a man fuzzy, I thought.

Judson simply looked forward in that faraway gaze, saying nothing. For a long silence, nobody said anything, and it felt so damn awkward I was ready to get up and go to the can, even though I didn't have to. But I didn't want to miss anything.

I sipped my whiskey, trying to make it last. This guy had me puzzled. It was too late for Halloween, and the boardwalk was closed for the season. Why would he be dressed up in this outfit on a night like this? Was the VFW planning a parade in the middle of the winter?

Not one to indulge semantics, Old Seamus went back behind the bar and poured a whiskey, serving the man, trying to ignore his blue uniform. Judson knocked back the shot in one motion, slammed the shot glass on the counter and asked for another.

"I'm from the South," he said smiling, then added "... South Philadelphia. Hit me again."

Old Seamus laughed, we all chuckled nervously. O'Halloran kept throwing darts at the target and missing. Old Seamus kept pouring them, and Judson kept drinking them. Last I remember he'd downed at least six shots, let out a loud belch, then farted.

He also asked for some kind of beer that Old Seamus didn't have – but was soon washing those whiskeys down with warm Guinness, and not looking none to happy about it. Apparently he was from a South much farther South than Philly, for the Irish tradition of warm Guinness didn't seem to be settling well with him, by the sound and smell of things.

The conversation twisted and turned through history. I didn't understand a helluva lot of it, I flunked history in high school so what I knew I'd learned from television and movies.

By the time the two men had gotten into the subject of the Civil War, it was clear each of them stood on two different sides of opinion. As the hour wore on, so did their agitated state increase, and before too long, Old Seamus was asking Judson to take his leave.

Turns out that Seamus's kin had fought in the Civil War, from right here in New Jersey – and though Old Seamus believed all men were created equal and always gave everyone a fair shake in his bar, agitators and rebel-rousers were always asked to take their leave.

Judson did not move an inch once Old Seamus had given his directive, and in fact, seemed to be savoring the moment. He looked forward into space, like he was mustering up the energy to implode.

After some moments, he said "You know, Seamus, you've managed to take a splendid turn of the century home here and turn it into cut-rate New Orleans style establishment more suited to amorous gentlemen and ladies of the night."

The comment rendered everyone silent, as if the clock stopped ticking. Old Seamus stepped up to the man and got right up in his face

"Mister Judson, I think you'd better make your exit or we're going to have to take this thing into the street."

The words hung in the room like icicles off high tension wires.

Noah Judson turned to Old Seamus, got even closer to his face, and said "I agree we should take it into the street, but I do think we're both getting a bit long in the tooth for fisticuffs. Word 'round these parts is you keep a box behind the bar. Inside that box are two antique pistols for just such occasion. Is this true?"

Old Seamus had the expression of a man who has fallen overboard but hasn't hit the water yet. How would Judson have known about the pistols? Was it that well known a fact beyond local circles? And just where the hell had this man come from anyway?

Now, I gotta interject I don't think Old Seamus ever intended to use those pistols for their original purpose. They were there for decoration, I figured, but a decoration that had real meaning. That was my spin on it. But maybe Old Seamus was wiser than we all gave him credit for.

Old Seamus thought about it long and hard, drank a swig, and answered carefully.

"Aye, that is true, Sir. I am in possession of two such pistols," he whispered.

"And, might these pistols be in good working condition, and have adequate ammunition?"

"Aye, Sir, they are, and do."

"Then, Mister Seamus McShane, as God be my witness and on behalf of the Confederacy, I hereby challenge you to a duel."

* * *

It was pretty damn foggy out there that night, and of course, freezing, with the wind whipping in from the northeast. I carried the heavy antique box of pistols, for I had been drafted, without warning or prior consultation, into duty as duel-master.

I was more than certain this was a very bad idea, not to mention three sheets to the icy cold wind, but when

Old Seamus gets his mind made up about something, and he's giving you numerous beers for a buck, you don't argue. Besides, it was his ass on the line, not mine.

Old Seamus didn't wear a jacket, just that natty old lime green cardigan sweater I think he'd found in a Thrift Store nearby in Rio Grande. Still, even with his limp and his twitchy eye he had a sense of gallantry. He demanded respect, like an old mummer that refuses to die.

Yet, Noah looked pretty spiffy in that duster coat and his Confederate blues, I had to admit.

O'Halloran followed lamely behind us, a stupid half-grin on his face. Wrapped in his K-Mart quilt winter coat he wasn't making any definitive fashion statements, but it spoke a lot about his character. It fit him like a mugger's glove.

Old Seamus was in the lead, his height rising and lowering with each limping step. He seemed to know where he was going. Judson followed behind him, smiling. I was third in line, with the antique pistol box. O'Halloran trudged behind all of us; a lost stray.

I figured Old Seamus or Noah Judson would call this thing off before it got too dangerous, but both men seemed determined and I wasn't going to try to talk either one out of it.

To me, it was just a silly barroom game of chicken. I doubted Old Seamus would back down. Anyone that jumps out of foxhole and mows down three enemy soldiers point blank in the face of exploding grenades gets my vote for the being the last one standing, I don't care how many years ago or how many miles away it was. That takes some mean cajones, in my book.

We walked. My eyes searched desperately for someone, anyone who might spot us and ask what we were doing, to bring some light of reason into this increasingly dangerous scenario. There were no pedestrians, no cars... it was downright creepy. I looked across the expanse of Anglesea's empty streets and parking lots. The night clubs were all boarded up tight for the winter, their windows shuttered like closed eyelids.

Harry the Hats was locked up tight, a large CLOSED FOR THE SEASON sign nailed to the wall. Cozy Morley's Club Avalon and the Red Garter were also shuttered up tight, hunkered down against the wind, frozen corpses in suspended animation. Even Moore's Inlet was in hibernation. That flashing yellow light was the only life out there, swinging frantically on its tenuous wire, its rusted aluminum frame clattering in the wind, throwing an eerie orange glow over the old buildings and foggy street.

Old Seamus stopped at a spot in the center of the road and we all paused, listening to that wind howl and the buildings creaking and that crazy light rattling away like an old skeleton.

"Here," Old Seamus declared, pointing to his feet. "This is where it happens."

We all looked at each other. Judson smiled from ear to ear, a toothy kind of crazy, teeth-baring smile, and nodded. Old Seamus had a grin too, but one of forced determination.

Both men turned to me, waiting for me to speak.

It took me a few seconds to catch on, but I finally did. I dutifully squared them off, back to back, in the center of Surf Avenue, two blocks from the Ocean that threatened to overtake the bulkheads.

"Are you sure you both want to go through with this?" I asked. Both men looked sideways at me as if I had uttered a blasphemy against both church and state.

"Do it!" Old Seamus growled through his beard, freezing droplets of rain slicking it down.

I looked over at Noah Judson. He didn't seem shaken at all, the wind and rain seemed to avoid him, and he had an otherworldly glow about him standing there in that weird light. And of course, that haunting smile.

I cleared my throat officially. I addressed what would have been an assembled crowd, had there been anyone there, secretly hoping the Wildwood Police would show up before this thing got out of hand.

"...um... Gentlemen," I started nervously, "...You will walk ten paces away from each other I will count your paces. When I get to.... to....."

"When you get to *ten*!" Old Seamus hissed.

"When I get to *ten*, you will turn and fire your pistols, and may the best man win."

My words hung in the icy air. I prayed to hear police sirens. I waited as long as I could before speaking. The only sound heard was the creaking of the swinging yellow traffic light. I could feel Seamus's eyes burning into my skull.

"Are we going to stand here all night, or are you going to present those pistols and start the *damn count off?*"

Old Seamus was getting pretty cranky out here in the sub-zero Arctic wind. I heard O'Halloran's teeth chattering, almost as loud as my heart beating in my chest.

With shaking hands, I opened the wooden box. Inside the ornate, hand-carved enclosure, on a layer of red felt, were two large antique dueling pistols, polished as the day they were new. Both were loaded with one round each. Both extremely deadly weapons. My hands shaking, I lifted the box ceremoniously to the two men, both of whom seemed deeply steeped in concentration.

"Um... Okay gentlemen, please take your pistols."

There was a momentary pause, like time had stopped, then both men pulled their pistols from the box. Noah Judson immediately allowed his arm to fall to his side, as natural as he had been doing this for years on the battlefields of the Civil War, or in parlors of houses if ill-repute, somewhere in the deep South.

Old Seamus turned his pistol in his hand, getting used to the weight of it, and cocked back the release, then, dropped his hand to his side in readiness. O'Halloran's eyes were open so wide you could sail battleships into them. I started the count. I prayed both men would their intended target and end this madness.

"Ah..," I stammered, "A-Al-right, gentlemen, get ready, the count is about to begin!" I waited again for the siren that never came, a sign from God, a stray lightning bolt, anything. I felt Old Seamus's eyes drilling into my soul.

"Stop stalling and *get to it*!" he grumbled.

The time had come.

I swallowed hard, my heart doing double time.

"Paces! One.. Two... Three...." I stammered.

Both men strode purposefully away from one another as O'Halloran and I ran for cover. Both of us took refuge behind

THE WITCHES OF WILDWOOD

a battered trash dumpster. We both watched intently while I counted. The relentless wind moaned painfully as it gusted and blew warning gales down the empty streets of Anglesea.

From behind the trash dumpster, I shouted *"TEN!"* as loudly as I could and watched in horror as both men turned, lifted their pistols and fired.

The first thing I saw was Old Seamus's cap fly off, the pellet just missing his skull. It caught the edge of the cap and flung it off his head. You could see a red pitted mark on his head where the bullet grazed him.

I could hear a coupla dogs start barking off in the distance from the backyards of several of the houses. Old Seamus's pistol went off in a flash of smoke and fire, the pellet that Old Seamus fired hit Noah Judson square in the chest. The impact caused him to fly backward in one quick jerk, his pistol dropping to the ground, both hands grasping the place where his heart should have been.

What happened next went beyond all reason or understanding.

As Noah Judson grasped at his chest, an eerie blue-white glow, like the arc of a spot welder, began to peek through the space between his fingers, and soon the glow spread to encompass his entire chest, lighting up the space where he stood and throwing a bright white hot nova of light around him.

It threw dark shadows of his twisting frame against the pavement and surrounding buildings, expanding outward as he turned, gasping, and in one blinding burst of energy, I saw the inner core of him explode out of his chest, the long duster coat breaking apart in the aura of energy that had surrounded him like a halo.

Noah Judson disappeared.

There was nothing where the man had once stood, not a trace of clothing, not a scintilla of evidence he had ever existed at all. All that remained was his dueling pistol, laying on the ground, smoking. For a long moment that seemed like an eternity, we all stood watching incredulously the place where Noah Judson had once stood, trying to make sense of what we had just seen.

O'Halloran and I jumped out from behind the dumpster, running our arms and hands through the air where we were sure Noah Judson once stood.

"Mother of Mary," muttered Old Seamus, blinking his good eye while the other twitched uncontrollably.

"Holy shit!" O'Halloran emoted, a dark wet stain forming in front of his crotch.

I blinked, tried clearing my vision, snapped my head back and forth, looking up and down the empty street, trying to ascertain where Noah Judson could have gone. Old Seamus still hung on to the pistol. His body sagged, like someone had let the air out him. He let out a sigh, then sat cross legged on the ground.

O' Halloran and I were motionless and speechless. The dark stain in the front of his pants expanded, then froze.

We all looked at each other. The only thing to be heard was the creaking, swinging traffic light, the crying of the howling sea wind, and the sirens approaching in the distance.

* * *

I never went back to Seamus McShane's Irish Pub after that incident. I stopped drinking altogether. Old Seamus never told anyone the story of what happened that night. Some stories you tell over and over and they become legends. This one was so unbelievable it was best left untold. Ten years later, Old Seamus died, taking the memory of that story to the grave with him.

After Old Seamus passed away, a real-estate developer bought the property and demolished that beautiful old Victorian. He sold the land to a fast-food restaurant investor. A few months later, they put up a Kentucky Fried Chicken where McShane's Irish Pub once stood. There's a plaque in front with a cartoon caricature of a man who styled himself after a Kentucky Colonel but had never fought in a war.

Me? I still live in Wildwood year round, in an upstairs apartment behind Sylvia's old coffee shop, just a few blocks from the strange happening which occurred that crazy winter's night. I walk a lot at night now, especially when I crave a drink, but I don't touch the sauce anymore.

Wildwood has changed a lot over the years. They closed up all the clubs and most of the restaurants. Even the spot where the old diner used to sit is empty and overgrown with weeds. I'm thinking someday soon they'll probably put a McDonald's there.

Sometimes when I'm walking at night, in the middle of the winter, when the streets are desolate and cold, the northeast wind blows in off the Atlantic. When the foggy mist is just right, I imagine I see the ghostly apparition of two men squaring off with dueling pistols in the eerie swinging arc of a rusty old yellow traffic light.

One of the men is a stubborn old Irish bastard that looks a lot like Old Seamus.

The other is a civil war soldier that looks a lot like Colonial Sanders.

The ghosts are smiling.

The Fortune Teller Machine

The day Augie Meyer took delivery of the fortune teller machine was the day everything started going to hell in a hand basket. What happened from that day forward is a tale which defies logic. I will attempt to tell it to you now. You can draw your own conclusions.

First out, my name is Wrigley Shepanski and I work summers in Wildwood, New Jersey at the boardwalk arcade owned by Augie.

Before we go any further, no, I don't know why my parents gave me the sissy name, other than my mother's grandfather had been named Wrigley. I go by Rig and if its all the same to you, please don't bring it up again because it's a sore spot.

It was 1987, the summer I started working for Augie. It's the second job I ever had. Just for the record, my first job I pumped gas at a wink of a filling station just off the coast road in Strathmere. That place went under, just like many of the small mom and pop businesses had been doing at the shore. I was happy to have a job, any job, even though if pay was lousy.

Anyways, Augie, who wasn't around half the time because he liked playing the ponies at Atlantic City Racetrack, usually left Barnsey in charge. Barnsey was Augie's right hand man, so to speak, though Augie was left handed. Barnsey was short and wiry and his hands shook a lot. I think he had been in prison once but it was just a rumor and if it was true, he didn't talk about it. He had a faint scar under his chin and his face was wrinkled in hard lines. Barnsey wasn't winning any beauty contests.

So, anyways, Augie was very excited the day the delivery truck came. All morning he had been acting restless and checking dark corners, like he was about to have a litter of kittens.

"Wait'll you see what I got coming," he was telling all the employees.

"It's a gem. An antique. A collectors item!"

He had this ornery look on his tortured, weathered face. He always reminded me of one of those old boxing trainers you see in the movies, stout, tough and kinda paunchy, except he was was short and now had a pot belly.

"When it arrives you're gonna shit your pants, Shepanski."

Laurel stood next to me, somber as ever, her thumbs hooked into the dirty pockets of her change apron. She never reacted to anything, kinda like your silent little sister, but had that.. I dunno... skeptical look.

Laurel was a solid, seemingly emotionless girl. She didn't say a lot. I knew she was smart and had an analytical mind, because she had graduated from high school with some kind of honors, but she didn't show it.

She measured things, took them in. There were spaces between what she thought and what she said, and when she spoke, which was rare, you listened. Calm, measured and a poker face. But a pretty face, in a tomboy sort of way. Tiny and strong, yet there was something about her I found attractive. But we were just friends, fellow employees and that was about it. We were exact opposites, and maybe that's why I liked her.

I was tall and gangly, like all my parts moved together but were out of sync. The guys in gym class called me *clickety clack*, whatever the hell that was. I definitely didn't like it, whatever it meant, and if any of them wanted to start something I'd punch them in the nose, especially that prick Barrigan. But I was talking about Augie before, and I got off track, so let me give you the skinny on him.

You had to take Augie with a grain of salt. He was always spouting grand ideas for making fortunes. Almost all of them ended in disaster, if they even materialized at all. There was the time he was going to bring back diving horses to the boardwalk, that scheme fell through.

Then he had a plan to sell frozen chocolate covered oranges on a stick - c*horangez* he would name them - as a food item to hot thirsty patrons on both boardwalk and beach. That was a disaster, it seems nobody had any hankering at all for a chocolate covered orange. Five hundred empty orange crates were still stacked out back, collecting pigeon-doo.

After that debacle, Augie hatched a plan to start his own tram car service on the boardwalk that would bring patrons right to his arcade, which I thought was a pretty good idea, but the City of Wildwood denied his permit four times, most likely because they already had their own tram car, thank you very much.

Though he faced continual failure, Augie was irrepressible, like a crackpot Edison. He was a man on fire with ideas — invention and innovation drove him, always in search of the next Big Thing. He was a true entrepreneur in that carnival spirit that was so common to men at the turn of the century, and I imagined him to be a sort of modern day P.T. Barnum.

"The truck is coming this morning," he yelled from the office in the back, "It's coming down from Coney Island. Don't go on your break, I'm gonna need your help," he yapped. Then was back on the phone, presumably with with his bookie.

Laurel looked at me in that immovable expression reminiscent of cemetery statuary. She was totally cool. Nothing got her excited. She didn't talk much but I knew her well enough to know she was smart, she just didn't wear her heart out on her sleeve like a lot of chicks do.

Me and Laurel always worked the floor making change. We wore black work pants and had purple tees imprinted with large black lettering, front and back. AUGIES ARCADE. Our main competition was the FUN CENTER, four blocks down on Atlantic - but that place had crappy machines half of which always seemed out of order.

Laurel and walked around with our change belts, monitoring the endless stream of teens which came to play air hockey, PacMan, Pong and Asteroids.

I'd make small talk with Laurel, often saying things like "It's slow today."

She'd stand there motionless, her gray-green eyes solid and unmoving. There was always a measured cadence of time when Laurel spoke, if she spoke at all.

"It's plenty busy", she'd say, never blinking.

Or if I said something "It looks like rain today," in my typical worried way, she'd invariably say "No. It's partly cloudy. No rain today."

She'd say things in a matter-of-fact way, and it was the final word, no room for wiggle. She wouldn't look at you when she said it, she didn't measure the reactions of people because I don't think she cared what other people thought. Her view was her view, and in her mind there was no other view, yet she wasn't adamant about it.

The entrance to the arcade was open across the length of two storefronts, with machines buzzing and dinging with lights and odd sounds, each machine a perpetual enticement to rubes with coins. That's what Augie called them, *rubes with coins*.

I think he got that term from his carnival days. He'd been involved in the arcade business all his life, and so had his father, back in Coney Island in the fifties, long before Coney took a nose dive.

To bring patrons in from the heat, he ran two large air conditioners in the back that made the place feel like an icebox, even though the heat came in from the boardwalk from the wide open front.

His electric bills were astronomical. A salesman came one day and tried to sell him on those long plastic strips that hand down from the entrance and keeps the cold in. Augie never went for it, he was too old school. "You gotta have face to face. The rubes with coins gotta see the machines, they gotta feel 'em."

"It's called 'open customer access,'" Laurel informed him.

"No," Augie would laugh, waving his cigar stub, "It's called bag a rube."

We had regular pinball, sure, but kids nowadays liked the

video screen games.

Augie still had Skee-Ball in the back, if you remember those. The long brown rows looked like antique bowling alleys capped at their far ends with round tubes where the balls would sink. Ghosts from a bygone era. Occasionally a couple or stray would roll a few rounds, but for the most part the Skee-Ball machines stood silent and empty, like abandoned houses.

The truck pulled into the back alleyway at exactly twelve noon. It was a big white boxy vehicle covered with graffiti. The brakes were almost gone and noisy as hell. When all the racket from the truck finally stopped you could still hear dogs barking in the distance. Barnsey was nowhere to be found, but my guess he was at Kelly's Irish Bar knocking back some cold ones.

The driver climbed down from the driver's cab with a metal clipboard with sheets of paper clumped to it. He was a short stout pugnacious man from the Bronx. He was impatient and seemed like he was in a hurry.

He placed a pen behind his ear and rolled up the back, revealing one large cabinet, about six feet tall. It was secured by belts and bungee cords to the truck wall and covered with padded storage blankets, like the kind they use to transport pianos.

The man lowered a wheezing pneumatic lift, then climbed up into the rear of the truck and removed the bungee cord and straps. Laurel and I stood there at the opening to the truck, watching like children as he uncovered the cabinet without fanfare or emotion, then angled a refrigerator dolly into place, wedging it under the lower edge of the cabinet. Augie came out into the alleyway to supervise.

"You're gonna shit your pants when you see her," he kept saying, "be careful bringing her in." He was nervous, like a proud father to be waiting for the birth of his first born. "she cost me a bundle," he added for good measure.

As the man angled the dolly with its strange cargo toward the rear of the truck, I could make out what appeared to be a glass and wood cabinet, about five or six feet tall, the features of what appeared to be a lifelike gypsy mannequin inside. At the top front of the cabinet printed on the glass in a strip of red carnival lettering was were the words:

ASK YOUR FUTURE

Below the glass, just above the coin lever were printed the words

GYPSY ROWENA

25 cents

It was a gypsy fortune teller machine.

* * *

According to Augie, back in the old days fortune teller machines were popular in coin arcades all over the world, particularly in tourist areas like boardwalk arcades.

Before modern video games and all the manner of distractions people had nowadays, the coin machines provided a means by which people could have their fortune told without having to interact with live fortune tellers, who often had a reputation for wheedling larger amounts of cash from their marks.

The cabinet was a strange curio – a throwback from an earlier era when people placed their faith in such oracles. One thing was sure, the thing weighed a ton. The driver worked the dolly and maneuvered the cabinet to the rear of the truck. Augie directed, waving his arms excitedly, while Laurel and I helped the driver get the machine out onto the tailgate lift. The driver looked like he was sweating frogs as he lowered the lift to the pavement.

We sort of cleared the way, leading him to where we wanted the cabinet to go, which, for now, was the back storeroom of the arcade.

"Right here, put her right here!" Augie exclaimed, pointing to an empty space in the middle of the floor. "Careful now! Don't damage the goods! She valuable!!"

The perspiring balding driver was swearing the whole way in. He didn't stop bitching until he had angled the dolly through the back door of the arcade. With the cabinet placed at the center of the floor, he yanked the dolly free with a flare perfected over years of practice.

Leaving the dolly standing next to the cabinet, he peeled a pair of dirty work gloves off, raising a metal clipboard. Pulling the pen from behind his ear, he snapped open the bent metal cover and handed it to Augie.

"Sign here," he said in a monotone voice, thick with Brooklyn accent.

Once he'd signed the delivery papers and sent the man on his way, Augie stood before the machine with a majestic grin on his face.

"This, my little chickadees, is Rowena, the Russian Gypsy

Fortune Teller. A relic from the last century. One of the truly iconic pieces of craftsmanship from Arcadian history."

As he stood there beaming, Laurel and I stood silent, observing the machine. It was pretty beat up, but now we could get a get look at it. As mentioned before, the thing was large wooden cabinet about six feet tall.

But now, uncovered completely and in the open light of the storeroom, where bright sunlight filtered through the dirty back windows and open doorway to the alley, the cabinet could be seen in all its battle-hardened glory. The upper part was surrounded by glass on three sides, the front and two sides, resembling a theater box office kiosk.

Inside sat a lifelike mannequin of a young girl, dressed in dark purple and gold gypsy clothing. What had once been a bright red scarf was now faded and tattered Her hands were suspended over twelve tarot cards which had been glued to a worm-eaten silk cloth in front of her. Her head was tilted down. Her expression was that of a real gypsy observing the cards before her.

She had a face which reflected a combination of sorrow and pain, yet somehow there was the trace of a Mona Lisa smile that bordered on seduction and promise, yet in the same instance was cruel and hard. If you ever seen pictures of Russian ballerinas you'd know what I mean. Tough beauty.

To the right of the card spread was an old crystal ball. The ball was really just a plastic dome set inside a small gold stand, and the dome had a crack running through it, most likely due to age and years of rough handling.

The mannequin was worn and faded, the flesh toned paint

chipped away leaving black specks. Her eyes were emerald and though her face was young and beautiful, there was something downright ominous and spooky about her.

The glass of the cabinet was smudged, scratched and dirty. A few small cracks ran in the upper corners of the front glass. There were also places where someone had shot it with a pellet gun - making it look like miniature moon impact craters.

The cabinet itself was burned in several places, like maybe it had been in a fire.

"Look at that craftsmanship," Augie beamed, pointing to the legs of the cabinet.

The cabinet's legs were like an old antique couch, ornate and hand carved, but dinged up.

"This was made by somebody who cared about his work. A master craftsman. Nobody builds things like this anymore."

I don't know how old it was, but it looks like it had seen better days.

Augie circled the machine excitedly, fingering its lines and contours lovingly. "She'll need some TLC," he pointed out, "Some restoration work is in order. She's been through a lot."

The cabinet was solid mahogany, with hand carved trim and edges. The finish was deep brown and rich. Even the legs were hand carved with art deco styling, kinda like you see in old movie theaters that were around in the thirties.

According to Augie, the machine had been designed and constructed by a Russian immigrant who had moved to Coney Island in the early 1920's. This man specialized in making handmade wooden pieces for amusement rides and had done restoration work for many of the rides on Coney until his death in the 1950's.

Augie told us that fortune teller machines had been popular throughout the thirties and forties, had started to fade from use in the mid-sixties, when pinball and more interactive electronic amusements were coming into vogue.

For years the fortune teller machines sat like silent sentinels in game arcades and merchandise markets - waiting patiently until someone would insert a coin into the slot and then the machine would come alive. Later models could with a pre-recorded message, move through some kind of ritual like a card reading, then deliver a printed card to the user with their fortune printed on it.

"Nobody makes these things anymore," Augie said, and you could tell by the way he said it that it saddened him.

He was right. All the arcade amusements were now made with lighter, cheaper materials, not made to last. Everything seemed to go that way, eventually. Take my old man, for instance, he had a 58 Buick. It was built like a tank and weighed more than the Titanic, and when you drove that thing down the highway you felt invincible.

"Now it's all tin and solder," Augie lamented. "But not this thing." He was beaming.

A proud papa.

Laurel and I looked on, happy for Augie but uncertain just where this relic would fit in at a modern amusement arcade.

* * *

That next week was a rough one for me. I'd come down with bronchitis, but I was determined to work. Augie was a man possessed. He worked all day and night on getting the fortune teller machine ready for the arcade, often staying up into the wee hours in the back room, which he had converted into a makeshift wood shop.

He'd laid plastic down all over the floor and put up a bunch of cheap clip-lamp work lights. Never the organized type, his beat up old tools were laying all over the place. He had an old disk sander that made so much racket it drowned out the sound of the air conditioners and made the lights go dim every time he turned it on.

"She needs a lot of work," Augie confided, "parts need replaced. Most of them can't be found anymore. I gotta make 'em myself. He spoke about the machine with reverence. When he referred to Madam Rowena, he talked about her like she was a real person. But Augie was right. The machine was in pretty bad shape.

Throughout the renovation Augie wore disposable masks the house painters use – peering out over his goggles looking like some demented Santa. He worked around the clock to bring Madam Rowena back to life.

I was out on the floor with Laurel, coughing and hacking and feeling like I was dying.

"You should go home," she said, never once looking over. She still never smiled.

"I'm fine," I said, "It's just a little cough."

She didn't believe me.

I couldn't take off work even for a day. Bucks were tight. I was already a week late on the rent.

* * *

When the week was done, Augie emerged from the backroom, damp sweat spread down his t-shirt and soaked through his overalls. He pulled the paper mask off, snapped off his goggles, then held his hand up to get everyone's attention.

"Okay gang, listen up," he cleared his throat for effect.

"I am proud to announce that the fortune teller machine is finished and ready for business! I want everyone in the backroom now for her unveiling."

All of us gathered in the backroom. Barnsey was there. In the center of the room sat the bed sheet-draped fortune teller machine.

Augie stood on an apple crate and cleared his throat loudly, assuming the posture and immediacy of a stumping politician about to make a speech of profound import.

"Friends, employees, fellow Arcadians," he imparted, dramatically. "Our business has seen the last of its greatness, the public has turned its back on the glory of the golden age. But I, Augie J. Meyer, have done my best to keep the old traditions alive."

Laurel and I stood together, near the draped machine. She watched the whole scene with her usual staid demeanor. Though expressionless, she was a keen observer. She surveyed everything Augie did with skepticism.

I, on the other hand, did what I could to hold back from coughing, but it wasn't easy, given I had to breathe. My head pounded and I wished I were home in bed. Augie nodded to Barnsey, who then clicked off the work lights and the main overhead light, darkening the room, now lit only by the lights now illuminating the cabinet under the sheet.

"So therefore my friends," Augie bellowed, "I present to you.... Madam Rowena!"

Grabbing the edge of the sheet which draped the machine, he yanked it off with the flair and aplomb of a stage magician.

With the exception of Laurel, everyone let out a collective gasp. I held my breath so I wouldn't go into a coughing fit.

There in the center of the room stood the gleaming fortune teller machine, completely restored – lit to the gills, with completely new, polished glass. The dings and cracks were gone, the mahogany finish buffed to a brilliant shine.

Even the metal parts like the coin mechanism looked brand new. The lettering had been restored to their original brilliance. But what really was shocking was the figure that sat within the box.

Madam Rowena seemed to glow with life - in fact, she seemed almost alive. Her beautiful, youthful features were now detailed and lively - her eyes brilliant and bright. Her clothing was brand new, bright crisp colors of purple and gold. Her turban had been outfitted with a brand new ruby jewel, fake but effective.

On Augie's nod, Barnsey dropped a quarter into the slot. You could hear how solid that machine was built by the coin dropping through its depths. The quarter clanked deep inside the solid steel encasement and suddenly the fortune teller machine whirred to life.

Inside the cabinet, Madam Rowena moved in animated splendor. Her head moved up and down, side to side, her hands running in counter clockwise circles above the colorful tarot cards. The crystal ball to her right lit up, glowing purple, dimming and ebbing like an old electric chair. Sparking sounds like electrical buzzing were audible.

Her voice erupted mechanically over a hidden speaker which seemed to surround the entire cabinet in deep rich tones. *"Madam Rowena will now command all of the powers of the Universe to foretell your future,"* she intoned, and you could hear the sounds of machinery moving inside the box.

Her voice, though mechanical, had the unmistakable accent of a Russian gypsy, or whatever a Russian gypsy should sound like, but the voice, like the girl inside, was young, mysterious, almost sensual, yet tinged with darkness. I really had to look closely to make sure there wasn't a living person sitting inside that box.

Madam Rowena looked so real I could feel the hair stand up on my forearms.

"Christ." I muttered under my breath.

Her hands then stopped over the card spread. Her arms came up, her torso and head moving slightly back, as if she'd made some profound discovery, and then she froze.

From the front of the machine, from a small slot, a tiny white card fell into a little pocket - then Madam Rowena's voice said *"Your future has been foretold on the card you see before you,'"* it said with prophetic certainty, *"Take it and use the knowledge you have gained from Madam Rowena."*

Then she was still once again.

Still as a corpse.

Her crystal ball had gone dark.

Only the lighted lettering from the box and and eerie

silence remained.

Nobody moved.

It was an awkward moment. Almost as an afterthought, Barnsey stepped forward and pulled the card from the slot, raising it, squinting as he read the printed words. Since he couldn't read, he handed the card to me.

"Read it, kid," he rasped in a froggy tone. I took the card with caution...like I was handling a snake. The card was ornate, the back of which had '*Your Fortune*' printed on it. The face of the card had one line set in 1930's style newspaper font.

"What has the prophetic Madam Rowena predicted, Mister Shepenanski?" Augie intoned dramatically from the apple crate. I tried clearing my sore throat and my lungs burned. I wanted to cough, but I managed to read the card aloud.

"'Be on the lookout for new opportunities,'" I read, shakily, "'you will soon discover riches beyond your imagination.'"

Augie seemed pleased. He waited for a reaction. It took a little longer than it should have, but we all clapped a sorry round of applause, made all the more empty by the fact there were only three of us.

All of us silently agreed the restoration of the fortune teller machine was an accomplishment - it's just that nobody really knew what to say. Laurel was the first to speak.

"You did a good job on this," she said in a measured monotone. "Where are we going to put it?"

As if he'd never even considered it, Augie's eyes narrowed and he thought for a second. His eyes lit up and he clapped his hands with one mighty crack.

"I got it! We'll keep her in the front near the roll up and every morning Barnsy will wheel her out front. She'll sit right on the boardwalk, a curiosity piece that will attract a crowd. At night we bring her in."

We were all dubious, but we agreed.

I had visions of vandals attacking the machine. I know Laurel was skeptical as hell but she wasn't talking. Madam Rowena would be the new mascot for *AUGIE'S ARCADE*.

Barnsey struggled with the machine, so I helped him. We titled it back, on two precision wheels Augie had mounted at the base rear of the frame, just below the wood-line, then pushed it through the arcade. I opened the roll-up door to the outside, the morning sun and ocean air streaming in.

A few early morning joggers and walkers passed by as we situated the machine to the right of the entrance way, back to the wall that separated us from Laura's Fudge Shop next door. The machine fit perfectly. Barnsey ran a bright orange extension cord from one of the inside outlets and joined the orange plug with the machine's own brown-colored power cord. The machine sprang to life.

The cadaverous frozen figure of the gypsy fortune teller looked innocent, but the little turns at the corner of her painted lips suggested what to me looked like a sinister mystery.

It's a mannequin, for crissakes, I reasoned. *A throwback from a bygone era, a has-been relic.*

Don't go projecting things onto an inanimate carnival dummy, Shepansky. Next thing you know you'll be waltzing Rowena across the boardwalk.

A few curious onlookers stopped to stare at the machine. Most just passed by without noticing it.

Madam Rowena had found a new home.

* * *

It rained almost every day for the next week. My bronchitis got worse. I managed to get to the arcade most every day, but believe me I would have rather been sleeping in my cheap boarding house room down on Atlantic Ave. I was taking NyQuil, Sudafed washed down with Alka-Seltzer, and was using antithetic spray for my swollen throat but nothing seemed to do much good.

I'd work my shift at the arcade, struggling through the days in a half-stupor while the day dragged on like a broken clock. Augie had come down with the flu also, and was spending much of his time either hiding in the office or was out God knows where. Knowing him he probably spent it on the phone with his bookie, or at the track in Atlantic City where the ponies were running.

Electrical problems caused the power at the arcade to become undependable, and on some days we had no power for hours at a time, while others everything would shut down for a few minutes and we'd be left in darkness, the silence deafening. The gamers would be snapped out of their trances and stare at the dark machines in disbelief the moment the blinking flashing dinging boxes went dead.

"Brownouts," Laurel would intone, but that didn't make sense since the electrical problems were confined to the arcade. At first we thought maybe Augie hadn't paid his electric bill, but Barnsey assured us he'd paid it.

Laurel never caught my flu. She was healthy as a racehorse. I imagined her immune system was about as bulletproof as she was, able to ward off germs at the cellular level even there with benign skepticism.

The Wildwood tourists stayed away on rainy days, many of them probably staying home rather than endure a week at the shore shuttered in a motel room with the kids.

The beach was gray and misty, angry waves dark and depressing, roiling into the darkened sands, bringing in long strands of brown kelp and horseshoe crabs.

It reminded me of times I'd visit the shore in the winter - an altogether different place in sub-zero freezing temperatures and the town and beach were stark and lonely, empty of almost all life.

Barnsey was grouchier than usual all that week. He'd developed a rash that left half his face with red splotches that looked like measles. He yelled at the employees a lot. He was always on my case. Sweep this up. Keep this area clean. Where the hell are you when the rubes need change. Clean the bathroom. It was like I was his personal pinata.

He never yelled at Laurel, though I don't think he liked her very much. Something about her intimidated him. I think it was her intelligence. Anyways, Barnsey always seemed to be in a state of constant tension and discontent, and now he scratched a lot, like he had fleas. Maybe it was crabs or something. But Laurel said something about exema. She always seemed to know what people had.

Every morning when we opened it was my job to wheel

Madam Rowena out to her appointed spot on the boardwalk and plug her in. On rainy days like this week we'd leave her just inside the entrance, but when it was only cloudy or sunny, I'd put her in the prime viewing spot outside.

People always stopped when the machine was out there, it had real curb appeal. What was weird, though, is hardly anyone ever stopped and actually put money in the thing. I think something about Madam Rowena gave them the creeps and they steered clear of giving her money. Maybe they were afraid of what she might predict.

Barnsey emptied the change tills every night for all the machines. Ever since we'd put her to work, he'd mutter stuff under his breath.

"Madam Rowena may tell fortunes but she ain't makin' us any," he'd mumble, and I sort of understood his feeling. After all, if fortune teller machines made money for arcades they'd still be in use, simple as that, right?

Still, the machine made a great attention-getter sitting out there. People found it a rather strange curiosity, even if they didn't feed it any quarters. A lot of kids and families would walk by and stare, but nobody seemed interested enough to drop in any coins.

On these gray depressing days there were hardly any people on the boards anyway, and the arcade was pretty much empty. Barnsey was out half the time, too, and I knew he was making trips down to Kelly's and swilling brews, even in the mornings.

By the afternoon when he'd come back he smelled like Guinness and cigarettes.

By Tuesday of that week I couldn't stand on my feet any longer. The bronchitis was kicking my ass. It felt like it was turning into double pneumonia. "

You should get that checked out," Laurel intoned with her usual emotionless concern. "could be serious."

"I'll be fine," I said, but inside I felt like crap. I launched into a lengthy coughing fit, which drew cautious stares from the rest of the employees. They kept their distance.

"Go home kid," Barnsey finally yelled from the back, "before you spread the black plague all over New Jersey."

Coming from Barnsey, the okay for me to go home was a pretty big deal. He never cut any of the employees slack even when they were sick.

"I need the bucks, Barnsey My rent is due."

"Forget about it," Barnsey said, We'll keep you on the clock. Just get yourself better. You're no good to me spreading germs all over the damn place."

I took his advice. I hung my change apron on my hook in the backroom. My whole body ached. As I walked out of the arcade I heard the fortune teller machine whir to life behind me. The scratchy mechanical voice of Madam Rowena said:

"Your future is at stake. Let Madam Rowena look into your soul."

I was too delirious to even look back. How she'd come to life without anyone dropping a coin in the slot was beyond me. I made a mental note to tell Augie about it later.

* * *

My walk back to the *Sea Mist* felt like the last mile of a death march. Everything hurt. My lungs were on fire and my head was pounding.

A cloudburst dumped new rain on the streets and drenched me before I'd even made it halfway back to my place. It was punctuated by a few loud rumbling explosions of thunder, deep and powerful, like a giant awakening from a long sleep.

Heat lightning flashed warnings of impending doom, erupting with such force that I could feel the heat on my face. Long bony white fingers shot down out of the sky over the ocean.

* * *

I slept the sleep of a dead man for the rest of the afternoon. A double shot of NyQuil had put me down for the count. Not even the fierceness of the rainstorm raging outside my window could rouse me from my tortured sleep.

The knock at my door came later. It was a short yet succinct rap of the knuckles, almost like a Morse code. I pulled myself from the bed, which took up nearly the whole room in the small cubby-hole apartment. I was on the ground floor, the front door wedged between the wooden steps which led up to the second floor of an ancient Victorian.

At first I thought it was probably the landlord asking for the rent again, which I did not have. But the knock was not a familiar one to me, and even in my sickness and delirium I knew it could not be him. I put on my robe, a mildewed relic from my youth that was now two sizes too small.

I felt like I'd been dragged down twenty miles of bad road. Every time I coughed, which was frequently, it felt like pieces of my lungs were coming up.

When I opened the door, Laurel stood there, her hands tucked neatly in her hooded black jacket. Solid, emotionless, her eyes locked on mine. It was dark and the rain was still coming down in buckets, yet somehow she was completely dry. Her words were calm and measured, like she'd rehearsed them.

"Bad news." she said, matter-of-factually. Her eyes never left mine.

"Augie's dead."

At first the words didn't register, like when you see a magic trick in front of your eyes, your logic tries to explain it but your brain can't process it. Laurel stood there motionless.

"What are you talking about," I said, irritably, holding back from coughing, watching her through the screen she looked like a ghost in the glow of the streetlight that shone somewhere high above to the left of her.

"There was an accident on the Parkway. Augie was killed."

I still couldn't make any sense of it. Augie was a man that would always live. I reached up and popped the screen door hook. It felt like I was moving in slow-motion playback.

"Tell me what happened," I said, pushing the screen door open.

She stood there as if contemplating if coming in was the right thing to do. Girls were funny that way. It took her a moment too long to reach out and take the door, but she did it. Once inside she just stood in front of the screen door. I left the main door open as the rain splattered down just outside the screen.

"He was driving back from Atlantic City," she said in a monotone voice. "The police said he lost control of his car and crashed into the guardrail. The car flipped over and he was killed."

There was no emotion in her voice but I could tell from the way her eyes were starting to well up she was affected. For Laurel, showing even that little emotion was a lot.

"Oh God, holy shit," was all I could say.

She remained silent. Her hands stayed in her pockets.

I instinctively hugged her and pulled her close. She was unyielding She didn't resist but she never moved a muscle. She seemed oblivious to my show of emotion, of my attempt to comfort her. I could feel her hard bony frame through the soft cotton of her jacket. Her hair smelled amazingly good, like she'd used a perfumed shampoo.

"Augie's brother is at the hospital in A.C., he's making arrangements. He said to hang tight, he'll keep us posted."

I released her from my grip and slumped into the kitchen chair.

"My God," was all I could manage.

* * *

Laurel didn't stay long. She simply stood in the middle of the kitchen floor, her hands stuffed in her jacket pockets. I went on and on about Augie - how yeah he had his faults but he was a helluva guy and even though he couldn't manage money worth a damn he was still like a father figure to me. That last part really wasn't all that true, but I said it anyway because since he had just died it seemed the proper thing to say.

Laurel stood, not moving. She never agreed or showed

acknowledgment, and I guess you could say she was a good listener, but it was more like she was aware of what you said she just didn't react.

It was never easy to tell what she was thinking, and easier still to project your own assumptions or insecurities as what you thought she was thinking. When I'd run out of words to say, I sat hunched over the table, feeling defeated and coughing a lot.

"I'm gonna walk for awhile," Laurel finally said. "I need to be alone."

That was a change for Laurel. Usually she didn't give any sign of emotion. I think Augie's death had put her in some kind of shock, but other than saying she needed to be alone, her face didn't change.

I didn't get up or say anything. She walked over to the screen door, opened it and let slam behind her. She turned and her face shone through the damp screen. "I'll see you later, Rig." she said, "I'll see you at work in the morning."

That was another thing about Laurel. She never called me Rig, she always called me Shepanski, kinda like a military thing. Like I said, she kept her distance.

She disappeared into the dark and rain, the din of countless leaking gutters and swollen rain spouts creating a cacophony waterfall sounds in the Wildwood night.

My head felt heavy and my body ached. I didn't bother to get up. I crossed my arms on the kitchen table and buried my head into the darkness, falling into a death sleep, the kind some people never wake up from.

* * *

My dreams were restless and disturbing. Images of Augie in his gold Cadillac crashing into a highway guardrail turned and twisted through my fevered mind.

I saw his terror-stricken face through the windshield, illuminated by the dashboard lights. I could hear the mechanical voice of Madam Rowena, sitting in the backseat of the Cadillac, dressed in her silks, free of the prison of the flashing glass box.

Cut to: Madam Rowena strapped securely by the tan colored seat belt, head swiveling back and forth, the mouth moving like a ventriloquist's dummy.

"Madam Rowena predicts you are going to die - die...die" then the word *'die'* repeating over and over like a broken record as the window in the car implode around them in a zillion shards of glass and rain.

Madam Rowena emitted an eerie blood curdling laugh, not the cackle of an old witch, but that of a young girl - but mad just the same. Her uncontrollable laughter was like the kind you hear in movies where a mental patient is locked inside a padded room and starts to lose it.

As she laughed the car was tumbling - everything turning over and over in a mad carnival ride - Madam Rowena remained strapped securely in the seat repeating her maniacal death laughter. Then the whole scene turned Topsy-turvy as the roof and dashboard caved in. The steering wheel crushed Augie's chest as the wrenching sounds of tortured metal within the confines of the car closed in on them. Augie was screaming.

* * *

I awoke from the nightmare sweating. My bed was soaked and my chest ached. My hair was wet with sweat and my respiration came in short gasps.

I dragged myself from the bed and limped to the toilet. I looked at myself in the tiny cracked mirror.

"Dear God," I croaked aloud. "I look like shit."

Splashing water on my face, I went back to bed, but I couldn't sleep. I twisted and turned for what seemed like hours. I kept having flashbacks from the nightmare, I kept seeing Augie's horrific face as the steering wheel crushed his chest, his eyes bulging out of their sockets. I kept hearing Madam Rowena's gleeful, terrible laughter in my ears. Down deep was the fear - the gnawing tension of knowing that something was terribly wrong.

Augie running off the road. Why? Was there something more sinister behind his accident? There'd been talk Augie had borrowed money to cover his gambling debts. Maybe the mob decided to put a scare into him, or worse? I imagined a bulletproof black LTD with tinted windows filled with angry mobsters, ramming Augie's caddy from behind on the Garden State Parkway.

Did Barnsey have something to do with the crash? Augie had no family, but Barnsey was like a brother to him. Maybe Barnsey killed Augie in an attempt to get whatever money Augie had left him in his will. No, that made no sense, either. Augie didn't probably have any money at all, in fact was in debt up to his eyeballs. He was leasing the arcade space, so I doubted there were any assets to speak of, certainly none worth killing a man for.

Then there was the matter of the fortune teller machine.

Hadn't everything had started going to hell when Madam Rowena arrived?

I'd thought about it long and hard then. People getting sick - including me. The financial woes at the arcade. And what about the weird electrical problems nobody could figure out?

All that stuff was non-existent before that 'thing' had come on the scene. I was never a superstitious person, and in fact didn't give much hoot to fortune tellers or tarot cards. If someone said to me you walk under a ladder it's bad luck or you see a black cat it's seven years of bad luck I'd tell you you're looney tunes.

To my mind, things happened as they happened, pure and simple. The laws of the universe were indifferent and balanced - you got what you got when you got it, my Dad used to say. But too much bad stuff had happened since we took delivery of her, there's no way it could be a coincidence.

Then there was the matter of Madame Rowena herself.

There was something in her face and those eyes that creeped me out. She seemed almost real. What bugged me the most, the thing that kept tugging at my conscience was this... attraction... I was developing toward her.

I was drawn in by her yet fearful. There was a terrible pain in those marble eyes, all the rage of past ages, a sense of betrayal. Augie said the man who had built her had modeled her on his young bride. He'd done a bunch of research on the history of the machine and said it was a fascinating but tragic tale.

The story was the man who built the machine had fled Russia and had sent for his bride to join him in America. The Kremlin had seized her and tortured her - and then killed her. It had destroyed him - driven him crazy. He'd spent years in his workshop building the thing. He had built the thing in her memory - what if he had also put her spirit into Madam Rowena?

Now you've lost it, I shuddered. I had to get out of the place, had to walk. If I stayed in that bed any longer, thinking the thoughts which raced through my fevered mind I would go the way of the Mad Russian.

I pulled on my jeans and sneakers, put my jacket on. The coughing was intense now, salty thick phlegm coming up in gobs from deep within my chest.

* * *

The rain had stopped as I made my way through the flooded streets toward the ocean. A light mist hung in the air. Drizzle continued to fall and a chill breeze gave the damp air an edge.

Hands thrust deep in my jacket pockets I walked briskly past dark Victorian boarding houses and neon-lit doo-wop motels, strange contrasts that were both the beauty and the novelty of the touristy enigma that was Wildwood.

It was just past 4:00am and nothing stirred inside those dwellings; the streets were empty of people and traffic. I stopped in the middle of Atlantic Avenue. I could see the neat rows of green traffic lights running as far as I could see in both directions, flanked by the periodic certainty of the neon signs of motels which slept on either side of the street. They faded off in the distance quickly in the mist, pastels in a Turkish bath.

I walked several more blocks, crossing Surf Avenue and walked, bent forward, leaning into the moist, cool breeze, my lower back aching. I looked up at the quiet empty windows of the boarding houses, rotting sentinels waiting out the seasons before their fall.

A block away I could see the *DEAD END* sign and the dark incline of the ramp which led up to the boardwalk.

It was eerily quiet. During the bright sunlit days I could see the throngs of tourists filling the boardwalk, the yellow tramcar trains. But now, in the quiet of early morning a tomb-like atmosphere seemed to pervade everything, the stillness punctuated by the low steady roar of the ocean off in the distance.

I walked up the boardwalk ramp and stepped out onto the slatted boards. I took a deep breath - my lungs smarting from the intake of air, the congestion causing me to let loose a barrage of coughing.

I looked north up the boardwalk, toward the direction of the arcade, which was at least twenty blocks away. The damp boards stretched away into the mist, barren and lonely. The amusement piers were silent and dead, the normally-active rides now just ominous silhouettes against the dark sky.

Not a solitary person on the boards at this hour - it would be several more hours before the joggers would begin to appear - and several hours more beyond that when the shopkeepers would begin the procession of opening up the boardwalk stalls.

Waves crashed from the darkness across the large expanse of beach.

A light drizzle fell as I walked slowly up the boardwalk toward the arcade, past the abandoned shops with their metal roll-ups shut tight against the elements. I tried blocking out the shock at what had happened to Augie, what it would mean for the future of the arcade.

He'd been like a surrogate father to me in many ways - for something to happen to him like this without warning made no sense. I kept thinking I'd go into work tomorrow and he'd be sitting there in his cramped office, his desk piled high with papers and junk, talking on the phone with his bookie.

What would happen now with the arcade, with Barnsey, with me and Laurel?

My head swam with doubt and fear. There was no way I'd get another job this late in the season, no way to make the boarding house rent. I'd lost a mentor, someone I'd looked up to, someone who'd shown some interest in me. Maybe I reminded him of himself so many years ago, during his first season at the shore, working his first job, trying to find his way.

Now he was gone.

Off in the distance there was a smudge of orange light on the empty boards. It was only then I'd realized the main streetlights on the boardwalk were out - leaving only black punctuated by the occasional glare of a white spot from the piers. This made the tiny speck of orange-yellow far ahead even more noticeable. As I walked closer the shape of the light turned to a more distinct rectangular square. There was a light coming from the direction of the arcade.

As I drew closer, the source of light began to come into focus and a chill shot through me, a premonition. That premonition became reality when, at three blocks from the arcade it had become all too clear what it was. Set back in its spot next to the graffiti-strewn metal roll up of the arcade was the fortune teller machine, lit up, spilling a soft-orange light out onto the darkened boards.

Madam Rowena sat inside, her hands poised over the cards - looking straight out in silent repose. Looking straight out when her eyes were normally looking downward at the cards. That was freaky. But maybe in moving the machine she'd shifted, I reasoned.

Yeah that must be it, Rig, 'cos Madam Rowena is a mannequin, you dummy.

How could Barnsey have left the machine sitting out all night like this? Perhaps he had gotten the call about Augie and had quickly closed up shop. Yes, that must have been what happened. He had probably locked up the arcade and driven up to A.C. like a bat out of hell, to see for himself what had happened to Augie.

I didn't have any way of reaching Barnsey. I had no key to the arcade. Laurel was nowhere to be found. She couldn't have done anything about it anyway, she didn't have a key, either.

Barnsey would likely be there at nine to open up. But it made no sense he'd left Madam Rowena sitting outside. Someone could easily vandalize or destroy the machine sitting out unprotected like this. I would have to stay and keep watch over it until Barnsey arrived.

And where the hell was Laurel? She said she was going for a walk earlier, to clear her head. She'd probably be sleeping now. I never knew where she lived, though she told me she'd gotten a room at a boarding house on Roberts Avenue somewhere, about five blocks from here. I'd never be able to find her in the maze of houses, unless she were sitting outside on one of the porches. Fat chance of that at this hour and in miserable weather.

I stood directly in front of Madam Rowena, staring at her through the glass of the wooden cabinet. looking into her eyes - they were cold and unfeeling, just painted on, yet they looked so goddamn real. I'd thought about the Mad Russian - imagined him working for weeks in a makeshift wood shop - driven by the grief of the loss of his beloved.

Had he sought revenge on the world in the making of this creation? What kind of mania would a terrible loss like this supplant in a man - to what levels would he go to avenge such an injustice? I was racked with fever as my mind flitted from one crazed thought to another.

Was the machine cursed, bringing pain, misfortune and misery to all who would possess it? Would death befall anyone wishing to place it on display? What had happened to the Mad Russian? Had he died some strange and unexplained death, or had he committed suicide? Or had Madam Rowena killed him?

My eyes could not leave hers. Despite my fear and revulsion of her, there was an undeniable attraction. She was young and beautiful, foreign and mysterious. She'd come from a world I never knew and could barely imagine. But just then I caught myself.

"My God, Rig, you are thinking about her as if she is real."

My own words, spoken aloud, shocked me, my own voice disturbing the silence.

A man alone on the boardwalk, staring at a fortune teller machine talking to himself, thinking horny thoughts about a mannequin. The fever is creating delusions. Must be. I continued staring into her eyes. She looked straight at me.

This was merely an assemblage of parts, a plastic and wooden mannequin. Weird thoughts swam in my pounding head.

The box she sat in is a prison, Rig. Would she not want to be set free?

It seemed like she could read my thoughts, that she knew every fevered vision that raced through my mind. It was as if she could communicate directly with me, telepathically with her thoughts.

Pain and longing seemed to emanate from her, black hatred, revenge and death co-mingled; energy potential floating like gases in the ether, not yet particles, circling one another, moving faster, speeding toward cohesion toward becoming.

Drop a quarter in the slot, my love, her thoughts whispered.

My hands went to my pockets, feeling for change. Nothing.

Hypnotized, I stood transfixed before her, a power and beauty radiated from her, from somewhere deep inside of her.

A stream of visions. Russian landscapes, tundras, cathedrals with pointed spires. I saw them walking, she and the Mad Russian, through snows and forests, deeply in love, the merriment of lovers – laughing, like innocent children playing in the snow - where no worry or care could reach them.

They are in the playground of the soul. The prized innocence of youth. Their skin glows with vibrancy, she runs and he chases her, they fall, rolling and laughing and kissing in the snow, making love. The whiteness of snow and the ice against their naked bodies drive them in the ageless dance of passion. Their lovemaking is urgent, their release sudden.

My vision pulls up and away from them - straight up into the sky and moving fast toward the heavens as they disappeared below me, two black dots surrounded by the endless whiteness of the tundra, with snowy forests giving way to the continent itself - a beautiful yet unforgiving place. The blackness of space then - floating in an endless sea of stars. Superimposed, fading in slowly from the blackness, a scene:

Rowena sits in a corner of a fire-lit cabin, at a round table. Before her are tarot cards laid out in the pattern of a cross. She is alone. She concentrates deeply on the cards. She begins to cry. Her cry changes to awful wailing sound, like a banshee in the throes of hell fire.

Her cry turns to laughter, an uncontrollable, almost gleeful laugh like some madman from a horror movie - a wicked witch hag of a laugh, then her young face turns to ashen gray, pockmarks of black grow larger. She ages and within seconds

MARK WESLEY CURRAN

she is a haggardly witch.

The fire goes dead - the room goes dark. Silence.

As if catapulted out of a nightmare - I am back on the boardwalk staring into the eyes of a mannequin. It is Madam Rowena.

Madam Rowena starts to move.

There was no mechanical sound of machinery inherent in her motion. Her hand and head movements seemed exactly the same as they always had, but now she appeared to be a real person sitting inside the booth. Her skin had taken on the same youthful vibrancy it had in the dream. Her eyes shot down to the cards before her - her fixed expression emotionless, then her brows arched and the corners of the mouth had turned sinister.

On what had been a gentle expression had now turned more intent. An imperious kind of concentration had fallen over her - and in that moment I felt dread welling up from inside of myself, a dread certainty that her determination would result in some final proclamation that would set the winds of fortune into motion.

As she read the cards my heart rate increased to an unbearable thumping. I felt my throat constrict. The intense throbbing in my head made all the more painful by the concentration of trying to make sense of what I was seeing. The speaker from within the machine came alive and crackled and her mechanical female voice emanated from the cabinet.

"Madam Rowena summons all the powers of the known and unknown universe," it said, then the machine began to vibrate, the internal and external lights ebbing and flowing,

172

pulsating, creating a most unsettling effect.

Madam Rowena stopped her hand movements - both hands suspended above the cards. She looked up from the cards and looked straight at me. Her mouth moved but it was no longer mechanical, yet her voice was electronic, crackling from the speaker like an old Victrola.

"Your fate has been determined," she said, the corners of her mouth turning up into a sardonic grin. A small ticket dropped into the slot. I was stunned into paralysis and could not force myself to move.

"Take it!" she commanded, and her face had taken on an angry expression.

Like a man forced to pull something from a raging fire, I edged toward the ticket, my eyes never leaving hers. The machine was vibrating heavily now, the lights flickering. I grabbed the ticket from slot and stepped back from the machine, wanting to get as far away from it as I could.

Madam Rowena began to laugh.

I looked down at the ticket - not wanting to read the stark printed words that stared back at me. I forced myself to focus - despite the madness that was occurring now with the machine - despite the fact that the laugh I was now hearing I had never heard before. A laugh that would have no possible function in a fortune teller machine unless the man that built it was a crazy person and had programmed it in as a joke.

My eyes narrowed as I read the words which said

LET ME OUT

When I looked up, Madam Rowena had placed both hands on the glass in front of her, framing her head between them, staring at me with mad, crazed eyes.

She was still - it was as if someone had arranged the mannequin in this position in that split second my eyes had left it to read the ticket. I dropped the ticket, backed away further still, a revulsion, shock and fear shooting through me in lightning waves, my mind was stuck between gears, a refusal to accept what was happening.

My eyes dropped down to the power cord which trailed from the back of the machine, the cord that would have met its orange extension, except the orange extension laid neatly curled up like a sleeping snake.

The machine was unplugged.

My eyes shot back up to Madam Rowena as she began to slam her hands against the glass, pounding with relentless fury as the cabinet shook with the force of her blows. The voice crackled over the the speaker yet came also from inside the booth - it came from her mouth, which now moved of its own accord!

The cabinet rocked as she pounded, then her mouth opened wide with a scream that sounded like it had emanated from the depths of hell, a loud, booming, powerful cry of forces being let out of their eternal prisons.

Her hands curled into fists as she pounded at the glass from the inside of the cabinet. Her voice boomed louder and the speaker blew out. Her hands thrust through the glass, shattering, pieces falling, tinkling on the cement slab scattering across the empty boardwalk.

The cabinet exploded in a blinding flash of light and smoke, glass and splintering wood flying outward - a nova white flare of fire in the center where Madam Rowena sat - her eyes now burning sockets of red inside a hot core of yellow and blinding white.

Propelled backward by the force of the explosion, I'd been lifted off of my feet and now sat facing her, my back against the steel railing of the boardwalk. Madam Rowena sat at the center of what was now left of the smoldering cabinet, the top of which was now gone.

She stood, for she was no longer just the upper torso of a mannequin. Her top half was dressed, the part of her that had been on display, but her bottom half was that of a department store mannequin, flesh colored, with hips and bone structure.

The plastic rippled and bubbled in waves of heat, with each successive wave now giving way to substance in the transformation of plastic to flesh. The creation of life from inanimate matter - something dead coming alive.

My legs were shaking so badly I could barely stand but knew I had to get to my feet and get the hell out of there as fast as I could.

The number one rule of preservation is that when a gypsy fortune teller mannequin comes to life and grows legs and is coming straight at you, you don't stick around for explanations. I turned tail on the gypsy and ran as fast as my shaky legs could carry me down the empty boardwalk.

At one point I stole a look behind me, I could see her, far behind me, trying to walk, her eyes blazing and smoke trailing off behind her, *ka-klump ka-klump ka-klump*, like only one leg worked and the other one was just attached for show. I could hear the hideous laugh coming out of her, and she didn't need the speaker anymore. What was worse, she was finding her sea-legs, because she was speeding up.

She was no match in speed for a frightened young man such as I - as if in a sprint race for my life (I was) I exited the boardwalk and down the darkened ramp at Surf Avenue where I did not slow down until I was sure that thing wasn't following me anymore.

* * *

A Wildwood Police car spotted me just off Atlantic Avenue and Surf, hung a U- turn and then pulled into the lot of the *Dew-Wop* motel. The window slid down only half-way. The policeman was male, short and stocky, maybe fifty or so.

"Officer," I said, winded, now doubling over in pain from my aching lungs. He said nothing, just waiting. Then he saw the fear in my eyes, sensed something was seriously wrong.

"Catch your breath - tell me what the problem is."

I tried talking between breaths, sitting down on a parking stall block, the hard cement digging into my butt cheeks. The cruiser door popped open and he stepped out of the car.

"Easy," he said. "What happened?"

He listened in disbelief, shaking his head, and even laughed a few times.

"Are you taking any medications, illegal or otherwise?"

I shook my head.

"How about psychedelics? Mushrooms? LSD?"

"I'm not on drugs," I countered.

"Okay kid. Show me where you saw this... gypsy. Let's go."

He walked back the car, got in and slammed the door.

I sat glaring at him. The name tag above his black shirt pocket was engraved with 'Montgomery.'

"Get in kid, I ain't got all night."

I pulled myself up, coughing, and got into the car, on the passenger side.

He was already on the police radio, calling it in.

* * *

The police cruiser crept down the center of the darkened boardwalk, the moist air barely moving yet cool and damp drifting in off the ocean. Montgomery rolled his window down and hung his left hand out of the car.

I sat in the passenger seat staring through the windshield and kept my eyes focused at a distance looking down the barren boards. The streetlights were all on now, lined in neat rows, disappearing off into infinity. I didn't even bother to tell Montgomery about the streetlights being off earlier. It would be just one more thing he'd figure I'd imagined.

"Whereabouts exactly did you sight it?", he finally asked, in a matter-of-fact tone.

I kept my hands jammed in my pockets. I felt like a little kid being taken home to my parents.

"Up ahead, toward Augie's Arcade," I said.

He put the cruiser's high beams on, throwing a wider path of white fanning out ahead of us. He was quiet. He guided the cruiser slowly down the wooden corridor. We stayed on the narrow strip of concrete that ran down the center of the boardwalk, where the tram car ran. The smooth cement glistened with the dirty wet sheen of sea-sweat. I could smell the salt-air on nights like this, close and muggy like a soggy glove.

When we'd reached the point at which I had last seen her, that final terrible image of her coming toward me, we'd just passed Mack's Pizza. I craned forward, peering through the windshield, now fogging up from the moist air coming in off the Atlantic. The orange lights of the boardwalk were a misty glare through the windshield.

Montgomery switched on his wipers. He reached his left hand up behind the left rear view mirror, where a silver hooded spotlight was folded neatly behind it. He pulled it back, directing it outward and turned it on, the intense beam shooting ghost-white light across the shuttered fronts of boardwalk shops and battered roll-ups.

I watched intently through the windshield, as if I'd expected that... thing... to come out of the darkness. My strained further down the boards, towards the arcade, now a half-mile off. Not a sign of Madam Rowena or the half-destroyed booth - not yet.

Montgomery continued pointing the spotlight up and down the boardwalk ahead of us with solemn intent, stabbing at the darkness. Once we'd come up on the arcade there was an empty spot where the fortune teller machine had stood. No sign of the explosion, no broken glass. Not a splinter of wood.

"Is this the place where it happened?" Montgomery inquired, flooding the arcade storefront with light.

"Yeah. This is it," I said, with the finality of a man who has been fooled by a magician's slight of hand.

"Stay in the car," he said, and unsnapped a long metal flashlight from under the seat.

Montgomery left the door open and the engine running as he got out of the car.

He slowly swept the flashlight beam up and down the arcade roll up. Turning his attention to the ground, he swung the beam downward, scanning the dirty boards. He stopped the light on her spot. Nothing but the gray slab of concrete where the booth had stood. Seeing nothing, he stepped back and into the car, pulling the door shut behind him.

Montgomery snapped the flashlight back into it's place under the seat, fastened his seat belt, and stared forward out the windshield He let out a long exhale, as if about to deliver bad news to a good friend, yet with calm deliberation.

"Nothing here. I don't see anything unusual. Are you sure it happened here?"

"Yes, I'm very sure."

There was a long silence. He then put the car in gear and we continued on for another half mile, then he swung the car around, heading back in the direction we'd come.

He said nothing more as we crept. He positioned the spotlight and shot the beam through the boardwalk railing, throwing shadow bars across the white sand. The light lit up the beach and bathed it in an eerie, ghostly-white luminescence I could see the rolling breakers off in the distance, the foamy white tops of the waves catching and reflecting the spotlight.

The beach looked desolate and lonely, a distant planet devoid of life. After ten more minutes of this, he finally snapped the spotlight off, folded the head downward, and closed the window.

"Whatever it was, it's not here anymore," he said, but I could tell he was skeptical.

"It happened," I replied in resignation.

It happened, hadn't it, Rig? My thoughts seemed to doubt their own sanity. Montgomery kept driving in silence. Only the sound of the police radio breaking in with routine chatter punctuated the quiet and the smooth running of the engine.

"I'll take you home kid," he finally said, before turning the cruiser down the ramp, exiting the boardwalk.

Other than give him my address, I said nothing.

* * *

I laid in bed the rest of the night tossing and coughing. The fever had subsided, but in its place an exhaustion such as I'd never felt before.

I'd drifted in and out of sleep, but just when deeper rest would almost come, the images of the incident on the boardwalk with the fortune teller machine would rise from the depths and devour me.

The haunting image of Madam Rowena climbing out of the booth through the broken glass flashed before me each time I tried to close my eyes.

The scene kept replaying itself like an old tape loop.

Strangely erotic, yet repulsive, the visage of Madam Rowena kept switching back and forth between a saintly Madonna, a beautiful yet sensual mysterious goddess, and an old gypsy witch.

Since she'd arrived she'd brought nothing but sickness, death and misfortune. She'd created havoc; now I was obsessed with her, and on some kind of unconscious level, I'd begun to fantasize about her.

When I'd finally managed to drift off into an agitated sleep it looked like thoughts of her had finally subsided. I tossed and turned in a restless horrid state of anxiety.

At some point during the night I'd come to consciousness, awakened by a sound.

I heard nothing but the ticking of the clock on the night-stand. I lay on my side, facing left when my eyes opened. As I came to awareness, I turned to my right.

I was face to face with the horrific rotting corpse of Madam Rowena.

I gasped and recoiled backwards, flailing outward with my arms and legs - kicking and screaming as I pushed the thing backward over the edge of the bed.

I heard it land, but from my position on the bed I could not see it. Panting now, my respiration at its peak, I laid there, paralyzed with fear.

I had visions of the thing, pulling itself back up on the bed, long bony fingers clutching the white sheets, but that didn't happen. Only silence. Steeling my nerves, I pulled myself over to the far edge of the bed, peering out over the edge of the mattress.

Lying crumpled on the floor was my pillow, wrapped in the top sheet No gypsy. No rotting corpse. Sweating and scared, yet feeling foolish I pulled myself up from the bed. I sat at the edge of the mattress, now soaked with sweat. My throat was sore and scratchy, my mind on fire with fever and anxiety. I pulled on my clothes.

* * *

Early morning dawn crept silently up from the East.

Reluctant purple-orange streaks stretched across the sky as I entered the beach from the boardwalk at Baker Avenue.

I avoided going anywhere near the arcade; was afraid at what I might find; afraid Madam Rowena might be waiting for me there, which of course was insane because Madam Rowena was an amusement arcade mannequin.

Or was she something else?

Gulls scavenged the shoreline, pulling and tearing at bits of detritus which had washed up on the sand. My bronchitis was getting worse, sitting heavy on my chest. I coughed up huge wads of phlegm, aching in every cell of my body and a pounding headache that never seemed to go away. Crazy thoughts plundered my fevered mind.

I walked for what seemed like hours, seeing only an occasional jogger. It was getting toward mid-season, the July-August heat delayed by the moisture brought on by the rains. Even the humidity seemed to be being kept in check by an odd cold front that had moved in from the north, and unusual weather pattern that the Philly weather- casters were saying rarely ever happened this time of year.

The salt air felt good on my face, even though I couldn't smell it. My taste had been deadened by the sinus infection, my energies used up in the fight against foreign attackers. A jumbled endless stream of paranoid thoughts besieged me.

What few people I saw looked tired, ragged. Run down, just like I felt now. I passed by Fun Pier, the waves crashing in around the wooden supports, above which sat a fun house called Dracula's Castle.

There was a huge gorilla towering above this, a giant amusement ride with King-Kong sporting long cables at the end of which were airplanes. There was a Ferris wheel and a merry go-round. All was frozen in stillness and silence. Everything looked used up and spent. Dead.

I didn't want to go back to the arcade. I was scheduled to work today, along with Laurel, but I dreaded it. I didn't even know whether our jobs would still be there by the end of the day. With Augie gone it was hard to say if Barnsey would continue to keep the arcade open. It was hard to say anything about anything. The future of the arcade looked bleak. I didn't want to work there anymore, anyhow, too much had happened.

It all seemed like the perfect summer only a few weeks ago. Working my first real job on the boards. Living in Wildwood for a season; the feeling of fun and excitement had elevated my hopes and fueled my dreams that past winter.

Wildwood was an endless party in the summer months. Kids came down from as far away as Canada and New York. For years this place had been the center of celebration; the clubs, the beach, the boardwalk were legendary, and for kids like me growing up in the suburbs of Philadelphia, a welcome reprieve from the hot, muggy inland summers.

My parents used to bring me down the shore for a week every summer, when my Dad took a vacation. Back then, in the sixties and seventies, the place was bursting with people, families, kids, excitement. The boards always seemed full and beaches so crowded you'd have to get there early to get a good spot on the sand.

But I had noticed with each passing year the crowds growing thinner; now it seemed like the beaches were becoming more barren of people, and even on the weekends the boards were dead. For me, it didn't matter. Wildwood was a place that fueled a kids dreams, a paradise where a carnival atmosphere would always prevail and the fun would never stop.

That had all gone to doggie-doo once Madam Rowena had arrived.

* * *

"Earth to Rig. Come in Rig," came Laurel's calm assuring voice from behind me.

I felt her hand on my shoulder, then it pulled away gently, startling me out of my funk.

I'd been sitting on the boardwalk bench starting out to sea for god knows how long. Laurel stood there with her hands in her hoodie jacket pockets, her hair so long and clean. She always smelled of soap and jasmine.

"You still among the living?", she tried, and sat down next to me at the far end of the bench. We both just sat and looked out at the ocean.

After a long time she said "Let's go under the boardwalk."

I can't say what motivated her to say that. The words hit me but didn't sink in. She'd leaned over and kissed me, then got up from the bench, took my hand like a playful child, and pulled me up from the bench.

"Come on!" she ordered.

She didn't have to coax me. Even dead tired I was not about to argue with the unexplained motivations and passions of a decided woman.

* * *

It was cavernous and damp beneath the boards. There was the smell of damp seaweed and brine as she pulled me along to a mound of dry sand between the pylons.

Empty beer cans and trash littered the sand around us, but there was a clearing that seemed almost prepared for us. A clean beach towel had been laid down, a large Budweiser label design still bright and unfazed, stared up at us.

Laurel sat down on the beach towel and patted her hand down next to her, a look of mystery in her eyes. I sat down next to her and she kissed me again, this time long and deep. Energy shot through me in pleasureful waves, feelings I'd never felt before. Overwhelmed, I pulled back.

"What's wrong?" she asked.

"Nothing. Just surprised, I guess."

"You don't like me?"

"Laurel, I'm into you more than you'll ever know."

"I already know that. A girl knows," she said. "I think you just need a shot of courage."

Smiling her Mona Lisa smile, it spread wider into a grin I'd never seen before, then playful laugh. She reached behind her and pulled at a maroon bottle cap sunk deep in the sand, pulling up a half pint of *Beefeaters* gin that had been buried next to her in the sand.

She pulled it up, knocked the sand off the bottle, unscrewed the cap, and took a long gulp. She swallowed it effortlessly, wiped her mouth, then handed the bottle to me.

"A toast...." she said.... "To us."

I looked down at the bottle for a half-second before taking it.

It already felt like a rite of passage.

I chugged it down, the bitter liquid burning my throat. She took the empty bottle from me and dropped it behind her, then she unzipped her jacket, pulling it off. She cross-crossed her arms over her head and pulled her tee-shirt off, revealing a black lace bra, then reached around and unsnapped it. As it fell, her breasts sprung free.

She looked deep into my eyes.

"Do you need a map?" she asked, playfully, and placed my hands on her breasts, and pulled me down onto the blanket on top of her. Waves of warmth entangled in light, a state in which the body held an integral part yet was somehow separate from it. Something held me back.

She wanted me badly and to be desired like that was pretty heady stuff; it was just happening too fast; seeing this side of Laurel as I'd never seen it before was intriguing yet scary.

It was like exploring a new world where the excitement of discovery lay just beyond your reach but you didn't know what monsters awaited you in the dark.

I pulled back from her.

"What's wrong?" she asked.

"You sure you want to do this? I don't want you to catch my cold."

She looked at me skeptically.

"If I haven't caught it by now, I'm not gonna catch it. And if I did, it might be worth it," a sardonic smile playing on her lips.

"Gimme a second," I feigned, trying to gather my thoughts.

I sprang to my feet, scrambling and fumbling to put my briefs back on, which was kind of ridiculous given we were alone and naked and nobody could see us.

"I gotta take a leak," I said, and left to find a spot to gather my thoughts.

You dumb shit, I thought. *You have the girl of your dreams wanting to make love to you and you are blowing it, big time.*

I found a spot behind a cement pylon and stood there, fumbling with my briefs, trying to focus. I wanted to cough, holding back. Ahead of me were dark shapes protruding out of the dank sand. Cans... bottles... trash---

Something didn't feel right. Call it an intuition. Then something else that caught my eye in the sand in front of me. The object appeared to be the back of a dummy's head, like a male mannequin, protruding just above the sand, but the hair looked dark and matted, with gray in it, matted down and sticky like Vaseline.

I tried focusing on it. I tried to keep my mind from its paranoid thoughts.

It's dark down here, man, I thought. *Your eyes can play tricks on you.*

I crept up on the head, with each closer step it grew larger and more defined. My heart was stuck in my chest, I came up on the mound to see it was the top of something larger buried in the sand. I saw that the other side of the back of the head had a face, unrecognizable at first.

Perhaps someone had buried a mannequin in the sand, I thought. *Get hold of yourself Rig...*

I kicked at the mound gently. A human hand was emerged. Now the top of a naked torso. I pulled the hand free, it was cold and muggy. I jumped back in horror, dropping the hand - as I did it fell back to the bloated and mangled corpse of a man. The throat was slit ear to ear, dried blood rusted brown smeared everywhere and crusted across the open slit.

It was a face that was contorted and compressed, the eyes clenched shut, like the remains of a kidnapped Mexican drug lord.

Recognition flashed suddenly as a lightning bolt.

It was Barnsey.

* * *

I staggered backward in shock, my stomach heaving. A scream was caught in my throat yet I couldn't make a sound, like a man in a nightmare that wants to scream but then discovers he has no mouth.

Staring at the corpse as if staring would bring some understanding to it, but it brought none. I listened for sounds but could hear nothing but the sounds of the waves crashing nearby.

There was no sound overhead as streetlamp light poked

down through the boardwalk slats. Just the sound of seagulls calling and a cool light breeze blowing through the openings looking out onto the white sand.

I forced myself forward, for another image had caught my eyes, one I did not want to see for it's unbearable possibilities.

Ten feet up from Barnsey, another dark mound, the top of which a fleshy gray patch appeared. I staggered closer to it, now a grim resolve dawning. I picked up a stick from the dirty sand and kicked and cleared the dirt and sand from around the mound.

It was the dead body of a man in his late seventies, the face putrid and splotched.

He was naked, his upper torso a blobby and bloody mess. His throat was also slit from ear to ear, almost decapitated.

The face of the man was unmistakable.

Blackness closed in around the edges of my vision as I vomited.

It was the corpse of Augie Meyer.

* * *

I hadn't finished retching and coughing as the scenes played out in my mind; flashbacks from living nightmares on a seascape of dread.

It was the dawning realization that Augie had not been killed in an automobile accident on the Garden State Parkway. He had been lured here to his death, as had Barnsey.

And so had I.

From just behind the pylon, a low guttural sound arose from the direction of the blanket where I had left Laurel. It was moving fast, a terrible laughter starting from a guttural low boom to a high pitched shrill, a familiar one I had heard once before.

Turning, I saw the naked body of Laurel running toward me in a mechanical, measured gait. Her face had changed from the neck up; she was no longer Laurel, she'd become a mannequin imbued with life, made all the more shocking by the long knife which dangled from her right hand, a knife blade encrusted with dried blood.

In that final instant, I knew the face. It contorted in a mad witches fury, eyes red and blazing, open lips flashing neat rows of stained, razor sharp teeth, spittle dripping from the corners of the putrid lips.

It was the face of Madam Rowena.

Jersey Devil

The sleek, black 1986 Lincoln Town Car shot South on the Garden State Parkway, clocking eighty and counting. New Jersey State Trooper Landy Trowler, parked in the meridian which ran down the middle of the highway, hit the siren and lights and swiftly took pursuit in his cruiser.

That the man driving the car would not slow down, even after Landy's lights and siren had gone on behind him, gave Trowler some cause for concern. But he also knew the car could not outrun him.

New York plates, Trowler thought while unsnapping the radio mic from its holder. *Probably a well-heeled geezer, but the car could be stolen.* The August heat was suffocating, even now as the sun was setting, a fiery dark-orange ball sinking into the Jersey marshes.

The Lincoln kept its steady pace - neither slowing down nor speeding up for at least two exits, then, finally, just past Exit 25, barely over the Upper Township County Line, it began to gradually slow. By this time Trowler had run the plates and already knew that the car had not been reported stolen and had verified the identity of the man who owned it. Both cars down the side, the Lincoln sat silent, dark black windows sealed tight.

Trowler stepped out of the cruiser, putting on his State Trooper hat, and made the slow approach to the vehicle. He kept his hand on the top of the handle of his gun as he tapped the darkened glass with his knuckle. It took a few seconds too long for the man inside to respond. Trowler felt his adrenalin kicking in, his reflexes tensing.

Finally the window slid down. The man sitting there was in his sixties, well-dressed in a black suit and tie, a comb-over patch of blondish hair doing a poor job at hiding the baldness beneath. The man stared blankly ahead, looking strangely disconnected, as if the window going down had been a curtain pull by a stage hand merely to reveal him.

"License and registration," Trowler said firmly, any trace of cordiality gone, given the man had not stopped till long after he'd been flashed.

The man stayed frozen, staring out the windshield, grim and defiant, a look of determination on his face. It was a face that still had lots of worry lines, despite the expensive beauty treatments that were the luxury of only very rich men – those still concerned with vanity.

The man was, as far as Trowler could tell, the one who matched the driver license photo he'd run, a man he'd seen in lots of magazines and newspapers and on television. It was none other than Ronald J. Tate, a billionaire real estate tycoon that had changed the face of New York City's skyline.

Tate had been in the news quite a lot as late, for he'd purchased vast tracts of land in Atlantic City in order to build huge gambling casinos.

Though not an attractive man, Tate was often seen with very young, leggy, extremely busty models on his arm; was the guest of honor at celebrity and society events worldwide. He even had his own reality TV show in which contestants would go toe to toe with him in make-believe business negotiations, out of which Tate nearly always emerged the victor, the climax of which the loser was thrown out the window of a high-rise office building. The show was aptly named *"Throw The Loser Out"* - and was a huge hit in the ratings for three years running. (There was even a rumor going around it might be up for an Emmy in 1987.)

Tate brought up the license and registration cards without looking at Trowler, flicking them up pinched between his index and middle finger. Trowler picked them out of his fingers, looking at them for several seconds.

"You know you were doing nearly eighty miles an hour in a fifty-five zone," Trowler stated flatly.

Tate spoke without looking up. "Do you know who I am?"

Trowler put the name to the face in that split second before handing the cards back.

"You do need to watch your speed, Mister Tate. Lotta families on the road down here. I'm sure you understand."

Tate said nothing, knowing he'd won.

"Everything seems to be in order, Mister Tate," Trowler said, then brought out a notepad and pen from his upper pocket. "One big favor. My wife's a big fan," Trowler said, "Could you sign an autograph?" Tate simply nodded as he took the notepad and pen and scribbled his name, handing it back to Trowler as if the trooper were begging for rice.

"You're a smart man, Trowler," concluded Tate, dismissing him.

The window slid up. The distance between the two men

could be measured in inches but they were a universe apart.

No speeding ticket had been issued, for the very rich and famous such as Ronald J. Tate were always given carte blanche.

It felt good to be in the top one percent. Hell, he was in the top one percent of *that* ten percent, for he was one of he world's wealthiest men. It took a handful of seconds for him to get the car back up to speed, this time pushing ninety, hurtling toward Cape May.

* * *

The Lincoln sped South down the Garden State Parkway. The expanse was lined with large leafy trees that sometimes gave way to views of vast open expanses of the South Jersey marshland. Pelicans and cranes strutted and flew among flocks of birds through the tall brown grass, clouds of mosquitoes drifted in golden-hued tufts, illuminated by the setting sun. Tate loved the smell of the salt marsh out here, for it was a welcome change from the smog of New York city.

The scenery sped past Tate in a blur. He rarely noticed the beauty around him. He analyzed open spaces in terms of cost per acre; their relative proximity to their population base and the relative economic demographic of that locality. Where others saw wasteland, Tate saw opportunity. It was that forward-thinking vision that had built him a considerable fortune.

So immersed was he in his thoughts that Tate missed his exit. The sun had just disappeared below the horizon when Tate's Lincoln zipped past the Wildwood off-ramp. The Parkway ended at Cape May, forcing him to get off the highway and onto the final interchange exit. *Exit Zero*, as the locals called it.

Tate pulled to the side of the road and looked around him, realizing he'd missed his exit several miles back. Cursing, he navigated the car back onto the Parkway, this time going North. *This time I'll watch the signs,* he thought to himself, clicking on the headlights as the sky turned to dusk and spread sinking blackness over the smelly marshes.

In a matter of hours, I'll be back in New York, Tate thought, *after I wrap the deal up with Zachary. When ten acres of prime Wildwood real estate will be mine. When I start the first step of the process that will be Tate TOWERS SOUTH.*

Zachary Wheeler was a wealthy restaurateur; had opened the wildly successful eatery known as ZACHARIAHS in the late 1950's to much hubbub; had even invented the ZACHARIAH COCKTAIL, a concoction of rum, coconut juice and 7-Up.

In a brilliant marketing coup, this drink became popularized by Wheeler who had masterminded the catchphrase 'Get Your Ass Zacharized', a rather controversial term in the conservative Fifties. By the eighties it had settled into a motto so familiar it had become a household word around Jersey and Philly and as far North as Canada.

Folks would travel from around the world to dine at Wheeler's sprawling ranch-style eatery, a place where the waitresses dressed as cowgirls, the bartenders played the role of cowboys. The entire staff would wear western style cap guns in holsters and assume old west mannerisms and accents, much to the delight of patrons, particularly kids, which were the true targets of Wheeler's marketing genius.

Wheeler was an old pro at promotion. He'd invented numerous promotional gimmicks to draw people to his restaurant, the apex of which was the SIRLOIN CHALLENGE, where restaurant goers possessed of great appetite and hubris would attempt to eat a 100-pound sirloin steak and all the fixins at one sitting; the reward of same being a free dinner but usually ended in indigestion.

Few could avoid the tsunami of advertising Wheeler unleashed during a typical summer season in the Wildwoods. Billboards lined country roads and highways throughout the entire state; the airwaves were filled with folksy home-spun cowboy style ads designed to appeal to the kids. Beach-goers along the South Jersey shoreline could not ignore the planes which flew hourly trailing long letters that spelled Z -A -C - H - A - R - I -A - H - S - ON - THE - BEACH! (Even though the restaurant was not on a beach.)

Wheeler's father had purchased raw land in North Wildwood back in the twenties, just over the bridge from Grassy Sound, back when the area was just a series of salt marshes. Today that land was worth millions, and by the time Tate was finished, it was going to be the center of gambling mecca that would only be rivaled by his properties in Las Vegas and Atlantic City.

Tate's mind envisioned glittering high-rise towers rising up out of the swamps of North Wildwood, palaces of sin and decadence that would be the source of great wealth for he and his cronies; the many crooked politicians and wealthy businessmen whose pockets he'd padded over the years with bribes of lavish gifts, cash payoffs and smokin' hot hookers.

Sure, there'd been a lot of opposition to his march toward wealthy imperialism, especially from the many poor people he'd displaced as he paved his way to wealth. Some fought him with enviable tenacity in the courts, but in the end the spoils went to the wealthy. Justice was almost always the province of those with the deepest pockets.

These were thoughts which raced through Tate's mind as he got off the exit and headed East on Rio Grand Avenue, accelerating to sixty on the empty stretch of road, unknowingly heading away from his destination.

* * *

Tate was oblivious to the scenery unfolding before him; a few strip malls and gas stations now giving way to wider stretches of marshy flatland, and then, finally, to large stands of trees which flew by in a dark green blur.

There were no road signs indicating he was getting any closer to Wildwood. *Something not quite right,* he thought, but put the notion out of his mind for the time being; *what a godawful waste of perfectly good land,* he thought, *This scrub looks worse than the swampy no-mans land we subdivided in Florida.* There was no traffic. The road got narrower and as it did, bumpier, yielding to a poorly maintained rural route that led deeper into thicker stands of trees.

Skeletons of tractors and broken down farm equipment sat in scrub-bush clearings punctuating the heavily wooded roadsides, rusting in the weeds.

As complete darkness fell, the sleek sedan rolled deeper into the thicket.

A sign finally appeared; *Welcome to Piney Woods!*

This can't be right, Tate thought, and pulled off to the side of the road. Checking the glove box for a map, he came up empty, pulling out the owners manual for the car and miscellaneous papers; a plastic flashlight; an old can of WD-40 and a stale Mounds bar. Cursing, he threw the contents back into the glove box and slammed it shut.

He'd sat for several minutes, the car idling at the roadside, headlamps on. There was no sign of life anywhere, not birds, not squirrels. Everything seemed dead, like he'd been traveling in some kind of purgatory.

A creeping paranoia slowly washed over him. He was not a man given to weakness and quickly dismissed it from his mind, but the flash of something in his mirror startled him. He glanced at the rear view, seeing nothing but the red glow of his brake lights illuminating the choppy road behind him. What ever it had been was gone.

Tate put the car in gear and made a U-turn on the highway, cutting tire marks into the soft ground, then gunned it, spinning wheels and throwing dirt behind him as the car rocketed back in the direction it had come.

"Piney Woods, New Jersey," Tate muttered to himself, "gateway to Nowheresville" he grimaced, and nervously whistled off-tune.

Tate now realized his mistake had been taking the wrong turn off the Parkway. He'd lost some time, sure, but no big deal. Soon he would be in Wildwood, having drinks with Zachary Wheeler and his wife, and enjoying a 100-pound steak with all the fixins, all, Tate was certain, on the house, of course. Why, he might even take the Steak Challenge and get his photo in the local papers.

As vision of cowgirl waitresses danced in his head, Tate was startled by the sound of wings above his roof - a flexible kind of wings, like the sound of parachute fabric. Very much like the sound of bat wings, only bigger. A lot bigger.

He saw the flash of something just above the ridge line of his windshield, only a shadow in the darkness, but a millisecond glimpse of what appeared to be a winged creature the size of two very large men, roughly fourteen feet long. It was flying.

A jolt of fear and disbelief shot through him. The acknowledgment of the fear itself bothered Tate more than the nightmarish sighting, for he was a man of courage second to none in business negotiations.

He shook the fear off quickly and stepped harder on the accelerator. The Lincoln shot easily down the two-lamer, the faint yellow lines shooting past at lightning speed. *I could not have seen what I think I saw,* Tate thought. He placed his focus on something outside his fear, something that always worked for him.

He thought of boardroom negotiations and large bundles of cash as he frantically hit the dashboard buttons on the radio, putting the station locator on auto-scan. He kept his attention focused intently on the road. Bugs and mosquitoes danced furiously in the headlight beams.

Static and distant voices crackled from the speakers as the tuner glanced from frequency to frequency, finding nothing but the vast radio wasteland of empty space. Finally the radio locked on a weak station out of Philadelphia, and jazz erupted through the noisy airwaves.

The saxophone of John Coltrane cut through the static, riding shotgun over cool piano and dreamy bass. It was soothing and mellow. Tate kept it there and let out a deep breath of relief.

I need a drink, Tate mumbled under his breath. *A really strong drink.*

Outside in the thick July humidity, a slight, cool breeze drifted in from the Atlantic, creating an almost imperceptible kiss of fog over the sleepy inland marshes.

High above the car, something circled.

Tate's mind wandered as he drove. He had come a long way since his early days growing up in Brooklyn. He'd fought his way out of poverty, had learned the language of the streets and found that the only way forward was by force of will and determination.

Being an only child of Irish immigrant parents, he'd learned from an early age that respect came not from being a nice guy but by trouncing your opponents and leaving nobody else standing. He never went to college, instead learned the ropes of the real estate business the hard way, teaching himself and saving every dollar he could to buy his first property.

Tate learned how to use psychology to intimidate his opponent, positioning himself in a more favorable position, then waiting for the right moment to close. The secret to his success was to find a weak spot he could use to his advantage. His key strategy was to always be able to walk away from the deal. It worked like a charm.

He would use the same strategy on Zachary Wheeler. He imagined the look on Wheeler's face when he told him he was going to buy his property at pennies on the dollar to build his next multi-billion dollar casino. Tate couldn't wait to see that look, and he also couldn't wait to see the look on Misses Wheeler's face when he dropped the bombshell.

His thoughts drifted to Mrs. Wheeler, as he entertained the thought of what she'd look like without her clothes on, or wearing black lingerie, one of the French jobs with--

Something dived down onto the car quickly, the edge of a blunt object slammed into the windshield, the sudden impact cracking the safety glass, leaving a spider-like shape of shattered plastic. The impact was so violent it startled Tate, causing him to veer off from the center to the right, the tires whirling up stones and dirt. Tate maneuvered the Lincoln back onto the road, looking around him, checking the rear view. There appeared to be nothing near the car.

The second attack came swiftly, this time a cloven hoof smashed into the glass on the passenger side, causing a baseball-size crack in the dark plastic. Tate undid his safety belt and leaned forward, looking upward through the windshield, catching a fleeting glimpse of what appeared to be a large winged creature flying up and away from the car.

It circled above the car again, then there was silence as Tate gunned the car hard down the highway, the strains of a mellow saxophone in grim contrast to the insanity that was now unfolding.

As Tate drove he glanced furtively out into the dark night around the car, a sick fear rising within him. His hands gripped the steering wheel in white-knuckled determination, his diamond rings sparkling from the glow of the dashboard lights.

His throat constricted against his tight collar, the perfectly knotted necktie straining against his pulsing jugular. Cold sweat broke out on his brow as he grabbed a red silk hankie from his upper pocket and dabbled at the sweat.

What God's name was out there? he thought, *some kind of creature... a bat?*

It looked like no bat he had ever seen. It looked more like a cross between a bird and a man, with bat-like features, but it was hard to tell in the dark and in the swiftness of its movements.

He'd heard of the stories about the Jersey Devil when he was a kid, but never paid them much mind. Things which could not be explained by hard science or proof did not interest him. Such folk tales were the province of weak minds, old wives tales; the fodder of story spinners. Better to set one's thoughts on the acquisition of wealth then the speculations of legend.

The third attack was sudden as two cloven hoofs smashed through the windshield, the shatter-proof plastic breaking out of the frame in a white-blue blur; the moist night air rushed in and blasted Tate, shocking him to sheer panic. He panted deeply in hard gasps, sucking in the dense air in gulps.

The car approached Marsh Creek bridge, a small wooden structure which spanned the length of five-hundred feet, below which lay a decaying swamp of a dead tributary. Tate searched desperately for any sign of life on the desolate road, yet there was nothing.

Is anyone alive in this shit backwater, Tate grimaced, *dear God someone help me...*

Up ahead coming toward him over the bridge, a set of headlamps cut through the night, shooting over the bridge, approaching fast. Tate felt a sudden surge of relief. Tate flashed his lights, honking his horn, attempting to wave down the truck. High beams flashed back at him from the pickup, as if trying to recognize him. Tate hit the button rolling down the window and waved frantically with his left hand, keeping his right hand on the steering wheel.

The pickup rattled past him, honking its horn as it passed. It looked like a young man with longish, sandy blonde hair, in his twenties. The truck had a sign on the side, BILL ANDERSON CONSTRUCTION. It kept on going, and as it did, a hand shot out the driver side window, giving him the finger.

Tate felt his hope turn to anger as he shot his own hand up, returning the finger. *Goddamn yokel,* Tate swore, guiding the Lincoln onto the bridge, doing sixty. *It would be a windy ride,* he thought, but he was determined to get to Wildwood, where he knew he'd be safe.

Something large and heavy hit his roof, likened to an army duffle bag filled with sand. Tate could feel the weight as it landed. The entire frame of the car bounced lightly on its suspension, and he now felt the ominous presence of the thing sitting on top of him, merely inches from his head.

Cloven hoofs smashed into the back window of the sedan, the third blow of which broke the window inward.

Tate let out a scream and punched the accelerator, trying to shake whatever was sitting on top of his car, but it was of no avail, for the Jersey Devil had attached itself with powerful webbed hands; hands well suited for climbing trees.

A chilling, banshee wail echoed out over the swamps and dense pine forests. Blind panic enveloped Tate as he momentarily jerked the wheel sideways, sending the car careening across the yellow line and smashing through the steel railing of the bridge, losing a front right tire as it cartwheeled over the side, plunging into the purgatory of moist swamp below.

The last thing Tate saw before losing consciousness was blackness.

Within moments the car disappeared below the surface of the swamp, the thick salty quicksand swallowing it whole. High above the trees, the sound of bat wings ascended toward the heavens.

A horrific silhouette of a grotesque winged creature shot out over the tops of the pine trees taking flight against the dark night sky.

Ronald J. Tate was never heard from again.

Werewolves Of Dennis

"Art, you're not serious." Cindy Mason said in disbelief as she gazed through the windshield at the dilapidated structure which loomed up before them.

"It's a fixer-upper," Art Mason replied, ignoring her cynicism, putting the Lexus in Park.

The old three-story Victorian mansion sat back against the woods just off Route 49, in a remote wooded area of Southern New Jersey in the tiny hamlet of Dennis. The was a sleeping giant, partially hidden by pine and oak trees. It sat on a heavily traveled rural route that wound its way through the thick woodlands that stretched to the sea.

During the summer months, when the trees were green and full, endless processions of cars flew past it. Vehicles filled with restless, expectant families and rebel party goers headed South to Wildwood; while a more tired line of cars would wind their way past the house Northward on their return from shore points all summer long; exhausted and spent from a hangover weekend or a week-long vacation. In the winters, after the season had passed, the road became like any other country road anywhere in America and the only cars one would see on it were made up of mostly locals.

Art and Cindy Mason first spotted the house back in the 1970's while en route to Wildwood, and Art grew fascinated with the decaying structure. For years it sat camouflaged by weeds and shrubbery. The only thing that set it apart from the scenery was the small handwritten FOR SALE sign out front near the road. That sign had been there so long it was faded with age and nearly illegible.

Each year they'd pass it, and with each year the place grew older, the weeds higher, and the couple got to thinking about buying it.

It had a high turret roof, surrounded by windows; Art knew right away it would be perfect for his broadcast room, and the surrounding acreage would be perfect for the erection of his radio tower. Cindy sighed and shook her head doubtfully.

"They're going to call us the Addams family," she said finally, and Art knew she'd already agreed.

* * *

Each evening at exactly 11:59 Art Mason took a deep breath, pulled the broadcast microphone toward his face and awaited the ON AIR countdown from his assistant, engineer Michael 'Sonny' DiScala.

Di Scala was a short Italian-American man in his twenties. People told him he looked a lot like Sonny Bono, hence everyone called him Sonny. He styled his hair in the same way as Bono's – a longish sugar-bowl cut that sported straight bangs that made him appear as if he'd been beamed forward in time from the late sixties. Sonny sat surrounded by an audio mixing board, a computer screen, and wore a headset microphone. He sat directly across from Mason in the adjacent room, separated by a control room window.

"In five! Four! Three! Two!... Cue Roll in!" Sonny would yell dramatically, hitting the button that would start the show introduction and music announcement. Just why he did this aloud and with such authoritative zeal was always a curiosity to Art, for the two men were alone and the verbal cue was unnecessary, but that was Sonny's inimitable style, so Art welcomed it, and in fact, looked forward to their nightly broadcasts.

The radio show music started.... a high pitched sound, a weird science fiction theremin that would give way to what could only be described as a spaceship landing as the deep voiced announcer boomed.

"The midnight hour is upon us, worldwide listeners. It's time for STRANGE HAPPENINGS... the show that brings you closer to the world of paranormal phenomena... with your host.. [voice dipping an octave lower]... Art Mason! From UFO's to the government conspiracies which hide them.. from psychics to science fiction... we bring you the *real* stories and *real* people behind the paranormal, both real and imagined! And now.... broadcasting to you live from the mysterious hinterlands of Dennis New Jersey... your host from on high ... ART MASON!"

Art always waited for the hand signal from Sonny: three fingers up, then two, then one... then Sonny would point with a flick of the wrist and Art would start the show as the opening roll in faded down.

"Good evening friends, welcome to Strange Happenings. I'm your host from on high, Art Mason." Art always moved in to the microphone really close at this point, so as to get intimate with his listeners.

"Tonight we explore urban folklore, as we are apt to do

from time to time. These are legends, modern urban legends, if you will, that have circulated, sometimes for centuries in small towns and big cities throughout the world. Often these folk tales become localized in the telling. My first guest this evening is folklorist expert Arnold Tomkins, author of the book 'Urban Legends Revealed!' Mister Tomkins, you're on the air!"

A timid voice piped in from a telephone line, on a signal which was now being beamed via satellite dish to over five hundred thousand listeners throughout the U.S. and Canada.

"Thank you, Art. It's... it's good to be here." The voice sounded unsure, shaky.

"Now, Arnold, in your book, you state that Urban Legends are often based on folklore that has existed for centuries, but given a modern spin. Can you give us an example?"

"Well.... yes, I can," Tomkins cleared his throat nervously, "One of the more persistent urban legends is that of the man who escapes from a local mental asylum and is on the loose, and at the same time, a young couple is parked in a car at a local.. [clears throat nervously] ...lover's lane, if you will."

"A lovers lane, as in a make-out spot, where teens go to get laid?" Art asked, in his trademark skeptical tone. It was a tone his listeners loved, a tone of doubt often used to play the devil's advocate to call into question the integrity of his guest. Listeners knew the purpose of our show was to bring on the latest and greatest in psychic and unusual phenomenon. It was also a platform used to debunk charlatans.

A common tactic Art Mason would use would be to corner his guest into some confounding argument which would lay to waste whatever credibility they'd had, and then Art would have Sonny close the guest's microphone, and Art would lay waste to the guest.

Arnold paused before answering. It was almost as if he were considering hanging up, for he knew Art Mason was trying to bait him. He waited for what seemed like forever in the short attention span of radio listener, a dreaded place called dead air.

"Are you there, Tomkins??" Mason asked in a mocking tone.

"Yes, I'm here."

"Well then, please go on." As always, Art was condescending.

"In the urban myth," Tomkins continued, "the lovers lane couple is inside the car on a moonlit night. At some point they hear what sounds like the scraping of a tree branch on the roof. The girl says to the boyfriend 'there's something out there, you have to go investigate,' and the guy says 'It's nothing, let's make love,' and the girl is insistent, she tell the guy he's got to find out what the noise is."

A long pause.

"I'm listening," Art Mason said in a disinterested tone.

"So the guy gets out of the car and turns to look, and when he does, he is shocked to find the corpse of a man hanging from a tree branch above the car, swaying in the night breeze, feet scraping the car roof. It's the escaped mental asylum patient hanging dead from the tree."

"Ooooooooooooooo scary!" Art Mason exclaimed in his mocking tone, then his voice getting serious and slashing as a verbal machete. "So whats the point, Tomkins?"

"The point is the stories are usually based on something true, which makes them believable. There is something in them that anchors them to the reality of now. But the rest of the story is myth, it doesn't exist."

"Well, Tomkins, as any physicist will tell you, it's been scientifically proven that nothing exists. Everything is an illusion."

"Yes, I've heard that," Tomkins answered, trying his best to avoid clashing with the mercurial radio host. "But I contend that there is a basis in reality for all urban myths. That in some way shape or form, each of them does exist in their own form of reality. It's the belief in them that makes them real. Real to the people who believe in them."

"Well that's just terrific," Mason yawned. "Psycho killers really do grow on trees."

"My book attempts to put into context some of the stories that have circulated for years do have a basis in truth," Tomkins asserted, his voice shaking in conviction.

Art Mason looked through the glass at Sonny and gave him the 'throat cut' hand signal, and the engineer disconnected Tomkins with a practiced flick of the wrist, an over-exaggerated move he did with a little dance-step of joy.

"There you have it folks. A quack who claims all urban myths are true. Arnold Tomkins gets.... a thumbs down!" Sonny clicked the mouse on the computer and the trademark thumbs down sound bite rolled, a combination of a crowd of hecklers booing amidst a chorus of quacking ducks.

"As you know, as your host on high I will always expose

the endless procession of quacks and weirdos that try to come on this show and separate you, dear listener, from your hard earned buck, and worse yet, try to betray your trust. It is my pledge to you we will explore the world of the paranormal together and we will separate the fact... from the fiction! This is Art Mason, you're on the air!"

The next guest was Miss Frenchy, aka Misty R. Caldecott, a New Orleans psychic from the French Quarter who was known to be 'The Astrologer to the Stars.' She'd been popular during the Sixties during the Kennedy era and had in fact advised both Jack and Bobby Kennedy during their administrations. She'd been a popular favorite of Jackie Kennedy and had successfully predicted his assassination a year before it had actually happened.

Back in the early days she'd graced the covers of national magazines, but those days had long disappeared. For a time she'd been featured on the tabloid covers, most notably the *National Ratquirer*, usually accompanied by unflattering photos of her with her hair in curlers and her face obscured by large sunglasses. Her star has definitely fallen, for even the rags had no interest in her anymore, and rumor had it she was a burnt-out alcoholic living in a trailer in some Florida backwater.

"Hello Art," came the voice, low and husky, sexy sounding but more the province of too many cigarettes and whiskey; "Miss Frenchy predicts a prosperous future, one of wonder and mystery."

"Why thank you, Miss Frenchy," chided Art with sarcastic sweetness, "and to what do we owe the honor of this most famous.... so called psychic... to the Art Mason show?"

There was a long pause, then Miss Frenchy, quite obviously hurt by the introduction, answered "I can see your are still your old self, Art," said Miss Frenchy in an asthmatic wheeze, "an ornery devil as always," she said. Art Mason assumed his authoritative voice, the voice of reason, the one his ego told him was the voice of the people, one who exposed those who would part the public from their hard earned dollar through the use of the claim of psychic ability.

"I am simply a crusader for justice, for the little guy who is working for minimum wage in Walmart and fast food joints all across this great land of ours," Art boomed, then countered with "So what are you plugging, Miss Frenchy? Something that will no doubt buy you yet another box of cheap wine? A psychic line? A paid subscription to a monthly newsletter? A book perhaps?"

"I do have a new book just coming out," countered Miss Frenchy, determined to go on despite the lambasting.

"And what is the title, pray tell?" chided Art Mason.

"It's called 'The Power of Energy Attraction.' It's a book about the power of intention and inner thought. It's based on the premise that we attract the same type of energy we put out. So if you put out love, love comes back. And if you put out hate, the hate comes back in the same amount of intensity as it was projected."

"Wow, that's just fascinating," Art Mason dripped, "and is this a book you thought up in some hungover state or were you three gills to the wind when you wrote it?"

"It's based on hard science. Physicists are now in agreement the power of attraction is a very real thing."

"Ahh. Physicists Those who make their living postulating and intellectualizing on theory and speculation, those who try to convince us we can hear the sound of one hand clapping?"

"I'm saying that modern science is affirming what sages and seers have been saying for centuries. Like energy attracts. We generate an energy field that attracts to us what we put out."

"I'm highly skeptical," Art Mason concluded, "And I wouldn't advise anyone to waste their money on such a book. Now tell us, did you ever give Kennedy a blow job?"

There was a long silence, then Miss Frenchy spoke again. Her voice was calm and cheerful. She wasn't taking the bait.

"Good night Art," Miss Frenchy laughed, "I love you. And thank you for having me on."

Sonny disconnected the call as Art went to a commercial break. "There you have it folks, another quack selling yet another bottle of snake oil. And speaking of snake oil, here's a word from our sponsor."

While the commercial spot played, (a spot hawking a CD package of 'The Best of Art Mason,' a compilation of his most popular shows), Art Mason popped a Valium and tried to rub away the migraine building in his throbbing skull.

Sonny watched Art through the glass with concern. His boss hadn't been the same in recent months. *Too many years on the air,* he thought, *too many battles fought.* It was a tough time for indie shows like Art's - in today's hardscrabble world of corporate owned radio stations it was getting harder and harder to find affiliates who would carry their signal.

Most radio stations had been bought up by large

investment groups, then forced to conform to the dictates of their parent companies. Boards of Directors now were in charge of programming. It was all about ratings. If you didn't fit a specific demographic and pull big numbers, you were a liability on a company spreadsheet and would fall to the ax, as many indies had before him. The Art Mason show was the last of the big holdouts, but he knew they couldn't hold out much longer. The ship was sinking and the times they were-a-changin'.

* * *

Art stared out the windows of the turret which sat high atop the ancient Victorian. Outside the windows overlooking the fields and woods, a full moon shone down on the sleeping township of Dennis.

Art harbored fear and anger. Anger at all the wrongs heaped upon him by the many enemies he'd accumulated over the years. Fear his wife would leave him, for the love had long gone out of their marriage. And the very real fear they'd lose the house, which was now seven months behind on the mortgage and in danger of foreclosure Rage had been a big part of Art's life for as long as he could remember.

Art was snapped out of his thoughts by the blinking light of an incoming call, lighting up the small phone panel next to his microphone. Sonny picked it up, then listened for a few moments, deciding whether to patch the call through to Art, or hang up, as he often did. Art watched as Sonny's eyes grew narrow, a relentless cold stare he'd perfected during a five year stretch in a New Jersey Penitentiary for forging checks.

Sonny's eyes widened, and Art knew they had a 'live one', meaning a caller that would engage the talk-show host in lively debate or a more serious debunking. Sonny made the hand signal to Art the call was live for pickup. As the commercial wound down, Mason swung the mic in at the last possible moment and picked up the fade on the backside, his smooth low voice riding up the falling crest in perfect cue.

"Welcome back to STRANGE HAPPENINGS - this is your host Art Mason," he clicked a switch on the phone panel, then boomed "You're on the air!" There was a long pause, the dreaded dead air broadcasters loathe, the seconds of silence that will lose listeners and send ratings plunging into the depths of hell. The voice was meek, yet angry.

"Hello again, Art." It was the shaking voice of Arnold Tomkins.

"Well hey there, if it isn't Arnold Tomkins, bupkis author of Urban Legends. To what do we owe this postmortem dishonor?" The voice was low and sinister, now, like a snake. There was a tortured quality to it, in pauses that contained poison.

"Have you ever heard of the werewolves of Dennis, Art?"

"No, I can't say I have, Tomkins. Why don't you tell us about them?"

"For centuries the locals in Dennis Township have reported sightings of an apelike creature, but standing upright, like a man."

"Uh huh." Art Mason feigned intense boredom.

"Every so often, when the planets align just so, and then there is a full moon, it goes in search of victims."

"I see," Art Mason replied with disinterest, "and when, prey tell, does this... werewolf... plan to appear next? In your next book perhaps?"

Arnold's voice dipped low and sinister.

"The planets have aligned. It's coming for you, Art. It's coming for you now, as we speak."

There was something in the voice that struck a nerve with Art, something desperate and angry.

He'd heard the tone before when several years back a young man had called in with a suicide call and shot himself on air over something Mason had said.

"Oh, I'm so *scared*," Mason chided, although he really had a bad feeling about this. He signaled through the glass for Sonny to disconnect the call.

"We'll let you know if we find these.. werewolves of Dennis... Mister Tomkins, and when we do we'll throw a hairy wolf party and invite you," he said, and clicked a button, cueing up a radio cart for the commercial. "We're going to go to a quick commercial break, we'll be right back," For good measure, Art Mason let out a wolf yell, such as one might hear in the night when wolves bay at the moon, while Sonny played Warren Zevon's *Werewolves of London'* as an exit piece.

The two men were always in sync with one another in that way, so long had they worked together they were like a well-oiled machine. They looked at each other through the glass, laughing as Sonny did a mock high-five through the glass, then made a circular Looney Tunes motion with his index finger around his ear, and Art followed suit.

Both of them heard the loud thump from the downstairs

of the house. Even through the headphones both men could hear it, and particularly feel it, for the vibration that accompanied it reverberated through the structure in a shuddering shock wave. Both men instinctively pulled the cups of their headphones away from their ears.

Art knew it could not be Cindy. She'd gone out of town to visit her sister in New York. From downstairs, there came a commotion of breaking glass and furniture being overturned and thrown. Even more disturbing than were the growling roars which accompanied it.

Something large and strong. Something not human.

Sonny's eyes were wide as dinner plates. Art Mason's face looked like a Van Gogh painting, the very definition of fear and confusion. The noise from downstairs was now moving upstairs toward them quickly, gaining in strength and volume as something very large and very angry bounded its way up the stairs, shaking the house as it went.

Both men threw their headphones down as Art exited the studio booth and ran into the control room where Sonny was already headed toward the door. Both men stood in the open doorway as the sound of a very large *thing* bounded toward them in gathering rage and fury.

Thoughts of home invasion and aliens raced through Art's head as both men stepped out into the dark hallway, a shaft of light illuminating the top of the stairway which led down to the lower floors of the house. A large shadow yawned across the shaft of soft white light, a shadow that looked like a cross between a large bear, a wolf, and a giant man.

It now stood at the end of the hallway, back-lit by the light from the floors below, red eyes glaring, it's immense chest swelled out in brute muscular ripples. Saliva dripped from its bared teeth, like a dog gone mad with rage and hate.

Sonny pulled his gun up from his waistband, a 9mm Luger, emptying the clip into the beast, the light from the firing gun erupting in bursts of popping fire.

The animal, now completely enraged, let out a blood-curdling howl, one which seemed plumbed from the very depths of Hell.

Sonny, realizing the clip was empty and had had no noticeable effect on the creature, hurled the gun, catching the edge the werewolf's pointy right ear, then the gun came to rest on the carpeted floor, a spent relic.

The werewolf broke into a run toward them, a mad sprint of determination and death.

The carnage was heard by listeners from coast to coast, resulting in the highest ratings of Art Mason's short-lived career.

The screams died down to silence.

Dead air.

Swamp Beast Of Grassy Sound

On a humid morning in early July, Eli Rogan awoke below deck of his battered boat, docked in the harbor of the tiny hamlet of West Wildwood. He was jarred awake after a restless sleep. The source of his disturbance still out of reach of consciousness, he fought the fog of sleep and lay silent in his bunk and listened. All was quiet now above him. He lay in the darkness as reality filtered in, his breathing returning to normal.

The dank smell of old cushions and weathered wood returned to him slowly. This and the sound of the water lapping gently on the sides of the fiberglass boat were the only things that revealed to him where he was. Sometimes he'd wake in the darkness of night and for a few seconds felt like he was floating in space with no sense of identity or location.

Rogan had been a fisherman most of his life. Now approaching seventy, he continued to go out each morning for his daily quota, more out of habit than of necessity, for fishing was his life and had been for the past five decades. The fishing life and the sea were really all he knew. The years he'd been drinking he'd had few other pursuits.

There was his stint in the Navy, when he'd seen action on D-Day, something he tried hard to forget, but he'd survived that, so few other things life could throw at a man could compare. Now it was only he, his cat Starsky and his boat, and memories best left forgotten.

The boat was named the *Lisa Marie,* a 1955 Eventide cabin cruiser, and, like Rogan, had seen better days. Both seemed weathered relics from an earlier time.

Most mornings in the early dawn, long before the sun came up over the ocean, Rogan would arise early and prepare a bowl of chopped fish for Starsky, a large orange stray tabby he'd adopted. He'd decided to name it Starsky, after the character in the popular TV cop show, though Rogan didn't watch much television.

Each morning for weeks the cat had waited for him out on the dock and would jump aboard, rubbing against his legs. An affectionate manipulator, it did not take long before the cat had endeared itself to him and soon Rogan found himself its chosen caretaker.

Rogan was usually awoken to the demands and scratching of Starsky at the cabin door, a cat that seemed to know each morning the precise time to rouse the sleeping fisherman from what passed for sleep.

Starsky rarely stayed the night, preferring to spend his evenings carousing the docks of the tiny hamlet, where fishing boats lined the small piers which jutted out from the bay side peninsula. But in the morning he'd scratch at the cabin door, meowing, awakening him and expecting his morning meal.

He didn't really mind the persistent cat. Rogan saw himself as a rugged individualist who was not dependent on others. But since Starsky had started coming around, the old man welcomed the company. Starsky gave him affection unconditionally and didn't ask a lot of bothersome questions. He found himself looking forward to hearing Starsky's meowing in the mornings, but on this morning, something was wrong. Silence.

It may have been Starsky was intimidated by the fireworks being set off the night before, just over the bay, and had sought refuge from the noise and light. Rogan understood that. Though he'd had many years to forget his experiences in Normandy, sudden loud explosions such as fireworks and even the backfires of cars still brought back sense memories he didn't want to think about.

In those few seconds before logic kicked in, Rogan felt the terror shoot through him. The horror of war, where a few explosive seconds could make the difference between life or death. Young men he'd come to know, men who'd stood right next to him in a split second turned to bloody husks with their limbs and faces blown off. These were memories he preferred to keep hidden below the surface, the monster in the box.

Rogan emerged above deck from the cabin. Something felt wrong. Out of place. He stood on deck and tried to get his bearings. It was still dark, just a few hours before dawn. He craned his head and looked heavenward. There were stars visible in the night sky. He looked down the neat rows of the harbor where the other fishing boats floated sleepily along the dock, illuminated by the eerie glow of the single utility light which shone down on the harbor like a plucked eye.

No one else to his knowledge slept on-board their boat as he did. He was completely alone out here most nights, unless one of the other fishermen was too drunk to go home or they were quarreling with their wives. Further down the inlet slept a small contingent of small homes; their porch lights serving as the only clue there might be any life out here at all.

Standing on the deck, Rogan noticed what appeared to be footprints tracked across the deck. They did not resemble human shoe-size tracks, but rather had a webbed triangular shape, much like a man who wears frogman flippers might make, but the edges were rough and jagged, like that which would be made by a large animal with furry feet. The footprints were dark, dirty and wet, leaving a trail across the deck toward the area where Starsky's food and water bowls sat.

Rogan's eyes stopped on the bowls, now overturned, with a small trail of Friskies leading out to the edge of the deck, disappearing at the side of the boat. Tracks of wet, dirty vegetation in the rough outline of man-size tree limbs soiled the deck and sides of the boat. Starsky was nowhere to be seen.

"Goddamn possums!" exclaimed Rogan, his voice breaking the stillness of dawn. But something didn't ring true in it, for he instinctively knew these were not the traces of something as small as a possum. He doubted a possum would climb over the sides of an anchored fishing boat.

They can be rascally bastards, them possums, he thought.

He called out for Starsky, whistling for him as one would a dog, but the only answer to be heard was the gentle lapping of waves against the sides of the boat.

He's probably out catting around, Rogan concluded.

He turned back toward the cabin. He looked down at his tattooed arms, his skin rough and wrinkled with age, the purple-blue ink faded with time. One was a woman; Betty Grable on his left forearm, with a winking eye and overly accentuated bosom, while on his right forearm was a crusty blue anchor and a cartoonish profile of Popeye, pipe jutting from his lip.

Rogan lived alone and preferred it that way. He'd lost Gert to cancer back in seventy five. That was ten years ago. Both his boys were in their thirties now, living near Levittown. He'd not seen or heard from either of them since Gert's funeral in Philadelphia, but he had it from a reliable source, (his sister in Fort Washington) that they were alive and well and had partnered in a car wash in Ambler. She'd given him each of their numbers and had encouraged him to call, but his pride would not allow him to. He missed both of them terribly but didn't want to admit it.

He didn't think about it much, but he always felt his sons held resentments against him for being gone all the time, and when he was home, his wife accused him of being emotionally absent. Thoughts of his sons impeded his daily routine as of late, perhaps because of his advancing age, or maybe just because, as he reached the twilight of his years, loneliness had begun to gnaw at him.

It saddened him how sometimes children went off in their own directions and never stayed in touch, but he was not often affected by emotion. He'd grown up in an era where men didn't talk about their feelings. If anything surfaced of any emotional import, it could easily be pushed down beneath the surface again. If a problem or emotion was particularly troublesome, alcohol had always been there to kill the pain.

He cleaned up the spilled Friskies and mopped the deck, finally going back below to make a pot of coffee. The java rig was the same one he'd used for years; a battered Brewmatic Jr. with a glass carafe that had never been thoroughly cleaned, its brown and black stained sides encrusted with the remnants of decades of use.

He used the tiny commode, taking his time, sitting on the cold seat and listening to the water gently lapping the sides of the boat. He felt old, worn out, tired. There were distances between his thoughts now, a nothingness that sometimes gave way to unpleasant memories.

One such memory had begun to surface when he heard muffled yelling from somewhere above. It was a female voice, shrill and urgent; a frantic cry for help.

Rogan pulled up his trousers, moving as quickly as he could out through the tiny closet and up onto the deck of the cruiser toward the direction of a commotion which had broken out somewhere just off the dock.

The sky was starting to lighten from the East from the direction of the Atlantic, a few miles across the peninsula. Rogan stood at the edge of the boat and peered out into the darkness in the direction of the noise. Four boats over there was a commotion. It was Fred Duffy's rig. His wife and daughter were on the deck yelling, looking over the edge. Their dog was barking off the edge.

Rogan hit the dock running. As he neared Duffy's boat, the *Chenin Blanc*, he could see Liz Duffy screaming, looking frantically over the edge into the dark water. Jagger, their aging German Shepherd, growled and barked, his paws slipping and scraping across the railing as his attention was fixated on some point below the surface of the water.

"What is it?" Rogan yelled down the dock, but Liz did not hear or acknowledge him.

He ran up the boarding plank and onto the boat, stopping at Liz's side as she watched helplessly over the edge into the water. Rogan peered over the edge but could see nothing. Liz pointed down into the water.

"It's Freddie he's..." her eyes wide, she shook with fear.

"Is he over the side?" Rogan was already pulling off his trousers, clad only in his briefs. In an instant he dove off the side of the boat, the water shocking his system. He could hear the dog barking and the screams muffled in aquatic layers through the water above him.

He struggled to see around him in the dark water but could not. He swam, reaching out around him blindly, trying to grab onto something. If Freddie was still near the surface somewhere, he might get lucky and latch onto him. Rogan swam desperately in circles, diving down farther, and continued until he could hold his breath no longer.

Breaking through to the surface, he sucked in air and went below again, continuing until he was exhausted. By now, several more boat owners and fishermen gathered at the edge of the dock, while one sailor, the red-faced Monty Reiser, threw a life preserver into the water on a long rope.

Once the men had pulled Rogan to safety, shivering and dripping wet, he strode to a waiting Liz, who had a towel ready for him. Her face was twisted in worry, her age lines deeply furrowed in terror and grief. It appeared she was going into shock. Jagger ceased his barking, though his whimpers and continual attention to the water indicated his concern for what he had seen take place just minutes before.

"I'm sorry Liz. I did all I could. You know I did."

Liz was silent, snapping her head from left to right as if trying to erase what was happening.

"Tell me what happened, what you saw," Rogan rasped as he wrapped the towel around himself.

"I can't explain it. Something took him over the edge. Something took him."

"You're not making any sense. What took him?"

Liz was inconsolable. Her shaking became uncontrollable before she fainted.

"Call an ambulance!" Rogan shouted to Monty Reiser, who was already at a dead run up the dock toward the payphone.

* * *

The paramedics and the police arrived quickly in response to the call. No one who questioned her could make any sense of the cause of Elizabeth Duffy's distress other than her account that something large and quite monstrous had come up over the side of the boat and taken her husband overboard.

Her own account was sketchy. She and her husband of forty years, Fred Duffy, were preparing the boat for the day's fishing when she'd heard a ruckus at the rear starboard side where Fred had been stocking the bait bin. She'd been alerted by Jagger's barking and had heard what sounded like a struggle and had ran toward the noise to investigate.

In the dim light she caught what appeared to be a large ape-like shape, covered with dripping vegetation, like sea kelp, pulling Fred over the side, and both had plunged into the water, disappearing. Jagger had managed to rip a piece from the thing's leg, which lay like a deflated football on the deck, surrounded by chopped fish bait.

Liz had screamed for help as Jagger barked incessantly from the edge of the rail, looking down into the darkness of the water.

Other than a story in *The Wildwood Times* and a mention on one of Philly's evening news programs, the incident was dismissed, but Rogan felt a sense of unease within the community.

* * *

Rogan went out each morning to fish, much as he had done for the past three decades, without fail. Even in his drinking days, when hangovers made the going rough, he'd prepare his bait and poles, throw lines and cruise slowly out of the narrow inlet long before the sun had come up.

You gotta suit up and show up, that's what his father always said.

Suck it up, boy. You gonna let a hangover steal your manhood?

The thought of his father made him laugh to himself, a wry, ironic chuckle.

Yeah, well, the old man died of alcoholism. Great advice, pops.

Out on the open ocean Rogan forgot his throbbing head. Back in the day, he'd bring a cooler full of beers and take his time finishing them. Somehow his problems seemed to go away when he was fishing, though he knew it was merely a distraction. His thoughts and fears were still there, somewhere below the surface, circling like predatory fish.

Rogan looked down at the deck where he used to place the beer cooler. It looked empty even now, even after these years he'd stopped drinking.

Ain't been the same since Gert died, he thought to himself.

He remembered when the hangovers had become unbearable and the depressions which followed them had left him nearly incapacitated with grief.

He'd quit cold turkey, just plain quit. It had taken nearly a month for the craving for a drink to finally subside, and once that had left him, it was just a matter of staying the course and just not drinking.

He'd attended AA meetings a few times, held twice a day at St. Vincent's church meeting hall, but he felt self-conscious and stupid among recovering drunks and hated reading out of the Big Book. He didn't need their help, he reasoned, and as long as he didn't drink, that was all that mattered, Bill W be damned.

Sometimes in his restless dreams he'd taken a drink; seen himself driving through Wildwood at night during the summer season when the streets and bars used to be full and fun abounded from every corner.

In his dream he'd stop in at Clancy's, his old whistle stop, where many of the fisherman drank. He'd seen himself sitting on his favorite bar stool and Clancy Dugan would pour him four shots of old Granddad whiskey, line them up neatly in a row in front of him, and place a frosted mug of draft beer on a cardboard coaster just at the edge of the bar.

In the dream, he'd remembered the way in which he agonized as he sat before those drinks, caught between the pleasure and relief he sought in the glass before him, and the conflict of his resolve to end the cycle of suffering drinking had caused him much of his life.

Thankfully he'd always awoken from the dream before he drank, and in those few moments when he'd come to consciousness, sweating and panting, he could not shake the fear and shame contained in those few moments of decision seated before the amber liquid.

Even in those last years of his drinking, when he left in the early mornings to fish, he'd brought a cooler with him on the boat and would drink beer slowly throughout the morning. In those days he'd prided himself on how he was able to control his intake, one beer per hour. He'd been in denial and he'd only been staving off the inevitable.

By sundown he'd be drunk and barely able to guide the *Lisa Marie* back into the harbor, and, once docked, he'd pass out below deck until morning without eating anything.

He'd often wake up in the middle of the night, head pounding, dehydrated and barely able to walk and would sometimes urinate right in the bunk.

He was ashamed of himself for allowing himself to sink to those depths, but was thankful he'd found the strength and resolve to quit while he was able.

Now it was late July. He'd usually stay out all day, just off the coast of Cape May, sometimes sitting for hours in one spot. He'd keep the fishing poles out on the brackets, where he didn't have to think about them, stretch out on his crusty deck lounger, pull his old fishing cap over his eyes and catch a snooze. Except for the incident that morning, it was a day like all the rest.

He awoke to the sound of the fishing reel winding out. To a fisherman there was no sweeter sound than that of the run of a reel and the knowledge there was a potential catch on the end of the line.

This one is large, Rogan thought, even before he'd unsnapped the pole from the clamp. It wound out fast and hard. Once he grabbed the pole and felt the weight of the fish he knew it would not reel in easily. A fish was pulling the line out fast, running like a streak of lightning beneath the water east toward the open ocean.

Rogan kept his cool and his hand steady, giving just enough tension on the line to keep it taut. For the next hour he would angle with his catch, wearing it down, until finally pulling it from the water into the boat.

But something felt wrong.

As he pulled the catch in, it became a dead weight, heavier and heavier on his line. He pulled and struggled with the fiberglass pole, bent nearly vertical toward the water. He pulled the weight toward the edge of the boat, then, locked the pole back into the support bracket.

He grabbed the long-hook, an aluminum pole that extended in sections, with a tip that ended in a sharp hook. He locked it off to its longest length and dropped it into the water, trying to snag the monstrous catch.

He squinted against the sun, stretched over the railing, nearly losing his balance as he attempted to snare the line. Finally hooking the edge of the line, and pulled with all might to bring the catch to the surface.

A dark shape slowly rose upward through the sunlit water. Something hideous and bloated. It was not a fish, that much Rogan knew. A white blob the color of the underbelly of fish slowly came into view. What rose to the surface came into focus as it became level with the surface, then bobbed out of the water like a rotted cork.

Rogan staggered backward, startled, dropping the hook into the water.

What stared up at him from the water was the putrid, decaying face of what was left of Fred Duffy.

* * *

Rogan awoke in a panic. In his shock he was no longer a man leaning over the edge of the boat. He looked down to see his own body at rest in the deck-lounger, sweating in a blind panic from the nightmare.

The fishing poles were just as he'd left them. Three evenly spaced fiberglass rods poked out over the water. He composed himself as his respiration returned to normal. He stood at the edge of the railing, looking down into the water.

The only thing he saw was trash and debris floating on the surface, something he'd been seeing with more frequency in recent years. Man did not respect the ocean, that much was clear, but then, the way of the world always seemed to be the pursuit of more profit at the expense of the health of the planet.

It had affected everything. Global warming and over fishing, along with toxic waste, had made making a living fishing difficult if not impossible in the past decade.

Disgusted, Rogan pulled the lines in and packed the poles up in the storage box, pulled anchor and pointed the hull toward Grassy Sound. As he steered the vessel across the gentle waves, he watched the Wildwood shore off in the distance.

The amusement piers had once been a beehive of activity this time of day, but no more. The shore-towns were dying as families had become more fragmented and air travel less expensive. What had once been the tradition of families down the shore had given way to a migration to more exotic locales like Hawaii and Tahiti.

He thought of all the summers on the ocean with his sons as they were growing up, their fascination with the sea. When they were young they seemed so full of innocence and wonder. Now their focus was on their own lives and values, with raising their own families. But it amazed him how quickly they moved on and seemingly forgot about their parents.

The hot summer sun was sinking just below the horizon on the bay side of the peninsula as Rogan guided his boat homeward, the cranes and gulls scattering out over the tall grass and reeds of the Sound.

Despite all of the changes, some ramshackle fishing homes still sat like ancient sentries on their stilts in the waving grass. Rogan wondered how much longer it would be before the developers had taken those, too.

* * *

The afternoon sun had already disappeared below the horizon as Rogan walked up the short expanse of dock to the gravel parking lot where his old pickup truck sat rusting in the impending twilight. Most of the boats were in for the night; their catches already delivered to local restaurants and stores.

Rogan fiddled with the keys in his pocket, finally slipping the longest key into the lock of the Chevy truck door, turned it, the lock popping up. It took four attempts for the engine to turn over, the tired relic in its last breaths of life. He sat in the parking lot, revved the engine and allowed it to warm, his thoughts on earlier days and times.

He'd thought of the many days when Todd and Eric would play in this lot as he and Gertie prepared the *Lisa Marie* for the day's fishing. Everything had seemed so simple then. Sure he and Gertie sometimes argued, but their marriage was solid and they both felt a sense of purpose in raising their sons.

Yet a distance had grown between he and his family, even then the spaces between them widening as the months and years wore on.

Something in his heart missed those days and longed desperately for them to return.

Memories are a canceled check, Rogan thought to himself.

A fly buzzed and banged against the passenger side window, seeking escape. Rogan watched it for a second, then cranked down the window, allowing the fly to soar through the window and out into freedom. He put the truck in gear and pulled forward, rolling slowly past the few parked cars which lined the lot, dust rising as the evening lights began to blink on.

Rogan drove through the streets of Wildwood, noticing

how thin the crowds had become in recent years. They could hardly be called crowds anymore. For decades during the busy summer seasons throngs of people would criss-cross the teeming streets, club-hopping to hear some of the East Coast's most popular groups.

In those days big name music stars came regularly to Wildwood, and for many it was considered the birthplace of Rock and Roll. Now it looked like a ghost town. Somehow its spirit had vanished. He wondered what it would look like ten years from now, probably a sleepy hovel of faceless condominiums and a generation too young to remember its glorious past.

A group of rowdy teens pulled up next to him at a stoplight. The driver was a sandy blonde haired kid with crooked teeth. In the passenger seat was a big stocky kid that looked like a bully wrestler, his big meaty head filling up the window frame.

"Hey old timer, why don't you get that shit-crate off the street before someone gets hurt?" he jeered, passing a smoking brass pipe to the driver while two other youths snarled and snickered from the backseat.

Rogan kept his eyes straight forward, ignoring them.

"Whatssamatter pops, hearing aid not working?" the kid tried again, a titter of laughter again from the backseat.

It took forever for the light to change, and as the seconds crawled by Rogan fought to gain control of his temper. The punks had no idea he'd fought for their freedom and put his ass on the line for them. During the war he'd watched close friends die so that future generations could prosper and their children would find a better way of life.

The light turned green and the driver popped the clutch, the Javelin burning rubber and leaving Rogan in the dust.

Fucking punks, Rogan thought, and gave them the finger through the glass.

He crept slowly along Ocean Drive, the old doo-wop motels, once alive with brightly painted pastel facades and faux palm trees, now they sat nearly abandoned. Some never reopening even for the few brief seasonal months, like they'd given up on life altogether.

Rogan had spent much of his life here, and on each street and nearly every building, restaurant or bar, he'd had some history. These were places in his youth where he'd met girls and drank and danced. The memories shared with friends, the times spent on the beach just over the boardwalk, now empty and standing in desolate silence.

He'd met Gertie on the boardwalk, remembered vividly the first time he saw her. He was introduced to her by Bernie Lowenstein, a friend he'd known from high school. He and Bern were barely in their mid-twenties, just back from the war.

Gertie had been standing in line to buy tickets for the amusement pier when Low had made the introduction, and Rogan remembered how pretty she was, and how his heart skipped a beat the first time she looked at him.

Rogan stopped his truck near the boardwalk ramp leading up toward the amusement pier, his mind lost in images of the past. In the shadows below the rotting boards he could see the huddled shapes of young men passing a crack pipe, their faces hard and angry.

Dear God how this place has changed, he thought. Saddened, he turned the truck away from the boardwalk. Wildwood just wasn't the place is used to be. Not anymore. He longed for a past that had disappeared too soon and a youth that had slipped by just as quickly.

He drove up Atlantic Boulevard, the yellow-orange streetlamps offsetting the broken neon signs which cast a garish glow through the mist now settling in from the ocean. He rattled past the old Lincoln Hotel, now converted to a modernized motel for families, and the bar that used to be his favorite hangout.

The parking lot was deserted. There were lights on inside and a flashing OPEN sign. It was on nights like these, in settings just as sinister, that bad things happened, Rogan thought. But the real tragedy of it was that he just didn't give a shit anymore.

Resist it... Rogan thought.

He passed the bar, continuing down Atlantic as the mist settled into fog. The town seemed empty and eerie. As he passed the side streets which dead-ended to the ocean, yellow stoplights blinked like beacons, illuminating the damp streets now bathed in a gray sweaty swirl of drifting fog.

He cranked down the old window, took in the dank sea air, heavy with humidity. The smell of salt marshes was thick and pervasive. It brought back sense memories of his childhood spending summers down the shore. He listened. He could hear the distant roar of the breakers as he turned left onto a side street away from the ocean.

Montgomery Avenue was barely visible, the tall Victorian-era rooming houses loomed up in the darkness, but no streetlamps marked the way. Most of the streetlights on this desolate avenue had burned out or the timers didn't work. Now the structures had morphed and taken on shapes from the past.

Sharks swam up from the depths of consciousness, memories Rogan had suppressed in most of his waking hours since the war. The buildings he saw through the hazy windshield were those of a bombed out European city, the faces of those buildings left standing dropped away to reveal multiple floors and stairways, their interiors left intact like dissected dollhouses.

The memory flashed back vividly from nothing, from a lost frequency now found. *Toulon, France, August 1944.* Rogan had gone into the apartment building on a recon mission looking for survivors and possible snipers. The krauts liked to hide in these structures and pick off the American troops as they walked through the just-liberated cities and towns.

Rogan had reached the second floor and entered the first apartment to the right of the stairwell, his rifle in front of him when a shape hard-tackled him from somewhere to his right. Both had gone down hard, the rifle had dropped and skittered just out of reach of both men, now fighting for their lives.

The German was heavy and strong and fought with a vengeance. The man grunted and cursed German obscenities, striking Rogan several times in the head and face with his fists as each fought to gain control over the other.

In the ensuing struggle, Rogan's strength and speed were superior, allowing him to reach down to his waist and unsheathe his bayonet knife. He brought the knife straight up, shoving it directly through the German's jaw, piercing upward into his mouth and nasal cavity, then pulled out and shoved it multiple times into the gurgling man's heart. Within moments the German was gasping on the floor, coughing up blood. Within a few moments, the man was dead.

Rogan lay panting on the floor. He'd watched the German die, the one of many men he'd seen die during the war, many of them his friends and comrades. His heart felt heavy as he turned his head sideways and threw up. He felt remorse and grief and a guilt that would never leave him. It had been his first kill, and he vowed it would be his last.

The memory clicked out of consciousness as Rogan snapped back to reality.

He guided the rattling truck slowly down Montgomery Avenue, valves tapping like skeletons on a hit tin roof. The mist was heavy and the buildings had morphed back to their normal facades. Empty dark windows and desolate porches lined the dark street. It did not seem like there were any living souls left here.

What if they are all dead?

Lost in his thoughts, he pointed the truck toward the bay and drove toward West Wildwood. Past dark empty summer homes, past the liquor stores and quiet neon-lit motels, Rogan longed for the solace and familiarity of the *Lisa Marie*.

The pier was abandoned and dark with fog that settled into a dirty mist. The boats were barely visible as he parked the truck in the gravel lot. He trudged to the pay phone at the wharf, the metal box exposed to the elements, dripping with moisture. He dropped a quarter into the slot to try calling Eric again. There was a metallic click and then an airy sound, an answering machine recording. It was Lisa's voice, Eric's wife.

Hi this is the Rogan residence, Eric and Lisa. We're not in right now but please leave a message at the sound of the tone and we'll get back to you soon!

Rogan didn't leave a message. He hung the receiver into its cradle, disconnecting the call.

He shuffled down the dock where the *Lisa Marie* floated silently in the dark water, thick dirty-white ropes looked like umbilical cords tying her to mother earth. Rogan wanted to throw those lines and sail her to the edge of the earth and disappear forever.

There were no signs of life anywhere, no cats or barking dogs. He looked around for some sign of Starsky. Rogan sensed that whatever had taken the Starsky had also taken Old Fred, and neither one of them were ever coming back.

There'd been rumors and stories over the past decade from local fishermen of a creature which dwelt in the swamps of Grassy Sound; something like a water-based Bigfoot with an attitude.

Rogan never gave much pluck to myths and rumor, but one thing was certain. There were a number of unexplained disappearances of fishing men over the years in the sound; most of the men had been older and at the end of their days.

He'd heard the talk in Clancy's, guys drunk on their ass. Words and phrases drifted back to him.

"Don't make no sense, people don't just disappear."

"Something come down from space to take them away."

"Weird science man, Loch Ness shit."

"I saw it one night, came up out the water like a hairy ape, then disappeared."

That last comment came from Sollie Brewster, about a week before he vanished. Nobody'd seen hide nor hair of him since.

There were frequent reports of pets gone missing, particularly cats. But even a dog or two had vanished without a trace since the stories started circulating, and one fisherman, Rusty Talbott, claimed he'd taken a photograph of it. He kept the tattered Polaroid square folded up in his wallet. If people bought him enough drinks he'd make a show out of pulling it out.

"Took this me-self," he'd say, in a down-low drunken whisper, like he was disclosing the secrets of the ages. Then he'd painstakingly unfold it, and each time he did it the ritual seemed to take longer. The story always changed slightly each time he told it, with frequent stops to drain his glass and let his listeners know he was getting thirsty.

The photo had run in a few UFO-sighting newsletters, underground photocopied publications with limited circulation. But the photo was too dark and grainy to really tell what it was in the image.

The shape it depicted looked like the monster in the movie *Swamp Thing*, a Roger Corman picture that had come out in the late Fifties. Though some claimed the photo was authentic, the progeny of some clash of nature or retaliation of the planet toward its toxic inhabitants, Rogan thought the photo looked more like a man dressed in a monster suit covered with wet leaves and seaweed.

He went aboard and stood at the railing, looking out at the narrow channel leading out toward the ocean. A bank of swirling fog drifted above the surface of the water, hazy lights of small homes and surrounding streets gave only a hint of illumination through the mist.

It was goddamn quiet. Rogan mused. *Too quiet.*

Rogan went below deck, peeled off his clothes, and left them in a crumpled heap on the floor. He climbed into his unmade bunk and lay staring at the ceiling. He clasped his hands behind his head. His body ached. He prided himself on not taking a drink, but his soul felt empty and loneliness ached in his heart.

I'm down here, Gertie. If you can hear me. Things ain't the same since you died my dear. Too many goddamn changes, too much shit under the bridge.

He fell asleep to the images of he and Gertie on the boardwalk rides all those summers long ago. When Wildwood had been so different. When values had been worth a damn.

* * *

Rogan awoke sometime past midnight to the sounds of something on deck above him. A scraping and dragging sound, something he could not quite make out. He fought out of sleep, trying to shake himself awake.

He thrashed around in the dark for the Coleman lantern, and it finally yielded to his touch. He clicked the switch and the cabin was bathed in a cold flashlight glow. He listened again. Above him the sound had become louder. *Thump. Swisshh. Thump. Swisshhhh.*

He swung his legs down to the floor, leaned forward and slid the bayonet knife out from beneath the canvas mat that served as his mattress. It was the same knife he'd used on the German. He listened again. Silence.

Prob'ly Starsky, finally come back... he thought.

He slipped the knife back under the cushion, then thought the better of it and slipped it out again. He stood slowly, his legs aching, grabbed the lantern, clasped the knife in his teeth like a pirate, and climbed the stairs up to the deck.

Above deck, as he pushed open the cabin door, a cool wind hit him. A storm had crept in during the night and a steady wind was blowing out of the North Atlantic. A cold mist hit his face as he walked past the wheelhouse and up onto the slippery deck. He could hear the creaking of boards from the pier being stressed by the steady press of wind. Boats banged against the dock, pulling against their ropes.

But there was something else.

It was a presence more than anything, something out of place. An uneasy feeling crept over him as he stopped, held his breath, and listened. *Thump. Swisshh. Thump. Swisshhhh.* ... It was coming from the aft of the boat.

Rogan removed the knife from his teeth and grasped it tightly in his right hand. He moved stealthily toward the sound, peering out at the darkness at the edge of the craft.

Then he spotted it.

It was a shape.

Something large.

Something that resembled the image in that grainy photo except without the grain.

The Thing froze, caught by surprise as Rogan moved into its line of vision.

Rogan held his breath and counted, trying to counter the shock which ran through him.

There were a few long seconds before the shape finally moved. It lumbered toward him. The closer it got the more astonishing and horrific it became. The size of a small ape, it appeared made of sea kelp, seaweed and wet leaves. It had two very large holes for eyes, with a thin membrane like a cataract over the openings.

It smelled like overripe fish and rotting vegetation. It was hard to make out detail in the dark, even at close range, but the thing moved awkwardly, as if in pain, as if land were not its first home.

Thump. Swisshh. Thump. Swisshhhh.

Before Rogan could make sense of what was happening, the shape was on him.

Rogan had tensed up in fear, his reflexes too slow. The swamp beast had him in a bear hug and emitted a deep gurgling sound from somewhere in its chest. Thrown off balance, Rogan was lifted from his feet as the thing edged him closer to the boat railing. He tried tightening his grip on the bayonet knife, now seeming a disembodied appendage.

Rogan tried to thrust the knife upward but his arms were locked by the immense strength of the beast, which squeezed him in a wet, rotting vise. The smell would have been unbearable had he been able to breathe.

They teetered at the edge of the railing, then the shape angled itself sideways. Though Rogan fought to regain control. he could not match the strength of the beast. The thing pulled both of them over the side, crashing into the dark water.

The shock of the cold water shot through Rogan like icy electricity. The thing was taking him down to the bottom, not letting go in its vise-grip of death. The beast seemed to gain in strength and agility once it had hit the water, gathering even more control in its natural habitat. This was, at its heart, a sea based creature, Rogan somewhere in his depths and panic instinctively knew.

Rogan found himself floundering in blackness and cold, yet the warmth of the creature, despite its death-grip, could be felt through its matted leaves, fur and skin. Oddly, he felt a sensation of security in the murky water, as if he was being held by mother earth.

His eyes stung from the murky salt water, a taste of warm mucous rising in his throat.

Thoughts raced through his mind. Scenes from a life well-lived yet full of tragedy and despair. He felt the sun on his face as he lay on the beaches of Wildwood with his family, his young sons playing in the sand.

The Ferris wheel where he and Gertie had kissed for the first time, high above Fun Pier, overlooking the open sea. A place in his mind where youth seemed eternal and possibilities were endless.

The faces of friends and parents, the boys he knew in the war, swimming past him in the freezing wet dark. He felt the struggle slowly drain from him.

The swamp beast held him like a lion holds its prey, with knowing tenacity and strength, its calmness in the knowledge of certain victory. The two were as one, sinking down fast as the bubbles trailed toward the surface above them.

It was taking him down to the depths. He tried to gain control of his hand, the one clutching the knife but his fingers would not move. Involuntarily his hand released the knife. It dropped below them in its race to the bottom. Rogan heard the muffled clink of the blade against the rocks on the bottom.

He felt his lungs exploding from lack of oxygen, felt his consciousness slipping away, his body going completely limp. In that moment of release and surrender, there was clarity. It was an inner peace he had never felt before, something which defied understanding. It was as if it were the feeling he'd been searching for since his birth, but it had eluded him until this moment of death.

As if in a dark tunnel, a great white ball of light, spun off in the distance, coming closer, and as it did, it enveloped him in great pockets of comfort. Waves of warmth flowed through him and a joy that defied anything he had ever known.

It had all become clear to Rogan in that instant. He'd been fighting all of his life. It was time to let go.

The ball of light exploded in his brain and what had been his body, a body full of tension, worry, anxiety and pain, had vanished.

He slipped from consciousness and ceased to be Eli Rogan.

From above, on the surface of the water, little remained of the struggle which had taken place below. There were only the traces of air bubbles as they broke on the surface of the dark water, diminishing in frequency, then disappearing altogether.

The Witches of Wildwood

A Novella

J az and her three sisters were still in their late teens the summer they moved into the Wildwood boarding house.

Their florescent green Plymouth Duster pulled into the dirt lot which adjoined the decaying structure. The girls looked up in wonder at the ancient pointed turrets. "Perfect. It's perfect," Jaz said. Her eyes were blank.

Zoey and Ali, both characteristically quiet, seemed in agreement as their pretty eyes scanned the exterior of the house, its black shingled skin the color of bats. They nodded in approval while their thoughts circled as crows around ancient eaves.

When they all piled out of the old car, all seemed to move as one.

All of them were attractive, their hair styled and streaked, blow-dried and precision cut. Their skin tight jeans and tank tops had been carefully selected to show off their young bodies. All four girls were agile and strong.

Jaz was the tallest among them. She towered over them, like a lanky basketball player, her straight black hair long and thin was halfway down her back.

Their makeup was applied with care, although none of them really needed it. They all were in exceptionally vibrant health; all of them would turn heads on the boardwalk.

Maya was the heaviest sister, her dark Joan Jett hair capped a cute but pudgy face, her black AC/DC tee barely holding in her large breasts.

None of the girls wore bras, their nipples clearly showing through the tight tees, but Maya was the most ample figured among them. Her widening hips would one day qualify her as fat. For now she was considered slightly heavy; thick as some called it. It was a look certain men found appealing and she used it to her advantage.

"It might work," Maya said, looking up, eyeing the upper windows of the house, her thick mascara eyes narrowed in that studious way she always looked at things. She said things quite seriously, for she never smiled, and was always the voice of reason among them.

They all stood together, in a perfect line, looking up at the long windows, each of them spinning their own thoughts, but all attuned to a frequency not heard by most.

All of them felt the energy which pulsed around them, all of them had knowledge of the world of the spirit. All of them were witches.

* * *

The boarding house was owned by Abigail and Jonas Mayfield, an aging couple in their seventies who had run the place since the 1950's. Both of them agreed that each season seemed to bring a younger and more rebellious crowd to Wildwood, but neither of them spoke much about it to anyone other than themselves.

The couple longed for the days when families would come and spend sedate summers, just sitting on the wide porches drinking lemonade and walking the few short blocks to the beach.

In the heyday of the 1950's and 1960's, when the resort town of Wildwood was in its golden age, the Mayfields hosted hundreds of such families during the short seasonal months, many of them regulars. But it was the eighties now, and things had changed. Along with Reaganomics had come the exodus away from local shores, but the Mayfields resisted the temptation to sell to the proliferation of developers that had started sniffing around.

The house was three floors tall and had thirty units. Some were single rooms, while others were small efficiency apartments for families. The attic had once contained sleeping rooms. How the couple used them for storage since they'd moved in to the house from their suburban home in Del Mar.

They'd tired of the commute each summer, of schlepping their belongings back and forth between houses, so when they had retired, they'd moved to Wildwood and had, up to now, been able to maintain a decent living with their retirement, his pension, and the rental income.

Many of the older residents agreed that each year the element of kids was changing. They seemed a lot more reckless now, using drugs, and drinking on a level that bordered on insanity. *It was as if the Devil himself had taken over the town,* Abigail often thought, but she kept it to herself.

Abigail Mayfield liked the sisters. She felt they were charming and seemed so innocent, and in fact reminded her of herself when she was just a young teenager and spent summers working the boardwalk and staying in rooming houses just like this one.

The girls were precocious and charming; Abigail had especially taken to Jaz, the tallest sister. Jaz seemed awkward yet possessed of some darker wisdom Abigail could not yet fathom.

They all seemed a like nice girls yet a little rough around the edges, though they would not enter into any dialogue about their family other than they had all grown up in Camden, which would explain their slightly armored exterior, she reasoned.

She more than noticed a powerful smell of incense, a musty, heady aroma that emanated from them, and the fact they wore no bras, but it was after all a new generation, one that followed its own customs and defiant attitudes.

The girls paid a month's rent up front, which impressed Abigail. They had come early enough in the season to have their pick of units. The sisters rented the largest efficiency, the one on the ground floor with an entrance way just below the back stairs.

It was a spartan accommodation, and, like the house, was a throwback to an earlier century. A miniature gas range had been installed along with a basin sink for dishes for the kitchen.

The four bedrooms were like closets, each containing only a small single bed and a mismatched thrift store dresser, with paper thin walls through which one could hear other tenants in the adjacent apartments.

The girls didn't mind - they were young and it was exciting to be living together at the shore. They excitedly carried in their old suitcases and boxes, while they played rock music which blared from a stereo they'd set up on the top of the

1960's-era Frigidaire.

It was still the end of April, and a slight bite of cold was in the ocean breeze even in the blazing sunlight. The girls didn't bother with jackets, and the moment they were unpacked they'd all headed up on the boardwalk.

The shore town was still mostly empty of tourists but there were signs of the Summer season approaching. As the girls walked past the boarding houses and motels, owners removed wooden boards from windows, washed down awnings, preparing for the summer.

The sisters walked in a line, four across, always, like gunfighters walking into a new town. Jaz, because she was tallest, was always far right. To her left was Ali, the next shortest, a diminutive blonde with a pretty yet almost masculine face.

Zoey, the youngest sister, always walked to her left. Though Zoey was the shortest of the sisters, she was the one who hit hardest in school fights.

Bookending the four on the far left was Maya - her dark bangs and purple eye shadow setting off her somewhat sinister goth look. Her calm demeanor was deceptive. She could kill in a heartbeat.

They strutted down the almost-empty boards like they had already taken over the town.

"It's great to be alive!" Ali yelled, both fists raised in the air.

"Fuckin' Aay!" followed Zoey, stretching to meet the sky.

Jaz and Maya simply stayed quiet, smiling with confidence, though Maya's anxiety could never really be completely hidden. She always seemed troubled by some nagging thought that bubbled just below her surface.

They walked with an exaggerated swagger that day, the sea gulls circling overhead, the boardwalk empty of anyone except for a stray jogger or cyclist. Most of the boardwalk storefronts were still shuttered, with the exception of Mack's Pizza, which always seemed to attract people.

Their tight jeans fit like skins to their young attractive bodies; their tops showing off their figures in defiant tones - always offsetting a minimum of jewelry, an ear stud here, a thin silver necklace there - a scattered ring or two, just enough to give a sense of style and femininity that spelled youth, hip vitality and sexual prowess.

Though invisible to all but their most intimate charges, each girl had a small red and black tattoo on her right thigh, just over the pelvic bone next to their pubic region.

It was a circle of red fire around a goats head, below which were imprinted three tiny red gothic letters, ant-like, so small as to be barely readable:

666

The entered Mack's Pizza, empty now but for one teen boy picking up a boxed large to go. He could not take his eyes off them, all four eyeing him like hungry wolves surrounding a pork chop.

The teen boy fumbled with his wallet as he paid an angry-looking Greek man and grabbed the edges of the box, but never took his eyes off the girls.

"Hey young lover," shot Jaz, seductively, overdoing it, winking.

Zoey put her hands on her hips and swayed them

enticingly at the boy, puckering her lips in a faux kiss, rolling her eyes at him.

The boy didn't know what to do, not realizing they were only playing with him - his confused thoughts racing and causing his hands to shake.

The Greek took the boy's money. He never looked up from the transaction but had in fact taken all four girls in in the snapshot instant they entered.

A new generation of girls coming up now, bold, sassy bitches... probably have AIDS, he thought, and put any further thoughts of them out of his mind.

Maya waited at the counter for the two to finish their transaction while the other three girls strode to the back of the shop.

"I gotta pee," Zoey giggled, as all three entered the rest room through a large gray door.

"You always gotta pee," chided Ali, pulling the restroom door shut behind them.

They always did everything together.

* * *

Having piled into a booth, they sat two and two and played with their straws until the pizza came, all seeming to communicate on some primal, intuitive level, finishing each others sentences.

When the pizza came, the sisters ate voraciously, pulling the pieces from the pie like hungry birds attacking carrion, hardly chewing they spoke through mouthfuls as a radio blared Bruce Springsteen from the front of the shop.

The girls didn't speak until the pizza was partway finished.

"Let's go to the Playpen tonight," Jaz said decisively, "Ya know. Shake the trees. See what falls."

"It'll be dead," Maya said, without missing a beat. The lines on her forehead always seemed furrowed in deep thought.

"Dead is good," Zoey laughed, an ornery smile punctuated with tomato sauce. Jaz reached across the table and wiped the sauce off Zoey's mouth with a napkin like a watchful mother.

"Fuckin' aay it is," mumbled Zoey.

"Kinda early in the season for trouble, ain't it?" Ali asked. It wasn't really a question. She was being sarcastic.

"Never too early for trouble," replied Jaz, the only one of the four that seemed to chew carefully before swallowing.

The Greek threw a mound of pale dough in the air, manipulating it into a spinning disk. He seemed bored, stoic, and as he threw he looked out over the glass counter and out into the distant horizon of the ocean. It looked like he was dreaming of being anywhere but here.

"How 'bout an old guy this time?" Maya suggested, watching the Greek.

"Old farts ain't got no mojo," said Ali, "We need 'em young. Dumb. Full of come."

"More power that way," Zoey mumbled thorugh mouthfuls of pizza.

The girls all giggled in unison, a viciousness beneath their laughter.

* * *

The moon was full but hazy that evening, sitting over the

Atlantic like a sleeping giant.

Inside the rooming house, the sisters had blocked the windows with tin foil, long shiny strips scotch-taped together to form a shield against prying eyes and moonlight.

Jaz stepped back and analyzed the work they'd done putting up the foil.

"I dunno," she laughed. "Whattaya think, Zoey?"

"I think it's tits, man," Zoey said, chewing her gum slowly, carefully examining the clean lines of scotch tape she'd lain.

"It's a work of art. Let's get this done," Maya said, her mind on the task at hand.

Ali seemed introspective.

"When we do this, it makes me think of mom," Ali said.

"She'd be proud of us, mom would," Zoey chimed in.

"You really think so? I mean, we just started with the killing," Ali said, "I think she would have liked it had we started younger."

"There's gotta be a reason, a purpose for it," Maya said sternly. "You don't just start taking people out on a whim. Mom never did and her mother never did, she always taught us that."

"I get sad when I think about her," Ali replied, and then went silent.

"She didn't have to die that way," Zoey said quietly, almost as an afterthought.

The girls often speculated how their mother could have died when immortality was all but promised to all who worked the magic properly. Perhaps, it had been suggested once, her faith was not strong enough to overcome the illness which had overtaken her.

"She could have entered someone else, stolen their body," Maya said as she began moving the kitchen table. "If she had she'd still be with us. That's what was supposed to happen."

Maya wheeled on her angrily.

"There's no 'supposed to happen' in this world, honey. You got to make things happen.'

The conversation cast a solemn pall on the proceedings, and the girls did not talk any more about their mother.

The sisters had moved the kitchen table and chairs and chalked a precise pentagram on the floor of the tiny efficiency. As they went through the motions of setting up the ceremony, their youthful enthusiasm returned. Within minutes their vibrant faces were once again aglow with the delight of a brethren decorating the family Christmas tree.

Once preparations had been made, incense and candles lit, the cloth and altar, the bell, book and dagger laid lovingly onto the black silk laden altar surface.

The girls were resolute; their smiles and laughter turned deadly serious, giving way to a divine but deadly countenance.

They now moved as one in the eerie darkness, lit only by the dripping black candles which flickered on the tiny makeshift altar.

The girls all wore thick black hooded monk robes, only their faces illuminated by the flickering candlelight. They chanted in a language only they seemed to understand, a chant so ancient even they could not fathom its lineage.

It was a low monotone, a rhythmic cadence of impending doom. Their young voices gave it an innocent vitality, a new life than from its eternal roots, echoing from their lithe young bodies from an ancient past too terrible to comprehend.

They'd learned witchcraft from an early age. It had been passed on to them by their foster-care mother who had taken them in as orphans when they were children.

She'd been a driving force in their lives, for until Maya had turned all of eighteen and the girls had left foster care, Lucretia had taught them the power to wield the dark forces of the universe to their own ends.

That they hardly possessed the darker wisdom needed to wield the forces responsibly, or that they could inflict terrible danger on themselves and mankind, did not matter to her.

She herself had been taught and raised the same way; in her case, through the auspices of a vindictive matriarch named Sarah Fowler; begat from an entire lineage of witches which ran clear back to the Mayflower.

The sisters moved counter-clockwise within the pentagram, their solemn chant and intense one-pointed concentration focused on the summoning of the black forces.

They'd done the ritual many times before, but tonight it took on special significance.

Tonight they were the supreme, the alpha-omega, in their earthly presence and conviction they were one power, one unity.

Their power relied on sacrifice.

They were, for better or worse, the Witches of Wildwood.

* * *

They'd dressed to kill, all four of them. Each one wore

their own rendition of the little black dress; a minimum of jewelry and just the right amount of skin showing.

They moved through the sparse crowd and stood near the to the front of the stage, while the popular group WITNESS performed their tribute to Jethro Tull.

Most of the crowd were male, hanging with buddies and a few strays, some had traveled down from New York.

A few of the males were workmen, young independent contractors with their muscled young bodies moving gracefully through the crowd, beers in hand, scanning the mass for a quick sexual connection.

The sisters drew a lot of attention, their power to attract and hold sway with only men but also women. Even girls who had heretofore only entertained a fleeting fantasy of exploring another female were flooded with thoughts of that possibility with any or all of the witches.

The sisters were selective, and in fact rebelled in the stirring and channeling of deep sexual desire, for longing and lust. Each knew the power of unfulfilled fantasy, the promise of sex, the illusion of the conquering of the flesh. It was powerful elixir, and always unrequited love at the heart of it.

For each of the girls could lure the object of their desire with a single look and capture their prey with a mere glance to set the wheels of want in motion.

"The pickins look pretty slim," said Zoey as they moved through through the club to the front of the stage, her eyes scanning the crowd.

"A bunch of yocal horndogs," observed Maya with a wry grin.

"Every dog has his day," giggled Ali.

Jaz remained quiet, her eyes flitting from body to body, looking for a prime cut. All eyes were on them, they knew that, and their confidence was supreme. As they walked they saw the men staring, while paired buddies whispered ear to ear, casting hungry eyes in their direction.

A few of the drunker strays approached them, asking Jaz to dance, for she was the prettiest among them, the one with the naughtiest eyes. Their heavy Philly-accented slurs carried the scent of whiskey and cigarettes.

"No thank you," she'd say, innocently, like a southern belle, batting her eyes, yet giving the man a look which suggested otherwise, a look of seductive promise.

The girls stood before the rock band as it blared and the leader pranced on the stage, dressed in a long English overcoat which hung to the floor. He sported a long haired wig frazzled out and played a long silver flute while balancing on one leg as the group pounded out an inspired version of "Locomotive Breath."

In the shuffling madness known as locomotive breath
Runs the all time loser headlong to his death
He feels the pistons scraping, sweat breaking on his brow
While God he pulled the handle
And the train it won't stop moving
No way to slow down....

The girls grooved to the music, swaying, their faces turned upward, eyes shut in semi-orgasmic pleasure. The band members did their best to pretend the sisters were not there but each of them returned their attention to the four, so very conspicuous, their perfect skin and classy sexy attire made them the energy center of the room.

Even the lead singer gave them an occasional glance, a cool sideways-down look, taking their energy and channeling it into his performance.

Zoey did her best to attract him. She didn't have to try hard, for she was naturally seductive in an innocuous, innocent way, almost organic. The four girls stood in sharp contrast to the groupies who followed the band wherever they played or who came to the Playpen almost every night the group played.

During the break, the sisters walked to the back of the club and made their way toward the makeshift ladies room - a place of dark passions and dripping plumbing.

The black painted walls of the club had been arranged so that the light from the ladies room would not spill out into the club, so a small box labyrinth had to be navigated to enter.

There was no door to either rest room, both existing side by side with an old couch lodged in the wall between both entrances. The girls entered the dimly lit restroom, which smelled of urine and vomit.

All four girls stood at the tarnished mirrors touching up their makeup. Two others came in, one of them giving Jaz poisonous looks.

"What are you looking at, bitch?" Jaz shot menacingly to the staring brunette. The brunette's eyes averted, as she entered a stall, while her girlfriend, a short, stout blonde with a leather jacket stood by, glaring at Jaz.

Jaz kept her eyes on the blonde through the mirror while the other sisters grinned to themselves, with the exception of

Maya, whose stone features were unchanging as she applied her lipstick, a shade of crimson the color of dried blood.

The blonde stood like a sentinel next to the stall, a cold empty edifice, staring back at Jaz through the mirror.

Ali spoke as she watched herself through the mirror.

"I think the bitch has a butch protector," Ali spoke.

"Yeah," Zoey added, "her own personal pussy guard. She needs one with a mouth like that."

The lock to the stall slid open hard as the brunette stepped out and stood next to the blonde, the height difference between them nearly a foot.

"Wow, she's a tall one," Zoey said, "beanstalk and pipsqueak. Guess height doesn't matter when you're laying down."

In that instant, both girls knew they were outnumbered by two and in completely over their heads. The power and fury that came off of the sisters could be felt in the air, and both girls felt fear shoot through them in waves of electric dread.

Two more girls walked in to the use the restroom, saw the standoff and immediately turned around and left, while an overweight girl in the last stall exited quickly without washing her hands.

Jaz dove headlong into the blonde, thrusting her backward into the stall where she fell over the toilet and instantly had the girl by the hair with both hands smashing her head repeatedly against the porcelain bowl.

Once the girl was sufficiently subdued, Jaz used her fist to break the girls nose, then stood up and thrust the girls bleeding head into the bowl and drowned her.

Maya and Ali held the other girl while Ali threw a barrage of punches at her face, and within moments the brunettes face was bruised and bloody.

Then Ali worked on blackening her eyes until they were swollen shut, while the girls mouth bled profusely. There was no emotion in their violence, but the fury and terrible ferocity of it belied their innocent youth.

Then, in one swift movement, Maya pulled out the switchblade and thrust it into the girls stomach, turning it, then withdrew the dripping knife. They pushed the dark haired girl, now just so much bloody meat, into the stall on top of her drowned friend.

Zoey locked the stall from the inside and slipped out under the stall. The sisters wiped the blood up from the floor then cleaned themselves up, lined up in front of the mirror like debutantes at a prom.

There had been no witness to the carnage.

* * *

"Nothin' like a little strangulation to get the blood circulation" chirped Zoey in her best Chucky-Doll voice.

Jaz laughed. She loved it when Zoey did her Chucky voice.

The sisters moved through the club as if nothing had happened. As they walked back to the bandstand, they grooved to the music, their respiration returning to normal in a remarkably short period.

They didn't stay long. They left the club quickly and were bar-hopping once again, long before the bodies of the dead girls were discovered.

The witches finally settled on a dive-bar near Wildwood Crest called The Sea-Spray. It was sparsely attended and didn't have live music but was more than adequate for their murderous aims.

Jaz had managed to seduce a young able-bodied contractor with long, sandy brown hair. He was a tattooed man in his early twenties with bulging biceps and a clean collegiate look.

Maya had gone home with Ray, a bartender barely in his thirties. His short, military-style haircut was a turn-on for Maya. It reminded her of their father, a man who had abandoned the family when they were four.

Zoey liked them young, so she had bagged a youthful boy barely fourteen, a string bean of a metal-head with an AC/DC tee shirt and not too bright.

Ali went for the quiet, reserved type, thus she had no trouble attracting the attentions of a man old enough to be her father - even grandfather if you wanted to push it.

His name was Wayne, and he drove a Federal Express truck that covered the Maple Shade area. He had driven down alone in his battered Ford Maverick to stay the night in Wildwood Crest, at a tropical-styled Motel called the Shanghai-La

All four men would be dead by morning.

* * *

That Cape May might attract witches was not a random consideration. It's said some coasts are set aside for shipwreck; that spirits coalesce in the eddies and tides of forgotten shores.

Such had always been the case for the Cape of May, past which explorers' ships sailed and intuitive navigators, who were guided by the stars, could sense danger.

Not a few sensed with their own inner compass a menacing shadow which stretched across those sands and over the wooded thickets which grew almost to the edge of the water.

Dutch explorers who had ventured ashore had discovered carvings of deities and devils in the soft bark of pine; had sighted the scattered and burnt bones of sacrificial lamb.

It had been speculated the native Indians may have placed these things strategically to ward off the imperious but superstitious Europeans was a matter of grand speculation.

Another folk tale had arisen that the early Europeans who had come ashore and attempted to settle the harsh and unforgiving land had brought with them practitioners of sorcery.

Most had avoided the Cape; but those hearty few who braved it brought with them their own spiritual warriors for they believed the only way to fight fire was with fire itself.

* * *

Reverend Billy Wilkes tossed and turned in the tumble of stained sheets which covered the dirty mattress.

His thin wiry frame was still muscular even though he was pushing sixty. He felt old. Older than his years, carrying ancient burdens even he himself could not fathom.

Being restless with the power of the Holy Spirit, Billy Wilkes hardly slept. It had always been that way for as long as he could remember.

Even as a child, his mother, a Pentecostal Adventist,

noticed his zeal for the Word, and thus encouraged his devotion, though she never would have imagined he would become a TV evangelist.

Billy Wilkes had memorized the Old Testament from the age of five. By the time he was twelve he was preaching sermons on Sundays at Mount Joy Pentecostal Church, a small congregation in the backwoods of Atglen, Pennsylvania.

At that point few would have doubted great things were ahead for the young preacher, but few would have guessed he'd end up with a TV ministry, however short lived it would be.

But that was long ago, when things were good and the Lord supplied him with abundance. Then the devil had tempted him, and things had all gone so very wrong. Then he had been cast out of Eden.

Wilkes pulled himself out bed. Shaking fatigue, he put on his robe and slippers. He finally remembered where he was; room 432 at a Motel 6 in Pennsauken, New Jersey, just off the Black Horse Pike.

The small round table was standard motel issue. On it were a large, battered King James bible in a tattered zip up leatherette case, open to Revelations.

A .38 caliber revolver.

He switched on the TV using the remote.

At precisely six pm, the broadcast came over the local news about the Wildwood murders.

The broadcast made clear the strangeness of six deaths within the same two day period, yet no suspects or motives had been found. That they were not related seemed unlikely, for murder in Cape May County was a rare occurrence.

No mention had been made of the sisters, nor had they been associated with any of the crimes, but Reverend Billy Wilkes knew better. A witchhunter always knew.

He knew the deaths were related and he knew who was responsible for them, but he would not be reporting it to the police. They'd never believe him. They'd want evidence. And of course they'd look into his own strange past, one filled with a lifetime of drifting and remaining anonymous.

He sat in quiet deliberation as the news unfolded, then turned off the television.

He showered carefully, then shaved. He dressed with care in plain slacks and a sport shirt, picked up the bible and the gun from the table and left the motel room.

* * *

The '66 Cadillac Sedan cruised slowly through the streets of Wildwood, it's tinted windows blocking the intrusion of prying eyes. Slumped behind the wheel, Reverend Billy Wilkes drove in silence, one hand on the steering wheel, the other other on the bible on the seat beside him.

On the dashboard, dead center, was the small plastic figure of Jesus.

The sun beat down in a noonday blaze, though only April one could feel the onslaught of summer in the crisp air.

Inside the car, Billy Wilkes kept the blower on with the air conditioning off. He decided to open all windows, hitting the buttons on the driver door armrest. The air rushed in, filling his lungs.

He'd had fond remembrances of Wildwood; his teenage years, though difficult without father, were book ended each summer season with a trip to the shore. His Mother read scripture to him on the trip from Philly on Route 47 and 49, and they'd count the minutes as the trees rushed past them, the golden open fields and colonial towns zipping by in a blur.

The anticipation of reaching the shore after the long drive was painful for a child, especially when he had to pee. He'd imagined what those towns must have been like when the early settlers arrived and started them, so full of life and fear; running always from persecution yet eventually becoming persecutors themselves.

Wilkes remembered reading in school the early settlers had fled from judgment to pursue their religious freedom, yet would establish their own religion and persecute anyone who practiced otherwise. It had been that way in the many small villages they passed, but almost all had forgotten.

Billy Wilkes cruised the empty streets, eyd with disdain the sleeping clubs on Pacific Avenue. *Dens of iniquity*, he thought as he drove. *Here sin was allowed to flourish in blatant disregard for the scriptures.*

His car slid past the neon motels where he imagined countless couples fornicated and untold scores of illegitimate children were conceived. He cruised past the aging boarding houses, crumbling in disrepair. Their paint had faded from years of coastal rains and wind, snow and salt air.

Wilkes wondered about the ghosts of former residents whose souls had stayed anchored to the material world, attached and chained forever to desire. He'd always had images like that. Visions, his mother called them.

He remembered her face, etched with the pain of suffering like some latter-day Jesus, the constant worry in her eyes. She'd been a good woman.

Wilkes clutched the rosary which swung from the rear view mirror, the Jesus pendant clanking against the chain.

"I remember you mama, and I'm carrying on your mission, you'd be proud of me. You'd be proud to know your boy has been fighting evil on earth in memory of you."

Wilkes face was reflective of memories of many years gone by. A look that was far away; images of a small boy and his long-suffering mother hanging on to each other as if their very survival depended on it.

A sharp pain impinged on his consciousness, shooting upward from his palm. When he looked down, he opened his hand, releasing the rosary, there was blood. He'd clutched it so tight it had cut into his hand.

"Blood of the Christ, blood of the father," Wilkes intoned aloud as he pulled the Cadillac into a beachfront parking lot. It was eerie and empty. He set the nose of the sedan pointed toward the beach and watched the waves in the distance crashing in. God's creation was the only constant - the distant roar of nature - unchanging and resolute in its judgment

As he listened to the waves he slowly dozed off.

LEFT OFF HERE

* * *

On a Sunday morning in mid-July the sun blazed cleanly and brightly across the parking lot of the Cavalry Baptist

Church in Millville. The town was a pastoral community which slept thirty-seven miles inland from the Cape May coast.

It was a small church, built in the 1800's, and it's congregation, rarely exceeding 100, was mostly older residents of the town.

Its minister, Harley M. Clemmons, lived next door to the church. He was white and a fiscal conservative. His wife, Gertrude, had died of pancreatic cancer ten years earlier.

Childless and alone but for his small congregation and a chihuahua named Nipsy, Clemmons was in the twilight of his years yet remained steadfast in his faith.

On this Sunday morning he walked briskly across the gravel parking lot in his pressed clergy linens, the liturgical collar tight around his neck as the humidity and heat enveloped him like a shroud.

He unlocked the front entrance of the church, swinging the tall oak doors open and secured them in their open position by the rusty hooks behind each.

Once inside, he walked up the aisle, past the empty pews, his footsteps echoing through the structure, the smell of liturgy and ceremony pervading all.

It is the smell of salvation, Clem thought, and as he walked he knew he'd never tired of the power and majesty of the church.

In his mind the words and theme of his sermon that morning were as one, coalescing into one of his trademark fire and brimstone orations.

He rarely used notes, would wing it in the true tradition of his trade, for on these very grounds had walked and prayed a long and faithful lineage of followers, a flock which dated back to colonial times.

He moved with an angled gait, the result of bad knees and arthritis, as if bent against the force of gravity that pressed an invisible wind of mortality against him.

Clem was a name that didn't fit him but he took it well. It was a lot better than the nickname he'd earned in high school as an overweight nerdy outcast; Bloatus.

He'd always taken pride that he'd made something of himself, while the cruel kids who had teased him had ended up drunks, gone to jail, or died a day at a time living lives of quiet desperation. But pride was not something he dwelt on, for pride was of the devil.

Clem entered the rectory, a sparse backroom which held only a small table, four chairs and a small bookshelf. The high ceiling and spare wooden floor amplified every sound, even the sound of Clem's asthmatic breathing.

He pulled a chair out from the table and sat, taking care of the folds of his vestments so they would not wrinkle. He opened his bible, marked with stick notes new and old, some so old they were dog-eared and faded.

He put on his reading glasses and opened to Revelations, as the sun, white hot, streamed through the dirty windows.

* * *

Clem had been immersed in the passages for at least thirty minutes when he'd heard the first steps of people entering the church.

That those arrivals were somewhat early had not really

registered, for sometimes followers came to pray before the service in undistracted silence.

The footsteps were of four people walking, and they did not stop inside the chapel. They continued through the church and then moved toward the rectory. There was no talking among them, something Clem found odd.

When four black robed young women, quite young and beautiful entered the rectory, he felt the immediate presence of evil. He could hear the faint incessant barking of Nipsy barely audible from the house. Fear gripped him as he stared at them entering, and the four of them stood in a clean line, as if each knew what the other was thinking.

All four wore sexy, dangerous smiles, except Maya, who never smiled. Allison spoke first.

"A directive has been given us by the powers of Darkness," she intoned. "It is time for you to die."

* * *

There was no doubt among the sisters that the murders were increasing their power. Each felt the surge of energy that coursed through them with each kill.

"I feel so alive!" Zoey exclaimed on the morning after they'd tied Harlan Clemmons to a chair and stabbed him multiple times through the heart, "like I'm plugged into some bitchin' electrical source!" she marveled.

The other girls felt it too. Both Jaz and Ali would lay awake at night and feel it running through them - bringing them even more vitality and strength than even their young ages provided.

Though the four had separate rooms in the boarding house, they all dreamed as one. That night, the first of their common dreams opened with them standing in a forest around a large bonfire in a clearing.

They were fully naked in the warmth as the sound of the ocean rumbled nearby - all moving in unison to some song of the cosmos - a rhythmic dance that was both primal and powerful.

Their trance-like state had evoked a group consciousness among them of the all-powerful something that had existed since the dawn of time and transcended birth and death.

Their chants were to the spirit energies and demonic entities which existed in the subtle realm and their focus was to coalesce spirit into matter; to harness the power of these dark forces to their own will. In so doing they would strengthen their own power on the Earth.

* * *

Wilkes came awake suddenly within the darkness of the sedan.

As the headlights of a car slowly approached, he looked up at the windows from his place on the backseat, watching the white light playing across the water drops which had formed on the glass.

He'd parked far enough away from the entrance of the cemetery so as to not cause any suspicion. As the approaching car passed him and turned into the rusted gates of the graveyard, he popped his head up, his eyes level with the window, and watched as the taillights of the car disappeared inside.

He could not be sure how many people were in the car, but he was certain at least one of them was one of the witches responsible for the recent rash of killings. The pattern was always the same. The graveside vigil would follow, he was certain, by a ceremony, and then transmission would be complete. He popped open the backdoor and swung his feet down onto the damp ground, tucking the gun into his waistband.

He ran his fingers through his greased back hair, the smell of day-old Old Spice and Vitalis pervaded him, and fought back his fear as he quietly pushed the door shut, making sure to make no sound as he made his way through the gate, the humidity and fog like a wet blanket, threatening to suffocate him.

* * *

"It's right there!" Zoey yelled. She was sitting in the passenger seat, pointing through the windshield to the freshly-filled grave ahead, her excitement palpable.

Allison drove, her expression stoic, while Maya, seated behind Allison in the backseat, stared blankly ahead. Jaz lit up a joint from the dash lighter, the orange glow illuminating her dark, mascara caked eyes, inhaling deeply.

"Nothin' like a little spirit communicatin' to get the blood circulatin'!" Zoey chirped in her Chucky-voice, taking the joint from Jaz, and laughed a mock insane-asylum laugh.

"You be one crazy bitch," Jaz exhaled," "Park here," she

told Allison, directing her to a spot near the road.

They sat in the car smoking the joint down to the roach, passing it back and forth.

"I feel amazing," Zoey said, enthusiastically. "Like I could live forever," she giggled.

"It was the preacher-man," Allison said, matter-of-factually, "They pack a lot of power."

"More bang for the proverbial buck!" exclaimed Jaz, coughing out her hit, her eyes squinting in pain.

"Men of God make the best sacrifices," Maya said. "You know that." She took the joint and sucked in the smoke, waiting a second in thought, then, almost reluctantly handing the joint to Zoey.

When the joint was finished, Jaz secured the roach into a small skull-head roach clip, and torched it with her Bic, inhaling deeply, making wet sucking noises.

The other three leaned in and shared the smoking stub before extinguishing it into the dash ashtray.

"Let's rock n roll," Allison said, popping open her door.

All four girls got out, with Allison leading the way, the beam from her flashlight cutting through the fog like a searchlight over a dead sea.

"I think this is the one," Allison said as they approached the tombstone, the flashlight beam stopping on the grey-colored bevelled granite.

Maya looked around nervously. "This place gives me the creeps," she said, straight faced.

"Like hell it does," Jaz laughed, "you're right at home among the dead."

The name on the gravestone read: *'In Loving Memory - Harley M. Clemmons - Feb 8, 1945 - July 9, 1985 - A Servant of God In The House Of The Lord.'*

"Awesome!" Zoey exclaimed.

Allison's face was somber as she pointed the beam of the flashlight to the adjacent stone.

"This one was his bitch," Ali said. "So touching they are laid to rest together."

"Yes, most touching," mocked Jaz, reading the adjacent stone. 'May Gertie and Clem frolic in the great Hereafter for-fucking-evermore," she said, and hawked up a flugie, hitting Harlan's grave dead center, the mucous dripping down the lettering like melted gray taffy.

"I have to pee!" Zoey announced, and was already undoing her jeans. She backed up to both graves and pulled down her white panties, a long yellow stream squirting out and hitting the stones.

"Bulls eye!" she squealed, and farted, twice, and all four girls broke into laughter.

"Let's get this done," Ali said, turning to Maya, tossing the keys to her. "Maya, get the shit from the trunk."

Ali tossed the car keys to Maya and Maya went to the car, pulling a cardboard box of robes out of the trunk. Ali placed the lit flashlight on the ground as Zoey pulled up her jeans, looking relieved. Jaz looked around in the darkness and inhaled deeply. "I love the smell of freshly dug earth in a boneyard," she said.

"Maybe you should write a fucking poem," panned Ali, as she tossed a folded black robe to Jaz.

The sisters climbed into their frocks with only the sound of frogs and crickets permeating the night air, and the distant sound of the ocean from far away.

* * *

Billy Wilkes kept his distance - was careful to maintain his distance from the four hooded figures which now danced in an eerie procession around the grave of Harlan Clemmons.

They were attractive and young, he noticed, and the girls held hands, the scene lit only by the flashlight which lay on its side on the ground.

Fog had wafted in from the ocean, only a few miles away, and the dampness in the air obscured and reflected the beam from the flashlight, getting dimmer with each passing minute.

The girls chanted something in Latin, almost liturgical, yet Wilkes knew its origin was dark and blasphemous. A sermon for the end of days for the soul of the itinerant preacher, a chant from ages past and the cries of millions that had gone before him.

The faces of the girls could be seen through the hoods, yet obscured, and at this distance unrecognizable. Wilkes lay on the wet ground, watching through the trees as the four girls moved in unison around the gravestone.

They then lit several black candles, placing them around them in a larger circle, while one of them took a small black bag, which it self was made of velvet or cloth and drawn with a drawstring of rawhide. From this the girl removed twigs and leaves, placing them on a polished stone disk.

Wilkes had seen this ceremony before. It always occurred

within three days of the death of the victim, and always at the burial site of the accursed.

Though his understanding of their rituals was not complete, he knew this particular one was used to help increase the power of the practioners. In his travels far and wide he'd seen it all. There were many more out there like them, Wilkes knew, for he had been hunting the likes of them for nearly twenty years.

* * *

The ceremony lasted for the better part of an hour. The girls had gone through their eerie movements in flashes of lighters, incense smoke and a low monotone drone.

Wilkes had considered a simple direct approach, walking calmly up to them and shooting each of them, ending the matter then and there, but he knew their power was formidable.

Four very strong young women, athletic in their prowess, who not only could overpower him physically, but their mental power could not be underestimated. Once they focused their power on him he had little chance against them.

He'd experienced it before, in an encounter in Indiana.

He'd been tracking two witches for nearly a year, after they'd cut a murderous scourge of terror in rural regions throughout the state. They'd fortified themselves in a grain silo. He'd entered it, knowing they were laying in wait for him, but even armed he was rendered nearly helpless when they'd focused their power on him.

His mind had immediately become clouded, then an intense apparition appeared before him, a dark shadow forming from the dust of the wind and then hovered, towering over him, and an intense cold moved through him.

Exhaustion had racked him in massive waves, then he had lost consciousness. Fighting it, he'd managed to crawl free from the silo, but he'd never forgotten the lesson.

The memory of that incident still played in his mind as he lay there on the damp ground, watching the four sisters moving eerily in that circle, their low monotone chanting the very embodiment of evil itself.

Using the element of surprise he might have success, but it was too risky. Not here, not now. His plan was to take each one out separately.

All he could do is watch. And wait.

* * *

It was half past three in the morning when the girls finally left the cemetery, through a fog so thick it enveloped Cape May in a blanket of dank black wetness, making visibility near zero on the roads back to Wildwood.

Wilkes made sure to keep his distance, far enough back that the girls would not become suspicious, yet he couldn't afford to lose sight of them.

Many times their car had disappeared ahead of him as he struggled to keep up. At any moment he swore his car would plunge over some abyss into the Atlantic, or crash into something stuck in the road, or worse run off the road completely without seeing it and ending up crashing into a tree.

He clutched the steering wheel in a white-knuckled death

grip, sweat pouring down his forehead and down his back, seeping through the shirt which clung like a damp rag to his body. Though it was not raining, he kept the wipers on, but they did little to erase the layer of moisture on the windshield.

It was not far back to Wildwood, but the road conditions had jacked his anxiety to an almost panic level. That and knowing the witches of Wildwood were up there, just ahead of him.

And the knowledge the murders would not stop unless he put an end to them. He glanced over at the passenger seat, the gun and bible lay there on the vinyl. They gave him comfort.

Praise the Lord and pass the ammunition, he thought.

He'd followed the car at a distance, then closed the gap as the vehicle crossed the bridge on Rio Grand and entered Wildwood. The sisters drove fast, and at times he had to push the old Cadillac to its limits to keep up.

The Duster pulled into the dirt lot of the old boarding house and the four girls jumped out, as Wilkes drove slowly by.

They didn't seem to notice him.

* * *

That night in his motel room, Wilkes had terrible nightmares. He'd been captured by a band of witches he'd been hunting, some Hades of a forest. They'd hung him upside down from a tree, by the feet.

There was a crowd of them in hooded robes, men, women and children, and all were chanting as he hung there, barely hanging on to consciousness.

There was a large bonfire, and the members of the coven had flaming torches. Demonic entities seemed to swirl in and around the fire, in a hideous orange mist that smelled of formaldehyde.

The leader, an ancient looking man with wrinkled skin, stared up at him with lizard-like eyes and was yelling Satanic passages in Latin.

The man yelled to the mass of people chanting and moving in unison around the fire, and they formed a circle around him. The man nodded to a middle aged woman who drew a large hunting knife and approached him, placing the blade against his throat. Then everything went black.

Wilkes awoke panting in a sea of sweat. The sheets had soaked through, the bedding in a heap from tossing and turning during the nightmare. When he came awake with a startled jump it was to a darkened motel room, the only light from the crack in the door of the bathroom, which he always kept closed but slightly ajar, with the light on.

It was habit he'd developed after years of sleeping in motel rooms, for he hated waking in a completely dark place. It reminded him too much of the closet his mother had locked him into numerous times when he was a boy.

He sprung to an upright sitting position in the bed.

It took a few seconds to some to his senses as he shook the dream from his head. His hand went out instinctively to the gun which he kept on the nightstand next to him.

Touching the gun was enough to provide comfort; his hand went to his throat next, feeling smoothness and a sense of relief there was no incision or blood. He laid back onto the bed, his hair wet against the sopping pillow. When his eyes adjusted to the darkness, staring at the ceiling.

He had the odd sense he was not alone in the room.

When his eyes averted back down toward his feet, he saw the silhouette of a young girl with long dark hair standing motionless dead center at the foot of the bed. The figure of the girl stood like a dark statue, watching him.

Wilkes went for the gun and brought it up quickly, placing a single shot to the center of the shadow. The gun going off in the silence and darkness of the room was like setting off a small bomb.

The bullet hit the dresser mirror and shattered it, pieces of broken glass falling in shards and breaking on the surface of the dresser, some of them tinkling to the floor.

Wilkes stared ahead, sweat breaking out on his forehead, his breathing heavy in the vacated silence.

The figure of the girl had disappeared.

* * *

Jaz stood excitedly before the full length mirror, admiring her body and the way the little black dress hung to her youthful curves.

"Hot, very hot" she spoke aloud to herself, though her sisters were in the room. Ali glanced over from her seated position at the table, twisting a curling iron though her brunette mane.

"Yeah baby. That should get some attention in the casino. But more cleavage. You need more cleavage." Jaz looked nervously up at her bustline. "Ya think so?"

"Show em off!" yelled Zoey from the bathroom, seated on the toilet, "Flaunt em, bitch!"

Maya sat at the kitchen table drinking Seagrams and Coke from an antique silver chalice. She wore a medieval looking dress with a tight corset, but accented with a bright purple scarf, her huge breasts bulging from the low neckline.

"That's my motto." Maya said emphatically, and quietly sipped her own drink from a child's Sesame Street cup, the Cookie Monster staring back at her through the faded design.

"Easy for you to say," Jaz answered, as she pushed up her small breasts, trying to make them look bigger through the top of the dress.

The toilet flushed and Zoey emerged, still clad only in a white bra and cotton panties. She walked to the closet and flipped through her clothes, selecting a white summer dress.

"I'll be the conservative southern belle," she said, holding the dress to her chest, and effected her best southern accent. "For I have always relied on the canned-ness of strain-jus," and batted her eyelids seductively. All four sisters laughed in unison.

"So what's the plan?" Maya asked, putting in her contact lenses.

Jaz's face went dead serious as she primped her self in the mirror.

"We go to Atlantic City and find some new blood, that's the fuckin' plan, girlfriend," Ali said matter-of-factually

"Fuckin' Aay!" exclaimed Zoey.

"Let's lure one up to the room, I need to get laid," Ali said. She got excited just thinking about murder, even more so than sex, though the sex ran a close second.

"I hear that," agreed Jaz. "see if he wants to take on all four of us, maybe we can give him a heart attack. A lot less messy."

"No sacrifices in the room, you know the rules," Maya said.

"I'm a one on one girl," said Zoey, pulling the dress over her head, "you guys get your own."

* * *

Behind the wheel of the Cadillac, Wilkes had stayed slumped down in the seat from his position across from the boarding house.

The sisters generally did not go out before midnight. When they did it was invariably to a local night club, either one of the rock clubs on Pacific Avenue, or one of the larger venues in The Crest.

Wilkes had followed them numerous times during the summer as they would hop from club to club, enticing men with sex, then luring each one to his death during or after the orgasm.

He had been unable to get them apart long enough to kill each one separately. They would all have to be sent back to Hell together, he reasoned, though he was uncertain how he would accomplish it.

He knew only that God was his ally in the fight against evil, and that Providence would prevail. For now he had to stay close to them, track their movements, and wait for his opportunity. Or die trying.

As the girls emerged down the rickety steps of the boarding house, they were laughing, and Wilkes watched intently over the steering wheel as they piled into the Duster, noting their high heels and dresses, and knew they were on the hunt once again. He also knew he had to make his move soon or others would continue to die.

He placed his right hand on the bible beside him and recited scripture. "Even as I walk into the shadow of the Valley of Death I shall find strength from the Lord in the face of evil..." He paraphrased, as he often did.

He turned the key in the ignition, waiting as the brightly colored green Duster roared past him, then placed the car in gear and slowly followed them as they turned onto Atlantic Avenue, heading in the direction of North Wildwood.

It was just past midnight.

The Witching Hour.

* * *

Wilkes kept his distance as the Duster moved fast through the green lights lined in neat rows down Atlantic. A light mist had drifted in off the ocean, giving the air a dream-like quality, but it was starting to turn to drizzle.

It was mid-week, with traffic to a minimum, and at this hour most of the families were sleeping, the houses mostly dark as they sped by, and the all-night neon of the motels and blue-lit pools standing eerily silent.

Wilkes focused his concentration on the rear lights of the Duster, keeping them just in sight ahead of him. They had driven well out of the club district now.

Nothing would be open in North Wildwood, with the exception of The Red Garter or Harry The Hat, but mid-week the crowds would be slim past midnight.

By the way the sisters were dressed Wilkes knew they were likely heading for Atlantic City. Victims there would be more plentiful, and a dead body left behind less conspicuous.

His thoughts drifted. Memories of a lifetime of witch hunting had left him weary and a dull ache throbbed in his head.

That he had descended from Christian Crusaders he had little doubt, for in his dreams he'd seen himself scouring the countrysides of ancient Europe when witches were once a scourge which had plagued the lands. There were flashes of images, of faces reflected in firelight, the anguish and torment of inquisition and the glee of death's vindication.

His thoughts were suddenly pulled back to the present as the bend in the road turned sharply left. He pulled the wheel hard to the left and the tires groaned as the large car barely missed going over the curb into the coastal rocks.

The Duster had shot around the sudden bend at the Hereford Lighthouse. He'd become lost in his thoughts. Not paying attention. He'd almost wrecked the Cadillac.

The Duster flew past the Red Garter just past Olde New Jersey Avenue and on into Anglesea, the dim lighting of the sodium-vapor streetlamps casting an eerie hazy orange glow on the road ahead of them as they flew past sleeping beachhouses that lined Hereford Inlet.

Spruce Avenue opened to unevenly spaced and more sparse housing as they sped toward the Marina. Wilkes could see far enough ahead the Duster had made the hard bend right on Route 619 toward Grassy Sound.

Old fishing shacks lined both sides of the old road and the smell of salt marsh assailed his nostrils. It was eerie out here on this section of road, a place Wilkes sensed the ghosts of old fisherman haunted the swamps.

Wilkes knew somewhere not far ahead was Grassy Sound Bridge - and beyond that the more populated areas and stoplights of the next beach town. From his previous explorations he knew now was when he had to make his move.

Stretching out on either side of the highway to his left were the wide open expanses of bay, nothing off in the blackness but open space. To his right, beyond the shacks the lights from the distant shore points. Wilkes took a deep breath and reached down, buckling his seat beat, pulling it tight. Fifty meters ahead was the Duster - moving at seventy easy.

Wilkes floored the accelerator.

The Duster closed in fast as the sedan hit one hundred.

Night and darkness obscured the passengers of the Duster, giving it a robotic identity that was not human.

Wilkes went into the passing lane of the two-laner as if to pass the Duster, but once alongside he whipped the wheel to the right, slamming into its side. He'd created a broadside crease in the Duster's driver side door and sealed it shut.

The Duster sped up now as both cars, moving fast, were side by side. Up ahead to the right was a faded broken sign *EDDIES BOAT RENTAL*' affixed to a wooden telephone pole, and just beyond that a dirt parking lot.

Wilkes pulled the wheel to the right again, forcing the

Duster off the road toward the approaching signage. The Duster tried countering left but the weight of the sedan overpowered it, forcing it closer and closer toward the approaching signage. If Wilkes maneuvered it properly, the Duster and its cargo of witches would crash head on into the thick utility pole, leaving very little chance of survival.

Wilkes was sweating, feeling the perspiration beading on his forehead. His underarms were clammy and his heart raced.

The Duster slammed on the brakes at the last possible second, then went into an uncontrollable tailspin off the road, sliding sideways into the gravel parking lot.

The rear right panel slammed the edge of the telephone pole, smashing it in. The right taillight and rear bumper flew off and came to a halting skid in the middle of the gravel, tires smoking.

Wilkes slammed the brakes on the Cadillac, doing a fishtail spin that turned it completely around and sat at a stop on the road. As the black smoke from burning tires and gravel spray cleared, the Cadillac and the Plymouth faced each other like gladiators in an arena.

The only sound to be heard were strained engines and the *tic tic tic* of overheated radiators. In that few seconds of silence a rage and fury mounted, a calm before the storm.

The Duster's rear wheels spun in the gravel as the accelerator floored, sending the car shooting forward toward the Cadillac.

Wilkes floored the sedan as both cars hurled toward each other head on. The Duster smashed head on into Wilkes, the impact sending him forward that without the restraint of the seat belt, would have hurled him through the windshield.

The bible and gun hit the floor but the heavy artillery-class steel of the Cadillac Brougham was nearly impervious to the lighter weight and materials of the Duster, crushing the front end of the Plymouth like a beer can.

The Duster threw in hard reverse, pulling backwards and away, the accelerator floored again and then a hard squeal of brakes - then thrown in forward gear and thrust forward like a battering ram, smashing violently head on into the sedan again with enough force the rear wheels of the Plymouth left the ground a full foot and came back down again, bouncing on its shocks. Wilkes was thrown violently against the restraint again, cursing aloud.

Not good, he thought. *So much for the element of surprise.* It was four against one, but he had the advantage of weight and power. The witches had speed and agility and the powers of darkness. He had a classic sedan and Christ on his side.

The Duster pulled backward in reverse again, it's front grill pulling loose as it caught the front edge of the sedan's silver Jesus hood ornament, tearing it off as the steel grill clanged and bounced on the road and the Duster shot backwards, the brakes slammed again and it fishtailed to turn facing away from the sedan.

An arm popped out of the driver side window, giving Wilkes the finger, then the accelerator floored again and the Duster sped off over Grassy Sound Bridge leaving a trail of radiator fluid and water on the road.

Shaken, Wilkes floored the sedan over the bridge, trailing them. By the time he'd reached the center toll booth - now unmanned and empty - he could see the rear lights of the Duster disappearing fast into the long stretch of dark ahead. Flying insects and mosquitoes swirled in the slicing rays of his headlights. Oddly it reminded Wilkes of a John Prine song, 'Christmas In Prison' - he sang the words, the edgy scared sound of his own voice startled him.

The searchlight in the big yard
swings round with the gun
and spotlights the snowflakes
like dust in the sun.'

He reached down and cranked up the stereo - Tammy Wynette, on eight track, country-western music with its twangy steel guitar and the crying voice of Wynette a fitting but ironic soundtrack to the terror raging around him. The Duster shot forward, gaining speed ahead of him.

Wilkes had gained on the Duster for two reasons: he'd kept the pedal as close to the floor as possible; he'd gotten a lucky break; the impact of the two vehicles just moments ago had jarred two distributor cables loose from the Duster and it was now running at lessened capacity.

The Duster swerved and fishtailed back and forth as the vehicles played cat and mouse. At these high speeds either one could lose control and end up overturning or sent careening into the dark waters. Several vehicles approached from the opposite direction, flashing their high beams, speeding by, horns blaring, barely missing a head on collision.

Wilkes continued his assault on the Duster, ramming it again and again as the rear bumper of the car dropped and drug along the ground, refusing to let go. Sparks flew out from the dragging bumper and shot backward and underneath Wilkes car. After repeated ramming by Wilkes the bumper dropped off and clanged away, bouncing up and out of the frenzy as the cars sped by.

Low lying swamp stretched out for an eternity on either side of the road as the two battered cars hurtled at high speed toward the lights of Stone Harbor and the shore points beyond.

Wilkes knew somewhere up ahead another bridge would take them over the bay into Ocean City. It was there he'd hoped to drive them off the bridge.

A blinking yellow light swung eerily in the sea wind as Wilkes approached the curve taking them out of Strathmere.

The crossroads was desolate, a boarded up ESSO station stood as an abandoned monument to what the Shore had once been, a frightening foreshadowing of what it was to become.

As Wilkes rounded the bend a shock ran through him.

The Duster was gone!

Wilkes slowed the sedan, looking around him at the crossroads, then stopped. He turned the stereo off, and hit all four electric window buttons.

The glass slid down into the doors, a cool yet balmy sea breeze blew threw the car. He paused and listened. He could hear only the distant sounds of sea waves.

Moving forward toward the Strathmere bridge leading over into Ocean City, his heart sank.

The bridge was up in a straight vertical position - the iron grid like a giant hand stretching up into the sky, lined with blinking lights.

Either the Duster had made it across to the other side before the bridge had gone up, or they'd turned around, Wilkes thought.

Wilkes did a U-turn and brought the sedan to stop back at the crossroads. In the near distance was the Deauville Inn, dark and desolate, it's parking lot empty. He could see the outlines of small boats lined in the small marina behind it.

Wilkes looked desperately in both directions.

The Duster was nowhere to be seen.

He slumped back in the seat - engine wheezing as he sat idling in the middle of the crossroads, just under the blinking yellow light.

He took a long breath, feeling like it was the first time he'd breathed since he left Wildwood. His blood pounded in his ears and his head hurt. If the witches had made it over the bridge they'd be halfway across Ocean City by now. He could wait until the bridge was lowered, take his chances on catching up with them, but knew he'd missed his mark.

There was a sudden movement from his left - then a gunning of an engine coming fast toward him - a dark metal shape from the ESSO parking lot.

The Duster, lights off, slammed into his driver side door with the ferocity of a freight train, throwing Wilkes sideways in a violent snap, the seat belt the only thing preventing him from bouncing around inside the car like a ping-pong ball.

The Duster pulled into reverse and rammed him again, smashing the driver side door in completely this time, the side view mirror clattering to the pavement.

Wilkes was knocked unconscious for several seconds - when his eyes opened he saw the faces of the witches through the windshield.

All four of the witches walked toward him in the swirling fog, illuminated by the headlights of the Duster.

Then everything went black as Wilkes lost consciousness once again.

Ali poked her head through the open broken window of the Cadillac.

"He's out cold," Ali said, examining Wilkes. "Pull him out from the passenger side." The girls yanked Wilkes out of the car like a rag doll.

Maya pulled an over-sized dog-eared wallet from his back pocket, sorting through it. She pulled out his license.

"His name is Wilkes. William. Registered in Salem Massachusetts, Now if that don't beat all. And a man of the cloth to boot!" Removing what little little cash he had, she placed the wallet back into Wilkes's pocket.

Ali and Zoey looked beat, their eyes were crazed with rage and mascara ran down their faces. Maya stayed calm and supervised.

"Jaz, grab his feet. Get him over to the parking lot, there's a boat shed there. "

"We should waste him now," hissed Zoey, seething with bloodlust and hatred. "He about killed us back there, fuckin' *dick!* "

"We're going to waste him, no question about that," Maya tried a forced smile. "Don't blow your cool. This is one we need to kill slow."

Zoey grinned viciously as she struggled with Wilkes's dead weight. "Fuckin Aye!" she squealed in delight as the girls carried Wilkes off into the ghostly pale light of the Deauville Inn parking lot.

The Deuville Inn was an historic landmark restaurant, built during the civil war period. It was a multi-level stone and brick Inn, with the lower half used as the restaurant and bar. Though the dining room had closed for the evening hours ago, at this late hour there was a small crowd still at the bar.

The lights shone from within and a handful of cars were parked in the gravel parking lot, but none were the wiser as to the sight of four teenage witches carrying the dead-weight body of a dressed-in-black preacher-man across the gravel parking lot.

At the rear of the Inn was an old boathouse, its rotting timbers and dank wood stank of dead fish, sea salt and brine. The main entrance doors to the boathouse were padlocked.

"Drop him here," Maya ordered. The girls laid Wilkes down on the damp gravel. "Zoey, pull his car down here, make sure it can't be seen from the road."

Zoey took off in a fast stride toward the highway.

"I say we should kill him now," Jaz reiterated disdainfully.

"Keep your skin on, Honey." Maya said. "Break that padlock."

Within moments Zoey had pulled the Cadillac behind the boat house.

"Pop the trunk," Maya ordered. Zoey switched the engine off, hitting the trunk release. The trunk creaked open. Maya peered in. The trunk light was broken. Enough light remained from the pole-light illuminating the parking lot to see inside, revealing a spare tire, a scattering of old newspapers, and a tire iron. Maya pulled a rusty tire iron out, smiling.

Satan always provides, she thought. Within moments she'd broken the padlock off and the boathouse doors creaked open.

"Get him inside," she ordered, and the girls complied, carrying the groaning Wilkes into the boathouse. He was starting to regain consciousness.

"Hurry up he's coming to!" Jaz hissed as she grabbed him under his shoulders and lifted, while Ali and Zoey each grabbed a leg and carried him inside.

The boathouse was musty and dank. Heat from the afternoon sun had remained trapped in the barn-like structure, giving off waves of humid stagnation. The smell of old boats and seaweed and rotting fish mixed with old oil and boat grease.

The only light was the ambient glow of peripheral illumination coming through the window panes from the far side of the structure.

"Get him over there," Maya directed as the girls carried Wilkes to a boat engine hoist. Several chains hung down from the rafters, attached to a pulley.

"String him up!" Maya laughed cruelly. The other three dragged him to the foot of the structure and looped the chains through his arms. While the girls held him up, his legs wobbled unsteadily, unable to support his weight.

Maya rummaged through a nearby crate filled with nuts, bolts and rusted nails. Wilkes groaned and began to speak unintelligible words.

"Shut the fuck up, preacherman," Zoey laughed, and

punched him square in the jaw, knocking him cold once again.

"Hold him up!" Maya yelled as she rigged two large bolts through the chains fastening a loop under each of Wilkes's arm, capping them with a large nut. The girls watched in ornery delight as Maya used the pulley crank to hoist Wilkes off his feet.

Wilkes came to consciousness with the four witches looking up at him. His feet dangled at their face level.

"Wake up, preacherman!" Zoey yelled menacingly.

The faint light of the boathouse began to impinge on his awareness. His head throbbed in pain. His entire body ached.

"Mister Wilkes," Maya began slowly, "...You've fucked with the fundamental laws of nature." She seemed tired, like she'd said it all before.

"As such, a price must be paid!" Jaz concluded.

Wilkes was fully aware now. His mouth was dry but he managed to speak.

"The Lord will have his vengeance upon you. His wrath will be mighty and swift. Evil must be stopped before it multiplies and destroys the earth."

Ali seethed hatred through her clenched teeth. "There will be vengeance, alright," she said, "except that vengeance will be visited on you."

"By us!" Zoey blurted out, barely able to control her excitement. "Unfortunately for you," Jaz said, "Death will be anything but swift."

Maya came forward with a large pair of bolt cutters.

"Get his shoes off," she ordered.

The three other girls quickly complied, pulling his socks off, leaving ten white toes exposed.

"Ten little piggies!" Zoey laughed gleefully.

Maya wasted no time in moving in with the bolt cutters.

She took off his left large toe in one swift motion, then threw the bolt cutters down. Wilkes screamed in agony as blood spurted from the open wound, then slowed to a steady stream of crimson pooling beneath him.

"And now there are nine!" shouted Zoey with unreserved delight. The sight of blood seemed to excite the girls even more.

"Ali, bring the car down," Maya ordered, throwing the keys to the Duster to Allison.

The witches watched in quiet fascination as Wilkes hung in agony from the chains.

Ali pulled the car up to the boathouse and carried in the box containing the robes and candles. The witches dressed quietly in their black frocks with detached abandon. Jaz lit the candles, placing them in a circle around the pool of blood beneath Wilkes.

Once preparations had been made, the sisters began their ritual as Wilkes hung above them, moaning. Terrible pain coursed through his body from his decapitated toe, stabbing up through his leg and into his body.

The last thing Wilkes remembered were the witches circling below him. Their low monotone chants echoed off the boathouse walls as the candles threw long ominous shadows flickering against the darkness.

He felt the darkness close in around him, then lost consciousness once again.

* * *

When Wilkes regained consciousness he was alone. He knew he had lost a lot of blood. He could see a giant pool of crimson beneath him. His vision came back slowly, but the outer edges of his vision curved in and out in waves, ripples of red heat that matched the throbs of pain now impinging on his awareness.

He knew he would die here. He also knew what it would mean were he to die and the witches go on with their scourge of death. For Wilkes, this was enough for him to begin struggling free from the chains.

He had little strength left, through which the pain was unbearable. It felt like a sword had been inserted into his leg and pushed upward through his foot toward his left hip.

Several black candles still burned below him, though nearly exhausted of their life. The chains cut through his underarm muscles. He remembered from his youth a trick Harry Houdini had once done to free himself when bound.

Slowly he shook his muscles while relaxing them, eventually jerking his right shoulder low enough to slip through the chain. He screamed in torment as he hit the floor, slipping on his own blood.

Fighting to stay alert, he ripped a piece of cloth from his shirt. Crawling along the floor, he made it to the workbench where an assortment of tools and scraps of wood lay scattered.

He found a pencil from which he assembled a makeshift tourniquet, twisting the strip of cloth around the base of what was left of his amputated toe. His foot had swollen badly, but he managed to staunch the bleeding enough to where he could slowly pull himself up onto his right leg.

Wracked with pain and devilish images swirling in his brain, and limped toward the door of the boathouse.

* * *

When Jaz and her sisters emerged from the entrance to the Deuville Inn, they were drunk and giddy. Having had four glasses of red wine each to celebrate their victory, they were rambunctious and rowdy, though they'd kept a low profile while drinking at the bar so as not to arouse suspicion.

"I could kill another one of those holy roller bastards right now!" Zoey exclaimed, her speech slurred, as the sisters walked to their car. Earlier, the girls had pulled the Duster into the main parking area, leaving ample distance between it and the boathouse.

"Should we check in on him?" Ali asked, nodding nodding toward the boathouse.

"Fuck him, Maya said, "Just leave him, he's probably dead by now."

Ali, the most drunk of the four, added "The longer he takes to die the better for us." Her balance was unsteady as she threw the keys to Maya. "You better drive," she laughed, "I'm a little shit-faced." "We're outta here!" Zoey said, as the four of them climbed into the battered Duster.

Maya sat behind the wheel, closing her eyes in silence.

"What are you waiting for?" Ali asked impatiently, seated in the right passenger seat next to Maya. In that few seconds of silence the other three knew what Maya was thinking and closed their eyes in unison.

"Mama would be proud," Maya spoke softly. Each of the

girls joined hands and Ali reached over the seat to take Zoey's. They recited a chant in low tones in memory of their mother.

Maya was the first to open her eyes. She turned and looked back at the boathouse.

"Ali, get the preacherman's car and follow us. We'll ditch it someplace else."

"Check!" Ali said, and climbed out of the car, making

an unsteady beeline toward the boathouse as the other three girls waited in the Duster.

Ali slid into the Cadillac through the passenger door and scooted over to the driver side. She kicked the bible which lay face down on the floor mat. The car keys hung in the ignition. The key ring was a black square lined with gold, in the center of which was a small white cross.

She gazed at the key ring in amusement, contemplating the white cross. The absurdity of the Christian faith had always intrigued her. Her eyes rose and fixated on the plastic Jesus statue protruding up from the center of the top of the dashboard.

She snatched the figurene from the dashboard "Won't be needing you, hey-zuess," she intoned, then tossed it over her shoulder into the backseat. She turned the key, firing up the Brougham.

She felt a presence loom up from behind her. A leather belt looped over her head and around her neck. She felt her head snap back as she struggled to breathe, fighting with all her strength to loosen the grip of the makeshift noose.

Ali clutched at the belt around her neck, her face turning red, then blue as she choked and struggled, veins bulging and her eyes like giant marbles trying to pop out of her head.

Behind her, Wilkes pulled the belt back with both hands as tightly as he could until she was dead.

* * *

It had taken far too long for Ali to return to the car. Maya sensed there was something wrong from the feelings of dread which pulsed through her like electric waves.

They all intuitively knew Ali was in danger. They were like a finely tuned power grid. Further, each affected the other in ways that could not be explained by science.

All of them exited the car as if in one unified motion. They walked swiftly toward the boathouse. They could make out the distinct shadow of the Cadillac illuminated by the single pole light, casting a hazy orange glow through the mist.

As they approached the Brougham they could see the car was empty. Maya pulled the Duster up to the Cadillac, almost touching bumpers, then turned the ignition off. They sat for several long seconds, hearing nothing but the low rumbling surf of the ocean far off in the distance.

"You two check on preacherman," Maya said, "Make sure he's dead."

Jaz and Zoey jumped out of the car and walked toward the boathouse. Maya investigated the Cadillac, opening the passenger side door. There was no sign of Ali. There were also no keys in the ignition.

Circling the car, she stopped at the tailights. The edge of Ali's blouse protruded from the lower edge of the closed trunk. She searched for something with which to to pry the trunk open. Finding the rusty tire iron, she inserted the lower edge of the tool into the lower trunk edge, and pulled upward.

The trunk flew open and Maya had only a split second of view to see Wilkes lying in the trunk next to Ali's dead body. They were side by side, like some bizarre civil war death photo, Ali's face puffy and purple, her eyes open and rolled back in her head.

Wilkes was very much alive. His eyes were open and cold, alert and precise. They were fixed on her as he fired the gun twice. The last thing Maya saw were the muzzle flashes then everything went blinding white.

The bullets caught Maya in the forehead, exiting out the back of her skull in a splattering of fragmented bone, blood and brain matter.

Wilkes struggled to climb out of the trunk. By the time his good foot had hit the ground, Jaz and Zoey were on him. Jaz picked up the tire iron and struck Wilkes across the temple, sending him backwards, falling back into the trunk. The gun dropped, bouncing off the back bumper and landed in the sandy gravel.

Zoey grabbed at the preacher's right leg to pull him out of the trunk as Jaz swung the tire iron downward aimed at his skull. Wilkes blocked the tire iron, grabbing Jaz's wrist while he'd worked his right leg free and kicked blindly out at Zoey. Zoey was propelled backward several steps, releasing him long enough that he could emerge from the trunk again.

Grabbing the gun, he pointed it squarely at Zoey as Jaz approached at a dead run from the boathouse.

"Stop or she's dead." Wilkes said. Jaz stopped a ten feet

from the standoff, measuring the cost of reaching him. If he missed they could both take him down. If he fired, it could cost Zoey her life. Or he could shoot both of them.

Wilkes waved the gun toward the boathouse. "Both of you inside. Now."

He followed the girls as they strode defiantly toward the structure. They could hear the laughter of patrons emerging from the bar next door.

"Move it!" Wilkes said in a menacing tone. The girls stopped at the doors to the boathouse, left open from Jaz's quick exit. "I said get inside."

"You're going to risk shooting two teenage girls in cold blood with a handful of witnesses?" Jaz's face was that of a pleading schoolgirl's, one put on for show.

"I'd do it in a heartbeat to rid the world of evil," Wilkes said. Zoey spat on the ground, her eyes on fire with hatred and rage.

"You won't end evil by killing us." Zoey laughed. "We aren't the only ones. There's more where we came from."

"Shut up!" Wilkes barked. "Inside."

Both sisters entered the boathouse as Wilkes slid the doors shut. He hooked the broken lock through the latch. It would hold long enough for him to get away.

He backed away from the doors and limped toward the Cadillac. The cloth wrapped around his toe was soaked in blood and the throbbing of pain was so intense he was ready to pass out.

Entering the passenger side door, Wilkes threw the gun inside the Cadillac onto the floor and slid behind the wheel, wishing he'd been able to kill both witches only seconds ago when he'd had the gun trained on both of them.

Only he knew the gun had been empty.

Starting the Brougham, he spun out of the parking lot and onto the coast highway, pointed back toward Wildwood, and floored it.

* * *

Less than fifteen minutes later, Wilkes lay in waiting for the witches. He'd left the Cadillac on the side of the coast highway and made preparations for the appearance of the Duster.

Scrub brush and marsh trees concealed his position, crouched at the ready. His throbbing foot and leg were a crucible of pain. Within minutes he heard the car approach in the distance, running full throttle.

One lone headlight streaked its way toward him. *Thank God there are no other cars on the road,* Wilkes thought. *Safety first,* he mused, and pulled the lighter from his pocket.

* * *

From inside the Duster, the desolate roadway looked like a black streak into purgatory. Damp and glistening from the sea mist and light fog, it reflected the single headlight which shone only well enough the illuminate a limited distance in front of it.

Zoey spotted the Cadillac first, from her position in the passenger seat, her neck craned forward, her nose nearly pressed against the windshield.

"There!" She exclaimed, pointing toward the Brougham, which sat isolated and abandoned, its dark windows showing no life within.

Jaz stopped the Duster in the middle of the highway. From somewhere just behind them they caught a flicker and flash from an orange flame. The crash of breaking glass was all they heard before the back windshield and trunk erupted into flames.

Behind them, Wilkes stood in the road just behind the Duster and lit the second Molotov cocktail. He approached the driver side and hurled the flaming bottle squarely at the Jaz's face peering out at him from the dark glass.

The Duster, engulfed in flames, sat burning for several seconds before the passenger side door flew open and Zoey emerged, shrieking in rage.

Wilkes pulled the gun from his waist band and fired, catching Zoey in the left shoulder, spinning her sideways as Jaz leaped from the car on the passenger side and ran toward him with superhuman speed. He fired twice, the first shot missing her by inches and the the second bullet hitting her in the right breast, blood instantly staining her cotton dress.

She tackled him straight on as the gun flew from Wilkes hand and both of them collapsed on the roadway in a grunting heap. Jaz went for his throat first, squeezing with both hands with every bit of strength she could command.

Wilkes grabbed her head by the hair with both hands and jerked he head back as hard as he could, then brought his knee up hard, jabbing her pelvic bone, forcing her to release her grip from his throat.

She yelped in pain. She brought her own knee up hard into his groin, crushing his scrotum, then rolled off of him sideways, making a mad dash for the flaming car as Wilkes lay groaning in agony.

Jaz had already climbed out of the Duster and come to Zoey's aid, helping her to the car. Wilkes fought through his pain and crawled toward the gun.

Both witches made it back into car. The flames had died out leaving only a smoldering and scorched surface of bubbled paint. Jaz took the wheel and floored it, fishtailing sideways with tires spinning.

She'd pointed the Duster and barreled toward Wilkes. Wilkes managed to fire off two more shots, aimed toward the front windshield, hitting it twice before he rolled sideways. He'd avoided being crushed by the killing machine by mere inches.

Thank you Jesus for being my Lord and Savior, Wilkes managed, grabbing the gun and watching as the Duster fishtailed back onto the highway. The smoking tires spun wildly as Wilkes emptied the gun into the retreating hulk.

He forced himself to his feet. Tucking the empty gun into his waistband, his legs shaking, he limped as quickly as he could and toward the Cadillac.

* * *

Wilkes caught up to them sixty meters from the bridge. He grabbed the gun and angled it out the window, shooting three rounds in rapid succession at the rear windshield of the Duster.

The first two rounds hit the glass squarely in the center, opening two spiderweb cracks, while the third pierced completely through, shattering the glass.

The rear windshield fell away and Wilkes could now see Jaz and Zoey looking backward at him through the opening. He emptied the gun's final three rounds in an attempt to hit one of them, any of them, but the shots missed their marks, ricocheting off the chrome trim of the battered Duster's window frame.

Fast approaching Sea Isle bridge, the Duster squealed as its bent rear axle crippled its escape from the predatory behemoth. Wilkes could show no mercy for his quarry, knowing what was at stake was the eradication of evil itself.

He rammed them just as they were entering the ramp to the bridge, smashing hard into their right rear. The Duster pulled left, drifting into the left lane. Wilkes ran the sedan alongside them, forcing the Duster veering toward the toll booth. The Duster tried to counter right but the sedan was like a tank, pushing it ever closer to the intended target.

The witches hit the toll booth head on doing seventy, off center to the right, folding what was left of the hood back to the windshield, throwing the sisters screaming forward inside the car. Jaz crumbled into the steering wheel, crushing her rib cage; Zoey catapulted outward through the front windshield.

The trajectory and velocity of the impact caused the Duster to flip multiple times across the left lane, skidding on its roof, then slamming into the steel frame of the bridge, bursting into flames, spinning backwards.

Wilkes almost lost control of the Bougham. The flaming

wreckage of the Duster slammed into what was left of his passenger side, bounced off the right lane guardrail and over the edge into the dark waters below.

Wilkes slammed on the brakes, coming to rest facing backward, pointed back toward Strathmere.

He pulled himself from the car and stood at the edge of the bridge, the gun hanging loosely from his right hand, like some lone gunfighter peering out into an abyss.

The Duster sank quickly into the dark water, then disappeared. Wilkes stood for long time watching the water, even as the sirens approached in the distance. The ripples on the surface of the water lassoed in ever-widening circles, then became calm once more.

EPILOGUE

Nearly a year had passed. Wilkes had remained quiet yet vigilant, scanning the global news media. A story had finally surfaced in central Michigan that caught his attention.

Reports of a string of murders, some of the victims men of God. The circumstances which surrounded the killings had triggered immediate suspicion in Wilkes the homicides were witchcraft related.

He arrived in Howell, Michigan on a cold November night, crossing the county line into the rural community, driving a battered Ford Pinto. His tattered bible remained at his side, resting on the seat beside him, next to the fully loaded .38.

Newspapers from the area were scattered haphazardly on the floors of the Pinto, along with empty sandwich wrappers and crushed soda cans.

All his belongings were packed in one lone Samsonite

suitcase he'd thrown in the back seat. The old suitcase had a broken latch, held together by a makeshift leather belt.

The road was icy and desolate. Naked trees with bare arthritic limbs lined both sides of the narrow strip of road as Wilkes's headlights cut a swatch through the blackness.

The figure of a girl appeared in front of his headlights without warning. Her eyes were zombie white, a reverse negative of horror, her hair a tangled mat of wet seaweed.

It was Ali.

The Pinto struck her full on. Her body snapped as her head slammed onto the hood with a messy splat, then she hit the windshield before tumbling over the roof of the car.

Wilkes slammed on the brakes, skidding into the stand of forest. When he hit the tree he'd crushed the hood of the car halfway to the windshield. He was propelled forward by the deadly impact. The seat belt was the only thing that saved him.

He came to consciousness slowly, the creeping dawn of awareness coming back in waves. The pain from his right shoulder told him it was dislocated.

The Pinto was totaled, the tree trunk ripped halfway up the hood. The only view he had through the windshield came from the only working headlight, still on, crookedly illuminating the scattering of skeletal trees which surrounded him.

He saw figures walking through the darkness ahead of him, coming toward him in the swirling smoke of the wreckage.

From behind him, through the rear view mirror, an eerie glow of red and white from his rear lights threw a glaze of crimson at the ghostly figure of a woman approaching the car from the rear.

The battered body of Jaz staggered toward him, her head a bloodied stump, what was left of her left eye staring blindly out.

Ahead of him he saw them, all of them, or what was left of them, for none of them seemed even alive. Covered with mud and seaweed, they came toward him with grins like painted funhouse clowns.

Zoey's shattered left shoulder had festered to a sickly putrid wound the color of rotted whitefish. Her eyes stared blankly out from a dimension not of this world.

Maya's face was a frozen mask of evil. Two bulletholes in her forehead were leaking oily pus. The back of her skull was completely gone, revealing rotting brain matter spilling down her torn shirt. She was a litany of festering wounds as she drug her broken leg behind her.

Jaz walked with a broken hip, throwing her pelvis out sideways as she ambled through the trees, her face a twisted and pus-seething visage.

The witches angled toward him with the staggered gait of the walking dead. He knew he had only moments left to live as he placed his hand on the bible, closed his eyes, and prayed.